Acknowledgments

Quotation from DRACULA WAS A WOMAN, copyright © 1983 by Raymond T. McNally. All rights reserved. Used by permission of McGraw-Hill Book Company.

Quotation from "All in the Name of..." by Nikki Sixx, copyright © 1987 by Mötley Crüe Music/Sikki Nixx Music/Bordelo Brothers Music, BMI. All rights reserved. Used by permission.

Quotation from Volume I of *THE COMPLETE MARQUIS DE SADE*, translation from the original eighteenth-century French text copyright © 1966 by Dr. Paul J. Gillette. All rights reserved. Used by permission of Holloway House Publishing Company.

Quotation from "Woman of Dark Desires" by Quorthon, copyright © 1987 by Quorthon. All rights reserved. Used by permission.

Z-ROCK is a registered trademark of the Satellite Music Network. All rights reserved. Used by permission.

She was laughing at him, but inside his head, without moving her grinning lips.

■   ■   ■

Her lips hadn't moved when she'd spoken either, he suddenly realized, and now she didn't look as solid as she had. Her image was beginning to waver, becoming semi-transparent and moving slightly, up and down like a helium balloon on a tether. Her feet were no longer quite touching the floor.

"I'm afraid I have some bad news, Phil," Liz spoke in his head again, her grinning lips still not moving. "I totaled your car. Your cousin tried to use her head to crack open the windshield when we crashed. The windshield won. She's dead. So am I. Just thought you'd like to know."

Blood began to squeeze out of her mouth between her grinning white teeth. Blood began trickling out of her eyes and nose and ears. Suddenly her forehead split open with a loud cracking sound...

■

Also by Dean Andersson

TORTURE TOMB

Published by
POPULAR LIBRARY

RAW PAIN MAX

DEAN ANDERSSON

POPULAR LIBRARY

An Imprint of Warner Books, Inc.

A Warner Communications Company

POPULAR LIBRARY EDITION

Copyright © 1988 by C. Dean Andersson
All rights reserved.

Popular Library® and the fanciful P design are registered trademarks
of Warner Books, Inc.

Cover illustration by J. K. Potter

Popular Library books are published by
Warner Books, Inc.
666 Fifth Avenue
New York, N.Y. 10103

 A Warner Communications Company

Printed in the United States of America

First Printing: December, 1988

10 9 8 7 6 5 4 3 2 1

This one is for the Bulldogians
of the Dallas/Austin/Houston/San Antonio Fantasy Fairs,
where early portions of this novel had their debut,
and especially for the Chief Bulldog,
Larry Lankford,
long may his Bulldog(s) bark.

Special Thanks to:

- Boobie Bondage and Wild Bill for the tour of Z-ROCK's Metal Bunker, and to the Satellite Music Network's Kristine Sites for permission;

- John Newsome for the Trans Am/Harley info;

- Tim Boone for selected muse-ical/inspirational atmospheres;

- Quorthon for the Erzebetional energy that helped blast many a chapter onto disk;

- And best wishes to Ms. Fanni Hall, her Aunt Gwen, her Cousin Phoebe, etc., all of whom Erzebet would have liked, a lot.

—Erzebet's Grins to you all.—

Note:

This is a work of fiction. The major characters and events are not meant to portray actual persons, living or dead, or any actual events, except for the historical ones involving the Countess Erzebet Bathory.

Erzebet (Elizabeth, in English) lived in Hungary from 1560 to 1614. If you wish to pursue Erzebet beyond the pages of this novel, her life has been explored in several books, among which I give Professor Raymond T. McNally's definitive study, *DRACULA WAS A WOMAN*, my foremost recommendation. I also suggest *THE BLOODY COUNTESS*, a fascinating historical novelization of Erzebet's life by Valentine Penrose.

In addition, you might want to view *DAUGHTERS OF DARKNESS* and *COUNTESS DRACULA*, two of several films inspired by Erzebet's legend, and to hear "Woman of Dark Desires," a song about Erzebet written by Quorthon and recorded by his Swedish Metal band named, appropriately enough, BATHORY.

Dean Andersson
Dallas, March '88

The supernatural and the unintelligible continue to play roles in the sex lives of most modern people, since human sexual encounters remain essentially mysterious. Things are, after all, rarely what they seem to be.

Raymond T. McNally,
DRACULA WAS A WOMAN:
In Search of the Blood Countess of Transylvania

PROLOGUE ONE

Hungary, 1614

Lightning flickered into a shadowy, high-ceilinged room through slits along the tops of narrow, bricked-up windows. Thunder rumbled.

Within the room, a Countess in a soiled and ragged gown paced back and forth, frantic with horror, trapped in a nightmare that was coming true.

More lightning flashed through the slits. Thunder crashed nearer.

The Countess cringed whimpering into a corner, staring with terror at a bare patch of wall where a mirror had once hung.

The storm reached the castle. Her nightmare came true.

The man who brought her meal the next day looked through the food-hole in the bricked-up doorway and saw the prisoner lying face down upon the dirty stone floor.

The date was August 21, 1614.

After nearly four years of solitary imprisonment, the torturer, the mass murderer, the Countess Erzebet Bathory, alone and insane, was dead.

But only, of course, for a while.

PROLOGUE TWO

America, 1968

Three hundred and fifty-four years after her death, the Countess Bathory was found by an eight-year-old girl in a public library in a small Kansas town, in Seabrook's WITCHCRAFT, in a chapter called "World Champion Lady Vampire of All Time."

The girl selected several children's books and checked them out along with Seabrook's to camouflage her find, then carried WITCHCRAFT home sandwiched between the children's books, the spine against her body so that her parents would not notice. Before falling asleep she used a flashlight under the sheets to feed her guilty fantasies by reading the Countess' chapter three more times.

That weekend, on a visit to her grandparents' farm, she caught a kitten in the barn, bound it to a milking stool with bailing wire, and, slowly, beat it to death with a stick.

PART ONE

Safe Sex

☐

For sex and sex I'd sell my soul...

Nikki Sixx,
"All in the Name of..."

1

Toys in the Playroom

*She was terrified and helpless, naked in chains, masked tor-
turers crowding around her, laughing at her, hungry to see
her suffer, anxious to hear her scream. One raised a hot
poker, brought the glowing tip slowly up between her spread
thighs. The torturer's mask fell away, revealing a woman's
hideously deformed face, the nose and lips eaten away by
bleeding cancerous sores. Writhing tentacles glistened
within the dark cavern of her laughing mouth as she pressed
the hot iron against her victim's sex and kissed the bound
woman's scream-distended mouth, chilled tentacles sliding
wetly down the pain-constricted throat . . .*

The ripsaw buzz of a digital alarm clock chewed up the
dream and jarred Trudy McAllen awake.

She groped for the clock and turned off the alarm, then
lay looking up at the ceiling for a few moments, trying to
remember remnants of the interrupted dream. Shortly thereafter, she forced herself to get out of bed, went into the
bathroom, and turned on the shower to let the water grow
warm while she did more urgent things.

Another work day, or rather afternoon and night, stretched
before her. The thought did not thrill her.

Marv, her boss, claimed she had a bad attitude. Where her
current job was concerned, he was right. She was grateful to
him for giving her a chance to get her life out of the gutter
and onto the curb. The sleazy work she did for him in Dallas
was a vast improvement over the even sleazier things she
had done to survive in New York during those first near fatal

years after running away from her home in Los Angeles. But being grateful to Marv did not mean she intended to devote her life to waitressing at his club or dancing half-naked on his stage and acting (sort of) in his perv-porn videos.

The gym where she worked out was another matter. After fighting back from being a physical disaster on the brink of death, she liked the idea of devoting her life to helping herself and others get stronger and healthier. Her before and after pictures were the difference between Ms. Anorexia and Ms. Olympia.

The gym's owner had suggested he might hire her if a staff position opened up. Whether he really would or had merely been blowing hot air to get on her good side, she kept telling herself it was possible he might, even with her less than savory background. Working there could give her life some meaning. And looking forward to a life that meant something more than mere survival was a hope she could not afford to abandon. For nearly eighteen months that hope and her regular workouts had kept her drug-free and sober. Occasional fantasy-fixes in her private playroom, with a partner or, if necessary, as it often was, alone, helped too.

Trudy got into the shower. As the water steamed around her, she leaned back against the tiles and toyed with the unraveling threads of the dream her wake-up alarm had interrupted. She caught a few vivid images and held onto them.

She kept thinking about the dream, about the helpless excitement of the naked victim contrasted with the sadistic excitement of torturer. She had been both in the dream, had felt the erotic bite of the chains even as she had felt the flesh-searing poker in her hands.

She closed her eyes and touched her breasts, then other places. A few moments later, she decided the dream had started feelings that were too good to waste.

She turned the shower off and walked back to her bedroom, dripping water onto the worn green rug as she went. From a bottom dresser drawer, beneath folded t-shirts and sweatshirts, she took a key. Then she went to the end of the hall, unlocked a door, and entered her playroom.

She flipped the lightswitch. A red light bulb she had installed in the ceiling light fixture came on. The beige vinyl floor, cool against the soles of her bare feet, was a lake of frozen blood in the crimson glow.

Trudy closed the door and locked it. There was no one else in the rented house. She lived alone. But knowing the door was locked had an enhancing psychological effect.

Against the wall opposite the door was a piece of special furniture she had constructed herself. Two two-by-fours, each seven feet long, sanded smooth, stained dark and varnished, formed a wooden X to which were nailed four buckled leather straps, one at the end of each arm. Beneath the X, two thick beams extended down to a heavy wooden base, holding the X at a solid thirty-degree slant.

A full-length mirror attached to the back of the door opposite the X forced/allowed anyone strapped to it to see a reflection of themselves.

To the right of the X sat a two-shelfed utility table on wheels. Upon the table's white enamel (made crimson by the light) shelves lay Trudy's fantasy toys.

Some of the toys were common things that her imagination put to uncommon uses. Others were expensive (to her) items she had purchased on those rare occasions when she could squeeze a little extra from her tight budget.

The most costly items in the collection were a pair of stainless steel handcuffs, a multi-speed vibrator to which could be fitted an assortment of interesting attachments, and a handmade, three-thonged whip.

The rest of the collection included several thick leather straps fitted with buckles, varying lengths and thicknesses of strong nylon rope, three dozen wooden clothes pins, spring clips from an office supply store, and a tray containing miscellaneous items from miscellaneous hardware stores.

She reminded herself that the fantasy session would have to be a quick one or she would be late for that afternoon's video shoot. She also reminded herself to not leave lingering marks any place on her body that would show in the as-good-as-naked costumes she would be wearing in the video and later at the club. Then she positioned herself against the bondage frame.

She hurriedly strapped her wide-spread ankles to the bottom arms of the slanting X and strapped her left wrist to the top of the upper left arm. The right wrist strap was already buckled, but loosely enough to slip a hand in and out. The utility table and its collection of toys was within easy reach to the right.

She slipped her right hand into the waiting buckled loop, then looked at herself in the mirror, a naked woman strapped to the X, damp skin glistening in the crimson light, waiting helplessly for her tormentors to give her pain.

Watching her reflection, she strained against her bonds, bowed her body upward, jerked on the straps as if desperate to get free. Leather and wood creaked. She moaned low in her throat, moving deeper into her fantasy, sexual tension mounting.

Fantasy tormentors approached her. The hooded men shamed her with insults, leisurely examined her spread nakedness, discussed what to do to her first, then made a decision, and told her what it was. She begged them not to do it. They laughed in response.

Panting softly, Trudy slipped her right hand free of its leather loop and reached for one of her toys.

2

Temple

Phil Hastings lived on the Dallas side of the Dallas-Fort Worth Metroplex, but he had not been to downtown Dallas for more than a year, not since the Commerce Street Newsstand had closed. He missed it still.

He had first visited the newsstand ten years ago, in 1978, in secret, a thirteen-year old kid defying his mother's authority, staring wide-eyed at the long rows of books and magazines and newspapers, some printed in exotic (to him) foreign languages.

His mother was doing her Saturday shopping in the original Neiman–Marcus on the corner of Commerce and Ervay a few doors up the street. He said he was going to the bathroom, but instead he snuck out of the store and went down the street to the newsstand.

He had noticed the newsstand several times before when they had walked by on their way to Neiman's, and several times he had asked to go in. But his mother claimed they had not lost anything in there and so he had never been inside, until now.

Carefully squeezing through the forest of adults that crowded the aisles, feeling like an intruder in a forbidden temple, he cautiously pushed deeper into the newstand and found a new paperback by a writer whose novel about vampires he had read and reread until it was falling apart. There had been an all-black cover on the vampire book. This new one gleamed like polished chrome. It was call THE SHINING, but it cost $2.50 and he had spent all but $1.25 of his weekly allowance on some STAR WARS stuff at the mall.

Reminding himself he musn't be gone from Neiman's too long, he left the chrome-covered paperback and explored another long row of books, then another, and another, until . . .

In the newsstand's innermost depths, at the back where the lighting was not quite as bright, he saw an open alcove. A group of men, some of them wearing suits like his father only wore on Sundays to church, stood packed closely together inside. None looked at another or made a sound as they concentrated, heads bowed as if in prayer, upon the books and magazines before them.

Curious, feeling he had reached the temple's holy of holies, Phil went nearer. A large sign over the entrance warned him that minors weren't allowed. He had heard of such places, of course. They were supposed to be Evil. Shrines of Sex. Pornography.

Knowing he was not supposed to go nearer, Phil edged defiantly closer, and closer, pretending to be looking at the books on the row that led to the alcove's entrance, until finally he was close enough to steal a secret peek by straining his eyes sideways. What he saw made him forget stealth

—magazines wrapped in clear plastic showing beautiful women, naked. The nearest one had long blond hair. She was lying on her back, frowning as if in pain, legs spread wide. One of the men in the alcove suddenly looked at him, grinned, nudged the guy next to him, and pointed.

Phil panicked and began frantically pushing his way out of the store through the long crowded aisles. Behind him, he heard the men who had seen him laugh.

As he hurried back to Neiman's, he kept glancing back, expecting to see the men come out after him, but they did not, and his mother never guessed where he had been.

He immediately began wanting to go back and see more. Days afterward he still found it difficult to think of much else. One night he even saw the woman on the magazine cover in a sweaty, disturbing/exciting dream. It was not the first such dream he had ever had, but it was the most vivid and had the strongest effect.

Deep down where words and warnings could not reach he began to accept that his soul had been claimed by the Goddess Sex, even before he had seen one of her priestesses on the magazine. Maybe that's what had drawn him away from his mother and into the newsstand in the first place. Maybe it was the Devil's work or just biology. But whatever it was, he might go to Hell for it or he might not, but Evil or not, Sin or not, he wanted, *needed* more.

So, there were other secret trips to the newstand when his mother went to Neiman's after that, and although he made a show of examining the other books in the store (feeling as if everyone was watching him), fleeting glances at the magazines in the Holy Alcove of Pornography were always his goal.

He fantasized about carrying one of the goddesses home, finding a secret place, stripping off her plastic wrapping, and studying her secrets.

At fifteen he slipped inside the alcove and spent several precious seconds there before someone noticed and ran him off.

By sixteen he had seen a few PLAYBOYs and PENT-HOUSEs a classmate sometimes snuck out of his dad's collection and to school, but to Phil those mags were only pale imitations of the ones in the alcove. Then one night at a party he saw and experienced the secrets of Sex in the flesh when a girl he was dating let him have more than just a look. And after that the forbidden magazines lost most of their allure. But he still wanted to take one home, just to prove he could.

A new driver's license and his first car giving him adult mobility, he worked his courage up for a week, then put on a bored adult expression and tried to buy a magazine call BITCH GODDESS. The cashier, a woman, took it away and scolded him as if he were still a kid and she his mother. He left the store red-faced with embarrassment but also highly pissed, more determined than ever to somehow beat the system.

He tried at other times when different people were behind the cash register, but always without success. He tried and failed once using a fake ID. Another time he offered a man on the street outside the store five dollars to buy an eight-dollar WHIPMISTRESS for him. The man said, "Make it ten." He did. And the man walked away with all eighteen.

He even considered attempting to steal one of the magazines. But the two-way mirror at the end of the alcove dissuaded him. He did not want one of the mags enough to risk being arrested for shoplifting.

And Phil never did beat the system at the Commerce Street Newsstand. Not until he was legal did he leave there with a domitrix fantasy porno mag in a sack under his arm. But he did beat the system at other places in other parts of town, foul-smelling, poorly-lighted sleaze parlors that the Dallas Police had now long since closed down.

Phil had not cared what happened to the sleaze joints. He had, however, cared deeply the day the Commerce Street Newsstand had been demolished along with neighboring, long-time downtown institutions to make way for an important new parking lot.

The temple with its hushed alcove where he had found the Goddess Sex and become a man was gone. And he mourned it still. But he did not mourn the goddess, because he saw her everywhere.

She ruled the world, he sometimes thought, and probably always had.

3

RPM

"Hi," grinned the leather-clad (barely) goddess. "I'm RPM. That stands for Raw Pain Max. But you can call me Raw. Or you can call me Pain. Or you can call me Max. *Or you can just fucking scream!"*

Raw held a black whip. She stood six-feet-six inches tall in calf-hugging, spike-heeled black boots, towering over a short and slender man bound between two chrome poles. His mane of long blond hair was heavy-metal-rock teased and tangled. Heavy metal music from a demo tape by a local group pounded from dual speakers in the background.

Raw was bare breasted and bare assed because she was wearing a skimpy, laced-up-the-front, black leather fetish corset and nothing else. Except for the boots.

Raw's hair was dark and long, her lips full, eyes large and brown, forehead domed, nose straight. The tanned flesh of her bare arms and legs rippled with iron-pumping muscles. Her large (unusually large, for a bodybuilder) upthrust breasts were tanned too, their aureolae dark, nipples protruding provocatively.

Raw cracked her whip in the air near her victim's chest. He winced and jerked on his chains. "Your wife hired me to teach you a lesson," she told him. "But she only paid for one hour. That was all she could afford. My services don't come cheap."

Raw moved behind the bound man. He craned his head

around, looking apprehensively back over his shoulder, straining to keep her in view.

"So, it's time to get started," Raw announced, "and we're going to start with . . . this!"

Raw's whip struck the man's bare back, leaving a streak of red. He convulsed with pain and jerked desperately on his chains as Raw's whip again struck his back, leaving another crimson smear.

An orange ball-gag strapped into his mouth turned his cries of pain into bestial grunts.

"Pig sounds from a pig," Raw mocked. "Working late at the recording studio with your precious band, were you?"

She struck again.

"Too busy with that groupie bitch to remember your anniversary?"

And again.

"And after all your wife's done for you . . ."

Again.

"Working to support you through the hard times . . ."

Again.

"Giving you a fine son . . ."

Again.

"Never once being unfaithful to you . . ."

And yet again.

Raw walked back around to face her victim, threw down the whip, and spat on the floor in front of his bare feet.

"You're such a disgusting, loathsome worm that I may throw in an extra hour, or two, for free."

She picked up a knife and laughed at the look on his face. "Your wife said she didn't care what I did to you, *or where*. Want to see what fun we can have with this knife? Was that a yes? No? You'll have to grunt more clearly, pig."

She hooked her left hand in the waistband of his jeans to hold him steady, slowly brought the blade toward his groin, touched him with the point, and held it there while she grinned at him, savoring the terror in his eyes and his gagged sounds of panic.

"For starters, I think I'll carve your wife's initials on your balls. Do you think that would help you remember your anniversary next year? You don't? Well, like I said, it'll just be for starters. Bet you hope I don't slip and cut 'em off, right? Could happen, though. We'll just have to wait and see."

Raw let him struggle a moment longer, then held the knife blade between her teeth like a Hollywood movie-pirate, unbuckled her victim's belt, unzipped his fly, and jerked down his jeans . . . revealing bright pink boxer shorts covered with large red hearts.

There was a moment of stunned silence, then Trudy took the knife from between her teeth and stabbed Phil's chest as she convulsed with laughter. "I should punish you for *real*, monkey," she said, still laughing as she eyed the joke shorts he had put on.

Phil made a gagged sound of encouragement and nodded that some serious punishment sounded like a good idea to him.

She stabbed him with the harmless prop knife a second time.

A burly, red-haired man wearing a faded Hawaiian shirt stepped into the light from behind a tripod-mounted CCD camcorder. "You think it's funny to cost me money?"

"That rhymes, Marv," Trudy commented drily, then laughed again when she saw Phil roll his eyes.

"Get those goddamned things off him."

"And the right ones on," Trudy added. "You did bring the right ones, I hope, didn't you, Phil?"

"Forget it," Marv told her. "I'm not going to waste time doing a reshoot. I'll just edit out those fucking shorts and jump to a closeup of you poking his balls with the blade."

"Whatever," Trudy agreed as she reached down to unsnap the painted aluminum manacles on Phil's ankles.

"Don't waste time!" Marv shouted. "Rip the goddamned things off!"

"Phil paid good money for them," Trudy replied as she went ahead and unsnapped the manacles, "and I owe him for a good laugh."

Marv cursed at her disobedience.

She stripped Phil and threw the joke shorts to one side, then resnapped the manacles, stepped back, and gave him a wink. "Ready to continue, you loathsome worm?" she asked.

Phil nodded he was.

"I was talking to Marv," she said, glancing at the impatient man behind the camcorder.

"Fucking comedians," Marv growled.

Raw went back to work with the knife.

4

Guests

"Want to grab a bite before going to the club?" Trudy asked as she crossed the parking lot with Phil toward his car and her motorcycle. Phil had a battered black Trans Am. She had a used Harley 1100 with extended forks and a black leather king-and-queen seat.

Her RPM gear was in a "Sweats" gym bag hanging from one shoulder. She was now wearing a faded "World Gym" t-shirt whose cut/ripped/torn tail hovered several awesome-abdominal inches above the top of a pair of tight black jeans, the pegged legs of which were tucked into scuffed black motorcycle boots. Her long dark hair hung free and straight past her shoulders, glinting with coppery highlights in the sunlight.

The hot and muggy summer air was a marked contrast to the air-conditioned interior of Marv's so-called studio. Distant thunderheads billowed in the west promising eventual storms, their tops glaring white in the late afternoon sunlight. A commuter jet making a final approach to Dallas Love Field screamed past low overhead.

Phil was looking at the thunderheads as he walked beside Trudy, dwarfed by her height. He'd had a thing about thunderheads since childhood. "Fort Worth's probably already getting it," he commented. "The thunderheads," he motioned when he saw Trudy didn't understand. "We're probably under a severe weather watch or something."

Trudy shrugged her disinterest. "Are you going to answer me or not?"

"What?"

"About getting a bite."

"I've got to run over to D/FW. My cousin from Kansas is coming in on a 6:00 flight from Wichita, remember?"

"Oh, yeah. I forgot."

"It's almost 5:30 now. I'll probably be late. You could come with me if you didn't have to start waiting tables before our first show."

"I could do *a lot* of things if I didn't have to wait tables," she commented. "Bringing cousin to the club tonight to see our act?"

"I doubt that she's up to it."

"How come?"

"You have to ask?"

"Did you also tell me how long she's staying?"

"I don't know myself. Only a few days, I hope. She caught me off guard or I would never have agreed. I started wishing I'd said no the moment I hung up the phone. Haven't seen her since we were kids."

"Bring her to the club. It can't be any weirder than being from Kansas, can it?"

"I remember visiting up there as a kid. Kansas has its good points."

"The borders?"

"Why're you anti-Kansas? Wizard of Oz warp you?"

Trudy shrugged again. "Never been there. Just stuff I've heard. I'll bet the club would do her good."

"I doubt it," he replied, then grinned mischievously. "But maybe I'll do it anyway. We'll see."

Phil got into his Trans Am. Trudy climbed onto her Harley.

The Trans Am looked like a wreck from the outside, but when Phil turned the key a healthy rumble came from its well-tuned engine. Phil gunned it a couple of times. He turned on his radio, loud. It was tuned, always, to Z-

ROCK's Dallas frequency, a 24-hours-a-day, seven-days-a-week, FM hard rock station fed by the Satellite Music Network. One of Z-ROCK's mottoes was, "If it's too loud, you're too old."

Slayer's cover version of Iron Butterfly's 60's classic, "In-A-Gadda-Da-Vida", thundered above the sound of the Trans Am's engine. There was a small Z-ROCK Zombies-que window sticker on the car's back window and a large white-on-black Z-ROCK sticker on the back bumper's left side. The Z-ROCK sticker was not lonely. Phil liked bumper stickers and had them plastered everywhere

One was an anti-littering sticker that said, "Don't Mess with Texas." And there were other Texas-themed stickers, too, such as, "Native Texan," and, "Beautify Texas: Put a Yankee on a Bus," and, "Love NY? Take 1-30 East." But Trudy's favorite sticker was the one that she had given him for his birthday. It said, "If You Don't Like My Driving Call 1-800-EAT-SHIT."

Trudy kicked the Harley's engine to life as Phil drove out of the parking lot.

Marv's rented studio was a vacant building near Harry Hines not far from the Lyndon Baines Johnson Freeway, alias LBJ to natives, a.k.a. 635 to visitors struggling with Metroplex maps. Phil drove north on Harry Hines then headed west on LBJ, windows down because his air conditioner was broken. Traffic wasn't too heavy, considering the time of day.

Slayer finished their tune, an ad promised Phil he could get glow-in-the-dark Z-ROCK Mugs and other Z-ROCK Stuff, including free bumper stickers, at Underground Records and Tapes. Then Wild Bill told Phil he was about to hear another Z-ROCK Blitz, including some mandatory Metallica, but starting with Mötley Crüe's "Girls, Girls, Girls."

Phil kept time to the music and an eye on the thunder-heads as he drove west, doing clumsy drum riffs on the steering wheel, watching the tops of the thunderheads flat-tening out, becoming high-altitude anvils. He saw distant lightning flash near a wall cloud formation at their base and thought about planes fighting wind-shear while trying to land at D/FW. He guesstimated he would be driving back to

Dallas in the rain and wished (as he had the last several times he had been caught out in a storm) that he had taken the time to replace his deteriorating windshield wipers.

When the Crüe finished with the girls, Motörhead began tastefully torturing the speakers with "Eat the Rich" while Phil kept driving west on LBJ, passing through pastureland containing shiny new high rise office buildings instead of cattle.

Motörhead finished, Venom did a tune, and then Boobie Bondage, Phil's favorite Z-ROCK DJ, gave him that day's edition of Z-Real Rock News. She had some hot news about Anthrax and Bathory and Leather Nun.

The road eventually curved south and the Dallas-Fort Worth International Airport stretched out ahead. Wild Bill said goodbye for the day and Madd Maxx Hammer took over, which meant that it was 6:00 and, if Phil's cousin's plane had been on time, he was late.

He took a time-punched ticket at the entrance, drove on through, watched gate-turnoff signs until he saw the right one, then steered the Trans Am into a parking lot, found an empty space, turned off the engine, and looked at his Timex Ironman digital. 6:13.

He got out and headed into the terminal, not hurrying, not in the least anxious to see Donna again. He liked living alone. It was a terrible thing to admit, he supposed, but he sometimes didn't even mind now that his mom and dad were dead. He was an only child, used to doing things alone, and after he'd gotten over the initial shock of his parents dying in a car crash a year ago, he had settled into a comfortable life in what was now *his* comfortable home and with a bank account swollen by insurance money—not enough to keep him from having to work for a living, but a comforting cushion that made him worry less about financial matters than would otherwise have been the case.

His low-stress, no-ambition, part-time job clerking at a convenience store paid most of his monthly expenses, along with what he got for his sex-fantasy work with Trudy on the videos and at the club, activities which he had somehow forgotten to mention when applying for his job with the we-don't-sell-porno-magazines-anymore convenience store.

He had only been working at the club a few months. Before that he had worked at a variety of jobs, some odder and more interesting than others.

He had met Trudy last year when she came into the convenience store. He couldn't believe his eyes and told her so. She had snubbed him and left. But she had come back a few days later, and other times after that.

They eventually became pretty good friends. They had even slept together a couple of times. And he had once spent a gloriously long Sunday afternoon at her place in what she called her playroom, playing with her toys, taking turns letting her use them on him, and then he on her.

But they had never talked about their relationship being more than just friendship and occasional sex. Yet. It might still happen. He sometimes guessed he hoped it would. Who cared if she were a few years older, nearly a foot taller, had a police record, and more muscles in one arm than he had in his entire body?

Grinning at a picture in his mind of Trudy as RPM carrying him across a fantasy honeymoon threshold (he would certainly never be able to lift her), Phil walked into the terminal and started looking for his cousin, wondering if he would even recognize her. Then he saw a young woman coming toward him and wondered if it were her. If it was her, she had grown into an attractive young woman, about his five-six height but slightly shorter, light brown hair neatly and fashionably coiffed, large gray-green eyes emphasized by skillfully but minimally applied makeup, a black and pink outfit hugging her trim body, pink workout shoes laced on her feet. A shoulder bag dangled from one hand. But something about the way her eyes looked made him wonder for a moment if she were feeling all right. Maybe she had been airsick. He hoped that was all it was. Having her around would be bad enough without having her sick, too.

He wondered how he looked to her. He hoped that she would think, as he hoped all young women thought, that with his slim build and long blond hair and pretty-boy good looks he might be a member of some scruffy Heavy Metal band. It was not an accident that his clothing contributed to the effect: tight jeans, scuffed cowboy boots, a well-worn Def Leppard "Hysteria" t-shirt, a large silver skull ring, and a leather wristband on his right wrist.

"Hello, Phil?" she asked, her voice curiously flat.

"Yeah, Donna? Sorry I was late. Worked later than I'd planned. Anyway, welcome to Dallas. You check any luggage through?"

"I'm not exactly alone."

"You're what?"

"Someone came with me. A good friend."

Phil started frowning, assuming she meant a boyfriend.

"You'll like her."

"Her? Oh. Well, it's just that I'm used to living alone, and . . ." His voice trailed away.

A woman with a long mane of strawberry-blond hair was approaching. Her hard, dark eyes were fixed on his. She was wearing a black, military-look zippered jumpsuit and high heels, was a couple of inches taller than him, and about Trudy's age, a few years older than his twenty-three. She looked like she'd just stepped out of a Billy Idol or ZZ Top fantasy-sex rock video. She excited him, and scared him a little, too, which only added to his excitement.

The woman was still coming toward him, still looking at him, and he suddenly knew she was going to be Donna's friend.

"This is Elizabeth Smith," Donna said a moment later, proving his guess correct. "Liz, this is Phil."

"Hello," Liz said with a husky, bedroom voice. She extended her right hand. Her grip was strong and warm and firm. Her dark eyes dug even deeper into his. He felt slightly dizzy and had conflicting urges to either run away or try unzipping her jumpsuit.

"Are you with a Heavy Metal band, Phil?" she asked him, prolonging the contact of their hands.

His chest reflexively swelled. "Not any more," he replied as if he once had been. He'd had that misleading answer ready for a long time, but Liz was the first to have asked.

"I hope our staying at your place won't inconvenience you too much," Liz said, finally letting go of his hand. His dizziness and urge to run vanished. Unzipping her jumpsuit still seemed like a good idea. And now he suddenly felt wonderful, anxious to please Ms. Liz Smith any way he could. He had an impulse to tell her she could damn well stay at his place as long as she damn well pleased, as long as she spent some of that time in his bed. But instead, he said, "There's plenty of room at my place, but I converted the second bedroom into something else, so there's only one bed. You can have it, though, and I'll sleep—"

"With us in the bed?" Liz suggested.

"What?"

"Isn't there room for three?"

"Uh, well, not side by side."

"That's no problem, is it?" she asked, then laughed.

"Did I look that anxious?" he grinned.

"Anxious for what?"

"I'm sleeping on the couch," he announced.

"How disappointing."

"Really?"

"You're looking anxious, again," she warned.

"No shit. Come on. I'll show you where to pick up your luggage."

5

Rain

Phil had been right about the rain. They made it to his car before the sky dumped on them, but only barely. His ragged windshield wipers struggled valiantly to give a usable view. Leaning down to peer through an inch-wide swath of wind-

shield that the blades were sweeping clearest, he steered out
of the parking lot and onto the road leading to the exit.
Donna sat in the passenger seat, Liz in the back. With the
windows up, it was uncomfortably warm and muggy in the
car. Lightning flashed. Thunder, very loud, followed, very
quickly.

"Are you feeling okay, Donna?" he asked as they neared
the exit gate. She had not spoken since introducing Liz, and
he was still wondering if she were sick.

"She got sick on the plane," Liz answered. "She'll be
fine, won't you, Donna?"

"Yes. I'll be fine," Donna agreed.

"What brings you to Dallas, anyway, Cousin?" Phil asked
as he kept peering through the clear swath of windshield.
"I'm sure you didn't come just to see me."

"Actually, it was my idea," Liz replied. "An old friend of
mine moved to Dallas. I'm going to surprise her."

"Oh. Donna didn't mention that when she called. How
long have you two known each other?" he asked.

"Donna and I? Or me and my old friend?"

"Donna and you."

"A few weeks."

"Where'd you meet?"

"Lawrence."

"That near Salina?" he asked, which was where he had
visited Donna as a kid.

"Not really. Donna was going to school at K.U."

"College? Kansas University?"

"No. University of Kansas."

"Then wouldn't it be U.K.?"

"No."

"Were you in class together?"

"I wasn't a student. We met in a supermarket. Donna
looked tasty. So I picked her up."

"You what?" he asked, wanting to look around at her face
to see if she looked like she was putting him on. But he
could not afford to take his eyes off the clear swath of windshield. It was raining even harder now.

"I picked her up," Liz repeated. "I'll bet you've picked up
girls at supermarkets too, right?"

"Uh, not recently. So, you mean that . . . you and Donna—"

"Something wrong?"

"Uh, no. I guess not. I just never thought that—"

"It doesn't mean I'm not attracted to men, too," Liz assured him, "if that's what's bothering you."

"Nothing's bothering me, except the damned rain."

"Want me to make it stop?"

"Sure."

"What is it worth to you? Everything has a price. Including making rain stop. So, what's it worth to you? Tell you what, Phil. I'll make it stop raining if you'll help me satisfy a fantasy. Maybe your fantasies will mesh with mine."

"I somehow kind of doubt that."

"Really? Well, here's my fantasy. I meet this good looking guy who plays in a Heavy Metal band, and I get him alone and tie him up, and then—"

"You do *what?*"

"Something wrong again?"

"You found out about the club, right?"

"Club?"

"The Safe Sex Club?"

"Intriguing name."

"Who told you?"

"Told me what?"

"Shit. Stop it. Level with me. You somehow found out about the act I do with Trudy at the Safe Sex Club. So you decided to—"

"What kind of an act?"

"Oh, come on, Liz. The one where I get tied up and Trudy—"

"Sounds like my fantasy."

"That's the fucking point!"

"Does she strip you naked?"

"Almost."

"And does she strip naked too?"

"Almost."

"And whip you?"

"She pretends to."

"But off stage, she has *really* whipped you, and other things, I assume?"

"That's none-of-your-fucking-business private."

"Which means she has. You're right, Phil. It *is* a lot like my fantasy. What a strange coincidence!"

"Coincidence my ass."

"Do you suppose Trudy would loan her whip, and you, to me after the show tonight? Say yes, and I'll stop the rain for you, right now."

"Stop the rain first," he countered as he pulled the Trans Am into the D/FW exit gate and handed the woman in the booth his entrance ticket along with a couple of dollars. When he drove out from beneath the overhanging roof, the rain had stopped.

Phil said nothing, shocked. He turned the struggling wipers off. Then he got over his shock. "You know what they say about Texas weather?" he asked with a laugh. "They say that if you don't like it, wait a few minutes and it will change."

"They say the same thing about Kansas weather," Liz replied. "Does that mean you don't believe *I* stopped the rain?"

"Yeah, Liz. That's what it fucking means," he said, laughing again as he reached to lower his window.

"I wouldn't do that if I were you," Liz warned.

"Why not?"

"Because I'm about to make it start raining again. It was naughty of you not to believe I made it stop."

"Please! Don't punish my wipers again!" he joked, then laughed, but stopped laughing a moment later.

"Christ," he cursed as he turned the wipers back on. It had suddenly started raining even harder than before.

"Say yes to my fantasy and I'll make the rain stop, again," Liz offered.

But Phil was tired of the game. He turned the radio on, let Z-ROCK pound the speakers with Alice Cooper's "Prince of Darkness," and kept peering out the small clear swath of windshield while Donna stared blankly and Liz smiled contentedly to herself most of the long and very rainy way back to Dallas.

6

Jilted

At the Safe Sex Club a couple of hours later, Phil made certain Donna and Liz had a good table, bought them each a drink, then hurried backstage.

"At last," Trudy grumped. "I thought I was going to have to whip myself tonight. Have fun with cousin? And why are you grinning like a naughty little boy?"

"Because that's what I feel like. I brought them, Trudy. They're out front. I hope we shock the hell out of them. But don't count on it. Donna seems like an airsick zombie or something, and Liz—"

"Slow down. Liz?"

"A friend of Donna's. Says she's going to visit an old friend here. And she somehow knew about our club act, because she said she wanted to tie me up and whip me."

"That doesn't mean she knew about the act. Lots of women want to do that to you."

"Get serious."

"Okay. How's this? Get your fucking costume on before we miss our cue."

Phil hurried and was ready with a couple of minutes to spare. The lights dimmed. A crimson spotlight came on. The announcer announced Raw Pain Max and Slave and got off the tiny stage. Sinister electronic music mixing simulated chanting with tormented moans began pouring from the speakers.

A towering Domitrix suddenly pushed her slender male slave into the spotlight. Phil stumbled forward and slid onto his knees. He was wearing a rip-away shirt and pants. His hands were locked in prop handcuffs, behind him. He was barefoot and acted terrified of the muscled, whip-toting amazon who loomed above him wearing a flowing black satin cape over knee-high, stiletto-heeled boots and a straps-and-studs black leather fetish outfit that showed her gym-honed body off to maximum advantage.

Raw Pain Max prodded her slave with the toe of her boot, berating him in the traditional ways, earning laughs and claps from the audience, then she chained him upright between two poles so that his body formed an X. From now till performance's end, Phil's main job would be to appear to struggle and jerk on his chains without ruining the effect by demonstrating how flimsy the prop poles actually were.

Raw ripped away his rip-away clothes, leaving him all but naked in his black sequined G-string. As always, the moment of humiliation, even though fake, excited Phil. Knowing that Donna and Liz were watching made it more exciting than usual.

Raw's whip came down across his stomach. The rouge-coated lash left a streak of red on his flesh. The soft material only barely stung, but he convulsed as if in agony, groaned hoarsely, then began begging her to stop, which of course she did not do, several times.

The electronic music changed to a gear-grinding heavy metal rock number, in response to which RPM removed her cape and began a hip-thrusting, breast-shaking dance around her chained victim, using the whip on him again every eighth beat, then every fourth, then second, until he was crisscrossed front and back with rouge streaks.

Her dance ended as the music went back to sinister chanting-moaning beneath simulated thunder and howling wind.

She stroked his body, making him heave and moan in his chains for different reasons. Then she produced a fake knife with a hollow blade that discharged prop blood (washable) through the point. She used it to pretend-carve R-P-M on Phil's heaving chest. Crimson dribbles slid down his torso toward his G-string.

Raw leaned forward and pantomimed lapping up some of the blood with her tongue, then she suggestively moved the blade toward his G-stringed genitals, gave the audience a wink, and started to insert the blade beneath Phil's sequins just a moment before the lights went out and the music suddenly stopped. In the silence and darkness, Phil bellowed a long, tortured scream, Raw laughed maniacally, and the act was over.

The audience applauded. The lights came on. Phil and Trudy took a bow, then left the stage.

"You gave it a little extra tonight, it seemed to me," Trudy teased.

"You should talk. Those extra moves in your dance nearly made me pop my sequins."

Trudy laughed. "Thanks for noticing."

Ten minutes later, Phil led Trudy to the table where he had left Donna and Liz. They weren't there.

Phil asked about his two guests and was told they had left shortly after the Domitrix number ended. They had not left any message for him. And the doorman had seen them drive away in Phil's car.

In the parking lot, Phil found that his Trans Am was indeed gone.

"Jesus," he grumbled.

"Looks like we've both been jilted," Trudy offered. "Pretty shitty of them. Can't say I care if I meet them now or not."

"Don't blame Donna. Liz is into game playing. Fuck it. They stole my damned car!"

"Come on, Phil. I'll buy you a drink. Then after our last show you can hitch a ride with me."

"What is she, a hot-wiring expert? How'd she get my car started? I didn't give them my keys, dammit," he grumped, fishing in his pocket to prove it, but his keys weren't there. "Christ," he cursed. "So much for being nice to people. Fucking pickpockets." He grabbed for his wallet in his hip pocket, found it (with relief), jerked it out and checked the contents. His money and credit cards were still there. "I hope they have a wreck," he said, sticking his wallet back in his pocket.

"Not in *your* car, you don't."

Phil followed her back into the club, complaining and cussing every step of the way.

7

Bad News

The last show was over at 1:30 A.M. Phil washed off the washable blood and was ready to leave by 1:45. Trudy had already gone out front. He opened the dressing room door and came face to face with Elizabeth Smith.

"Going somewhere, Phil?"

"I . . . where the hell did you go? And who gave you permission to use my damned car? You're lucky I didn't call the cops on you and—"

She was laughing at him, but inside his head, without moving her grinning lips. Her lips hadn't moved when she'd spoken either, he suddenly realized, and now she didn't look as solid as she had. Her image was beginning to waver, becoming semi-transparent and moving slightly, up and down like a helium-filled balloon on a tether. Her feet were no longer quite touching the floor.

"I'm afraid I have some bad news, Phil," she spoke in his head again, her grinning lips still not moving. "I totaled your car. Your cousin tried to use her head to crack open the windshield when we crashed. The windshield won. She's dead. So am I. Just thought you'd like to know."

Blood began to squeeze out of her mouth between her grinning white teeth. Blood began trickling out of her eyes and nose and ears. Suddenly her forehead split open with a loud cracking sound. Cold blood and brains sprayed into Phil's face.

He gave a hoarse, strangled sob and jerked violently backward, hitting his head on the dressing room door.

The ghostly image blinked out and was gone, but her laughter echoed in his mind a few heartbeats longer before stopping.

He leaned back against the doorway for support. His heart jumped and jerked in his chest, his mind and body shock-stalled, head aching. Nausea welled.

A few minutes later, Trudy got tired of waiting and came back to hurry him up. She found him still leaning against the doorway, face pale, eyes glazed. "What the hell's wrong with you?" she asked as she reached him. "Sick or something? Marv's out front and wants to talk with us. God, you look awful. Phil? Hey, you're scaring me now. Phil?"

She gently took hold of his shoulders. He responded by looking at her. "I saw a fucking ghost," he whispered slowly, thickly, struggling to form the words. "Donna's friend, Liz. She said they were both dead, that they'd totaled my car. I have to call the police or something and report it. And—" He touched his face, then hesitated, looking puzzled. "I thought there was blood. Where's the blood? Trudy? Where's the damned blood?"

"Phil, come on. This is not a funny joke."

"This isn't one of my jokes. She turned transparent and floated above the floor. And her horrible grin, the way she laughed . . ." His voice trailed off, eyes glazing again.

"Snap out of it, Phil," she ordered, squeezing his arms. "You just had a dream or hallucinated or something. For Christ's sake, stop scaring me. Come on. I'll take you home and put you to bed. Can you walk or should I carry you?"

"You could, too," he said, rubbing his throbbing temples. "Carry me, I mean, like a damned baby. Fucking muscles. Wish I had some."

"Start working out with me. I've invited you often enough."

"Just get me home."

As they walked, Trudy watched Phil, ready to catch him if he started to go down. Marv, wearing a powder-blue polyester leisure suit from the 70s and a thick gold neck chain got down from his stool by the bar. "You found him," he noticed. Nobody stated the obvious better or quicker than Marv. He took a puff on a cigarette.

"Jesus, Marv," Trudy said, walking with Phil toward the bar, "Smoking again. You've got the will power of a lemming. If a two-pack-a-day smoker like me can stop, anyone can. Except, of course, maybe you."

"Don't get smart with me in my own club."

"What do you want, Marv?" Phil asked. "I just saw a fucking ghost and I feel like shit."

Marv frowned at him. "Always making with the jokes. Real comedian. To hell with it. I worked out a sweet deal with some people tonight to distribute the RPM video after they saw your midnight show. Told 'em to imagine the act realer and nakeder, then took them into my office and showed 'em a rough-cut slip. But they're movers and want delivery day after tomorrow."

"Marv," Trudy replied, "there's no way we can finish it that quickly."

"Just shut up, Trudy. I told them it was already finished."

"But it isn't!"

"It will be. I want the two of you at the studio by nine. These people aren't the kind who like being lied to. We've got to finish it quick and dirty."

"You mean quicker and dirtier, don't you, Marv?" Phil asked. His head was aching worse and worse.

"You should have asked us first," Trudy added. "Believe it or not, you don't own us."

"No? Let me put it this way, then. Either you two show up and work your respective asses off helping me get the video finished, or you and your paychecks are finished here at the club. Then you can both go back to being ordinary shits instead of semi-famous ones."

"Big fucking deal, Marv," Trudy responded. "I appreciate your giving me a job when no one else would, but if you're going to start playing dirty, so can I, because I don't *need* this gig," she lied. "I have a standing offer to join the staff at the gym where I work out."

"I bet the gym would have second thoughts about you if I showed them a few hot clips from your videos and mentioned your police record."

"Fuck that too. They know about my act here and the videos and my past. So don't threaten me with any of that crap."

"And maybe we've both had a gut-full of your sleazy

club, anyway," Phil added, head pounding with pain. "Maybe we should take our act to a *real* club. Maybe somewhere over on damned Greenville Avenue. Damn if my head's not ready to fucking explode," he groaned, rubbing his temples.

"Stop gawking and get Phil some aspirins, Rita," Trudy ordered a waitress who'd been enjoying the show instead of cleaning tables. "And bring a Coke with it. The caffeine will make the aspirins work faster."

"If you're done playing nurse, Trudy, I'm waiting for an answer," Marv said. "What's it gonna be? Nine o'clock? Or squat?"

Trudy took a deep breath. "I might consider it for an extra five hundred. Each. How about you, Phil?"

"Sounds about right," Phil nodded, "plus what I'd regularly earn at my clerking job. I'm docked a day's pay when I call in sick."

"Like hell I'll pay either one of you anything more."

"What's an extra thousand to you after the video starts bringing in the dough?" Trudy asked.

"It's one thousand dollars," Marv explained, grinning.

"Wrong. It's a finished video versus trouble with those people who don't like lying."

Marv thought about that, then said, "Three-fifty each. Or I'll tell those disappointed people whose skin they can take it out of."

"Christ, you're a cheap bastard," Trudy growled.

"Guess you're right. I hired you two cheap shits, didn't I? Well, is it yes or no?"

"Phil?" Trudy asked.

"Okay. Sure. Just get me home and make my head stop hurting."

"Thought you *liked* pain," Marv commented, grinning again.

Phil ignored him. Rita arrived with the aspirins and Coke. Phil took three and chased them with the Coke.

"Three-fifty each, then," Trudy grumbled. "See you at nine."

"On second thought, be there at eight."

"Don't hold your breath."

8

Sorceress

Outside the Safe Sex Club, the night lights of Dallas were reflecting pale orange from overhanging clouds. The air was muggy and not much cooler than it had been that afternoon.

"Damned Gulf air," Phil mumbled as he watched Trudy climb on her motorcycle. Then he climbed on behind. He put his arms around Trudy's trim-muscled waist. "Why can't the damned Gulf air stay in Houston where people *like* year-round saunas?"

Trudy kicked the engine to life. She headed for his house. Traffic was light at that time in the morning. The wind in his face made Phil begin to feel better. Ten minutes later, Trudy turned down the residential street leading to his house.

Phil's parents' home, and now his, was in a section of Dallas that had once been a lot ritzier. The money had since gone farther north. Much farther. But it was still a nice neighborhood and Phil's house, like the others up and down the tree-lined street, was aging gracefully.

Lights were on inside his house. His car, undamaged, was sitting in the drive.

"So much for your ghost," Trudy commented as she pulled to a stop beside his Trans Am.

"I don't know whether to laugh or cry," he replied. "What made me see what I saw? Am I cracking up? I think I'm kind of scared, Trudy."

"You aren't on anything, are you?"

"No way. Just the aspirins tonight. And just one beer between each act."

"How's the head? Still hurting?"

"Yeah. But not as bad. Come in with me, will you? Even if you don't want to meet them?"

"They'd better have a good explanation, leaving the club and upsetting you like that."

The front door was unlocked. Donna and Liz were in the living room on opposite ends of the sofa, watching an old movie on TV. Donna was still dressed as she had been at the airport. She sat with her hands in her lap, watching the TV, and did not turn around when they came in. Liz turned and raised a half-empty bottle of Corona Beer.

"Hi," Liz said. "Want a beer?"

On the coffee table in front of Liz were two empty Corona Beer bottles, a slice of squeezed lime inside each. Nearby on the table was an open bag of taco chips. Liz's black jump suit and high-heeled shoes lay on the floor. She was wearing only a skimpy black bra and micro panties.

"Having fun?" Phil asked. "Making yourselves at home? Find the fridge okay? Have fun driving my damned car too?"

"You sound pissed," Liz noted. "Aren't you just a little happy to find out we aren't dead?" she asked, then grinned the same grin Phil had seen her ghost use at the club.

"What the fuck are you talking about?"

"Short memory, Phil? I'm talking about telling you we totaled your car."

"I . . . you . . ."

Liz laughed at his expression. Donna just sat and stared at the TV as if no one else was there.

"I guess you have to know sooner or later," Liz said, taking a sip of beer. "I'm a sorceress in league with a demon. I can do all kinds of scary things, such as making people see things like you saw at the club. And lots more. Lots worse. But, hey, aren't you going to introduce me to the breathtakingly luscious Raw Pain Max? No? Hiyathere, Raw," Liz added, saluting Trudy with her beer. "Great abs. Great ass. Great *everything*. Yum."

"The name is *Trudy,* but I don't *want* any introduction to you, bitch. Phil's a friend of mine, and I don't like people scaring and hurting my friends. If you want me to throw her out, Phil, I'll be happy to oblige."

"Temper, temper," Liz scolded, standing up. "I might not be as easy to throw out as you think, Wonder Woman."

"Let's find out," Trudy said, and started forward.

"No damned fights in here allowed," Phil warned, "but I appreciate the offer, Trudy. She sure as hell has it coming."

Trudy returned to his side.

"Come on, Raw," Liz encouraged, beckoning with her hands. "Going to let your slave-wimp stop you?"

"Don't you ever call him that again. And if he says no fights in here, there'll be no fights. It's his house, his rules."

"My, my, what a speech."

"But," Trudy added, "if you don't mind getting the shit beat out of you in the back yard, I'll be more than happy to oblige."

"It's my back yard too," Phil added.

Liz laughed. "Who's the slave, Trudy? You or him?"

"Neither."

"Liar. I'll use my sorcery to send you a bad dream tonight if you don't tell me the truth."

"Boy am I scared. Look, bitch, I don't know how you tricked Phil at the club tonight, but I'm not falling for any of your mind-fucking I'm-a-sorceress shit, and neither is he. Right, Phil?"

"Damned right."

"Suit yourself," Liz shrugged. "For now. But don't say later I wasn't up front with you about my powers."

"Hear that, Phil? She's psycho. She's rotted her mind with drugs or something. I'm not going to leave you alone with her. Come to my place for the night, what's left of it. I won't get any rest for worrying about you if you don't. Then we can go straight to the studio in the morning."

It sounded like a good idea to Phil, and he started to agree. But then he saw Liz grinning at him again and he felt frightened again, but not just for himself. For Donna, too. He didn't want to leave his cousin alone with Liz anymore than Trudy wanted to leave him. His stubborn streak decided to show itself.

"I'm staying," he announced.

"Then I am too," Trudy replied without hesitation.

"No, Trudy. Really, you don't have to—"

"I'm staying."

He saw something in her eyes that said she was honestly

concerned about him. He made a face to conceal how it touched him.

"Donna," Phil said, "we'll be in the bedroom. I've changed my mind about letting you two have the bed. Sleep on the couch or floor or wherever. You don't seem to give a shit about how your friend is acting, so I don't give a shit where you sleep. But if you need help or anything, call and I'll come running. We're still family, even if your taste in friends need improving. Okay, Donna?"

Donna just kept watching TV, did not even look up at him.

"What the fuck's wrong with her, Liz?" he demanded. "What have you done to her?"

"Oh, it's *my* fault she's a zombie, is it?" Liz asked. "Well, as a matter of fact, it is," she added, then laughed. "You see, I tortured her to death, absorbed her blood, then brought her corpse back to life. Sorry if you liked her better before."

"Fuck that shit. Listen, if you hurt her in any way, I swear I'll find a way to make you sorry."

"I swear it too," Trudy added, "or if anything else bad happens to Phil."

"I love it when you're manly," Liz laughed, "*both* of you."

"I meant what I said," Phil insisted. "Short cowards like me can sometimes be a lot more dangerous than heroes. Guys like me don't always play by the rules because the rules have bitten us in the ass once too often."

"I don't believe in rules either, Phil," Liz replied, "but biting asses is another matter entirely."

"You can stay here tonight," he went on, "because of my cousin and because dawn's not that far away. But I want you out of here tomorrow. Donna, you're welcome to stay, though, if you wish, but without your so-called friend."

Donna didn't respond.

"Sleep tight, Phil," Liz said with seductive sweetness. "I'll make certain you dream about me. You too, Trudy," she said even sweeter, then slipped off her minimal black bra. "Either of you like what you see?" she asked, stretching her arms over her head. "Mmmm?"

"I'll dream about you all right," Trudy responded. "I'll dream about beating the shit out of you."

"Whatever turns you on, darling," Liz said, and slipped out of her minimal back panties too. "Where do you want to hit me most?" she asked, slowly putting her hand between her legs. "Just make a fist and show me, lover."

"You'd better get me out of here, Phil," Trudy urged, "or I'm going to change my mind about breaking your rules."

"Me too," Phil agreed, and headed for the bedroom.

Dreams in the Bitch House

On one wall in Phil's bedroom hung a Mötley Crüe poster. Another wall was decorated with a poster of the horror movie hostess Elvira. She was wearing a laced-up-the-side, black leather Domitrix outfit and holding a whip. Phil had stuck a small black and white bumper sticker onto the upper left corner of the poster that said, "Sticks and stones may break my bones, but whips and chains excite me."

"I still say we should have an RPM and Slave poster made," Phil mentioned. It was a subject they had discussed before. "Haven't changed your mind?"

"What do you think?"

"I still think it's a good idea to have a poster made. Especially with the video coming out and all. It would be—"

"Can we please not have this conversation again? Not tonight, anyway. Okay?"

"Okay. Sorry."

He started to get undressed. So did Trudy.

"You tired or anything?" he asked.

"No. How about your headache?"

"It's about gone."

"Good."

They took turns using the bathroom across the hall. Phil brought a condom with him when he returned to the bedroom.

"Forgive me for asking," Trudy said, "but can I assume you haven't caught AIDS or anything from anybody since our last time?"

"There hasn't been anybody since our last time. How about you, while we're playing twenty questions?"

"Me neither."

"Really?"

"Really."

Trudy pulled back the bedclothes and stretched out naked on her back. It was only a double bed. Her feet hung over the edge.

Phil put on his condom and then stretched out on top of Trudy.

Afterward, they slept, holding hands, and began to dream.

Phil dreamed he was at Marv's studio, chained between the chrome poles. Raw stripped off his shorts, leaving him naked. She kissed his lips and pushed her tongue into his mouth while she reached down and stroked him, making him grow hard. But when she pulled back, she had become Liz and had a knife that she proved was real by pushing the blade beneath one of Phil's toenails until blood oozed.

Liz licked blood from the blade and grinned at him. "Your blood's a bit flat," she told him. "Needs more pain." Then she used the knife on his chest, cutting her name deep before squatting and going to work on his testicles and penis, cutting him again and again, deeper and deeper, while she laughed and he screamed and screamed and . . .

He woke up bathed in sweat. He saw a shape in the bed beside him and jerked away, then remembered about Trudy. He was glad he hadn't awakened her. He glanced at his bedside clock. He'd only been asleep about an hour.

He got up and went across the hall to the bathroom. He heard the TV still going in the living room.

He used the commode, then splashed cold water on his sweaty face and looked at himself in the mirror.

"Liz told you to dream about her *and you did,* you shit," he whispered to his reflection. "Fucking great."

He went back to the bedroom.

His bedroom was filled with fog. Torchlight flickered orange within it. He inhaled smells of damp decay. Chains rattled. A whip cracked. A woman screamed. A woman laughed. Invisible hands jerked him inside and slammed the door closed behind him.

Phil's heart stuttered with shock and fear, then his mind compensated by telling him he must still be dreaming.

The fog thinned. His bedroom had become a torchlit dungeon. Trudy was hanging naked, suspended from a chain attached to wrist manacles. Liz, dressed in Trudy's RPM outfit was standing below her, holding a whip. Donna, naked beneath an open black cloak, watched blank-eyed nearby.

"Welcome to the Bitch House, Phil," Liz smiled.

Trudy's tanned and muscled skin already bore several whipmarks. Liz cracked the whip again, this time across Trudy's back, making the tip curl around so that it snapped against a breast. Trudy cried out her pain, then cursed Liz while swinging helplessly back and forth like a gigantic pendulum.

Liz offered Phil the whip, handle first. He shook his head no.

Liz's eyes glowed purple for a heartbeat, stabbing cold light into Phil's brain.

Robbed of his will, he could no longer refuse the offered whip. His hand closed on the handle.

Liz's eyes stabbed into his mind again.

He began using the whip on Trudy, kept trying to stop but couldn't, saying over and over how sorry he was as he continued whipping her, tears pouring down his cheeks while he struck her again and again and . . .

Trudy's sounds of pain changed, became nearer.

The scene wavered, reformed, was suddenly his bedroom again. He was standing with his back to the door. In bed, Trudy was writhing and moaning in her sleep.

Phil rushed to the bed and began trying to wake her up.

After several tries, he succeeded. Her cries and struggles stopped.

"It's okay now, Trudy," he soothed, stroking her sweaty hair.

"Phil? God. Liz was whipping me. Then you took the whip and started lashing me too."

"Uh . . . *I* was whipping you?"

"Yeah. But you kept moaning about how sorry you were all the time. It was just the kind of thing you'd do, monkey," she said, reaching up and taking hold of his hand.

"Trudy, look, I . . . had a dream too. Or an·hallucination. Or something. Just now. The same dream you just described. Can two people have the same dream at the same time?"

"Only on Elm Street."

"What? Oh. The Freddy and the dreamers films. I'm serious, dammit."

"Phil, you can't have had the same dream I had."

"I *know* that, Trudy. But I did. And before that I had a dream where Liz was cutting off my balls. Listen, I'm beginning to wonder if she isn't *really* a sorceress. Shit. Listen to me. I sound crazy. And scared. I *am* scared."

"Look, Phil. Don't let her mind games start getting to you down deep. If you want to believe something farfetched, let's think of a different explanation than the one she wants you to choose."

"Such as?"

Trudy thought for a moment. "Okay. How about telepathy? Some scientists who've done tests even believe in it. You told me so yourself after you read that book on it, remember?"

"So?"

"Well, maybe I was dreaming and you picked up my thoughts and hallucinated my dream or something. That's a better explanation that Liz's sorcery, isn't it?"

"But she *told* you to dream about her, and you did."

"That doesn't prove shit."

"But I dreamed about her in a different·dream before I entered yours, or whatever happened."

"That doesn't prove shit either."

He was silent a moment. "You hungry? I am," he finally said, hoping down-to-earth food might help restore equilibrium.

"Eat if you want to. I'm not hungry."

"There's some ice cream in the freezer, if Liz hasn't eaten it, that is. I'll get it and bring it back to bed."

He slipped on his jeans and headed to the kitchen. The TV was still on in the living room. But Donna and Liz were no longer on the sofa.

He went into the kitchen, telling himself he didn't care where they were or what they were doing, but with his hand on the fridge's handle curiosity got the best of him and he started looking for them, careful to be as quiet as he could.

When he finished looking, he cursed his way back to the bedroom, forgetting his ice cream.

"They're fucking gone," he told Trudy back in the bedroom. "So's my car. I didn't get back my keys. Don't I just take the cake for the stupidest bastard to ever—"

"I was just getting back to sleep," Trudy interrupted. "I'm sorry about your car, but I don't want to hear you piss and moan about it anymore right now. Okay?"

"Hey. You forgetting whose bed you're sleeping in?"

"You forget that I can get on my Harley and vanish into the night?"

"Shit," he said after hesitating. "Okay. I'm sorry for losing my temper. It's just that—"

"Come back to bed," she said. "I'm sorry I got mad too."

In the morning Liz and Donna and his car had still not returned.

Trudy and Phil shared a hot shower and ate a bowl of cereal each. Phil called in sick at his convenience store job. Then they went to Marv's studio and became RPM and Slave for a very long and exhausting day.

Not until after eight-thirty that night did Marv finally decide he could cut a complete video from the tape he'd shot. Trudy took Phil to the club. They did their shows. Then she took him home.

His car was still not back, and the mess in the living room was just as Liz and Donna had left it the night before.

"I'm worried about Donna, Trudy. I've been thinking about all this, and I think I should call the police."

"And what? Report your cousin missing? Or your car stolen?"

"Yeah. Both. What else can I do?"

"Phil, I can see your calling the police about your car, but not about your cousin. She probably hasn't been gone long enough for the police to be interested, anyway. And if the police pick Liz and her up for car theft, Donna will be arrested the same as Liz. Is that what you want?"

"Shit, no. I'm not even thinking clearly anymore."

"Didn't you mention that Liz was going to visit someone here in Dallas?"

"Yeah."

"Well, then, they must be there, right?"

"I'm still worried about Donna."

"God. Next you'll be wanting to call her parents."

"Might not be a bad idea."

"I never dreamed there was a mother-hen side to you. I think it's kind of sweet."

"Thanks. Sweet's what I always wanted to be."

"Bad word. How about endearing, then?"

"Much better. I'm going to clean up this mess."

"I'll help. Gonna call the police?"

"Guess not. You're right. They're off visiting that other friend of Liz's. Better they make her miserable than us and eat her food and drink her beer instead of mine."

"That's the spirit."

"I just hope Donna's okay."

"Look, Phil," Trudy said as she helped him clear the mess, "I want you to come home with me tonight. Okay? I don't want you here alone if they come back, and my bed's bigger than yours. My feet won't be hanging over the edge all night."

He laughed. "Deal."

They finished cleaning up the living room, then Phil put on a clean black t-shirt with "Z-ROCK Militia" on the front (and the Z-ROCK DJs' signatures on the back), a clean pair of jeans, and his scuffed cowboy boots. Then he threw some things from the bathroom, including a couple of condoms, into a zippered plastic overnight bag, and was ready to go to Trudy's.

10

Holly

The house Trudy was currently renting, off Plano Road south of the LBJ Freeway, had a living room with a fireplace, in front of which was a sprawling sofa.

Beneath one of the living room's windows stood a small K-Mart special bookcase. Placed on top of it to get light from the window were several potted plants. Elsewhere in the bookcase were books on bodybuilding with names on the spines like Schwarzenegger, Everson, McLish, and Ferrigno. There were also separate stacks of magazines such as FEMALE BODYBUILDING, MUSCLE AND FITNESS, IRONMAN, MUSCLEMAG, and WOMEN'S PHYSIQUE WORLD.

One corner of the living room held a Joe Weider "Master Blaster" weightlifter's bench. On the floor next to it was an impressive collection of chrome bars and black cast-iron free-weights. A framed poster of the reigning Ms. Olympia, Corinna Everson, hung on the wall over the weight bench.

"Staring at Cory again?" Trudy asked. "Trying to make me jealous?"

"How many times did you say she's won Ms. Olympia?"

"Four. I read an article recently that said she may be the greatest female athlete of all time."

"Guess she can have my vote."

"Mine too. Hungry? Sandwich?"

"Sure."

"Turkey pastrami on eight-grain okay?" she asked, heading for the kitchen.

"You and your funny food. *Turkey* pastrami?"

"Laugh all you want. Less fat in it than regular pastrami.

And I have unsalted potato chips cooked in peanut oil to go with it."

"Got any non-fat beer to wash it all down?"

"Phil, you know I'm an alcoholic and don't buy beer."

"Damn my mouth. Sorry. Really, I—"

"You're forgiven. How about some all natural fruit juice? It's really good. Mix it with Perrier and it even fizzes."

"Sounds fine."

He mixed them each a fruit juice fizzy while she made sandwiches, then they took the food and drinks into the living room and sat down on the sofa. There was a small Unitech radio/cassette stereo combination on an end table near the sofa. Trudy switched the radio on. Like Phil's car radio, it was set to Z-ROCK, but with less volume. A band called L.A. Guns was singing the "The Bitch is Back." Then Faster Pussycat began a tune.

They talked and ate while various Metal bands came and went, then they stacked the dishes in her dishwasher and headed to her bedroom. The first time Phil had seen it he had been a little disappointed. There was no black leather in sight, nor a whip nor a chain.

The bedroom walls were painted off-white. The bedspread was forest green. So were the sheets. Trudy had bought them to match the worn green carpet after she'd moved in.

They got undressed, Phil put on his condom, they made love, and went to sleep. The sound of a car pulling into Trudy's driveway woke them around 3:30 A.M.

"You awake?" Trudy whispered.

"Yeah. Sounds like my Trans Am."

"I'll take a look," she said and reached for her bath robe and a baseball bat she kept beside the bed. "If you were thinking of turning on a light, don't."

"I'll go with you," he decided, feeling for his jeans on the floor.

"You tell Donna and Liz where I lived?"

"No way. But you're in the phone book, and in my address book at home if they looked there."

As they crept through the living room toward the front door, the living room lights suddenly came on. Liz stood smiling at them by the door, which was ajar.

"Christ!" Phil exclaimed, jumping a step back as Trudy reflexively lowered her six-two frame into a fighting crouch and raised the baseball bat.

Liz laughed at them both and leaned back against the wall near the light switch, arms crossed on her chest. She was again wearing her black, zippered, military-look jumpsuit. "Gotcha," she said, grinning at them.

Trudy lowered the bat and Phil pulled himself together. "Where's Donna?" he demanded.

"Donna who?"

"Still playing games, bitch?" Trudy growled. "Well, not *here* you're not. This is *my* home, my rules. I can beat the shit out of you here and Phil can't stop me."

"You're welcome to try."

"How'd you get inside my house without a key? There's a deadbolt on that front door. Or rather, more important, how fast do you think you can get back outside again? Because that's where I want you. Outside and away from my home. Now!"

"Trudy, please," Phil said, "let's find out about my cousin first. Where is she, Liz?"

"Outside, with Holly."

"Holly? The friend you wanted to see in Dallas?" he asked.

"No. Just someone we picked up at a supermarket for a few kicks. We thought we'd have them, and her, here. I'm going to make you join the fun. Kind of an initiation."

"This is my lucky day," Trudy said. "Thank you, God, for making her think she's going to stay, so I can finally get my wish and beat her to a fucking pulp." Trudy threateningly raised the bat and started forward.

Liz spoke several tongue-twisting guttural words in some foreign language. As she spoke the words, her breath emerged as a glowing purple mist. The glow shot laser-straight toward Trudy, momentarily engulfed her head, vanished into her skull.

Trudy staggered, managed to take one more step, then stopped. Her grip on the bat began to relax. She fought to keep her hold, sweat breaking out on her forehead, muscles trembling. The bat fell to the floor. She could no longer move. When she tried to talk she discovered that the paralysis extended to her voice, too.

"What the hell?" Phil asked, "Trudy?" Trudy still didn't move, but the agonized and trapped look in her eyes made Phil feel sick, and scared. "Whatever tricks you're playing now, Liz, let Trudy go. I mean it."

"Or what? *You'll* pick up the baseball bat and attack me?" she laughed.

"Yes. Yes, I will." He reached down for the bat.

Liz mumbled something else. Purple mist engulfed and sank into the baseball bat, which then leaped into the air and shot sideways, struck the framed poster of Ms. Olympia, and shattered the glass.

"You fucking bitch!" he cursed, terrified. But he was angry too, and his temper took control. He ran toward Liz, reaching out to grab her arms, intending to turn her around and push her out the door.

Liz waited for him to reach her, then casually gripped his shoulders with her slim-fingered hands. Pain shot through him as what felt like steel vises clamped his shoulders.

She grinned at him as she effortlessly increased the pressure, forcing him inch by painful inch down onto his knees while he cursed and clawed desperately at her gripping hands. "Making pacts with demons makes you stronger than you look," she explained as she kept pushing him lower, still increasing the crushing pressure.

"God . . . damn you! Stop it!" he managed through clenched teeth as his knees touched the floor. "You're breaking . . . Aaah! . . . my . . . shoulders!"

She gave him a final shove that sent him sprawling onto his back at her feet.

"Just . . . who the hell *are* you?" he panted, rubbing his shoulders as he stared up at her from the floor.

"A sorceress, for starters, like I already told you."

Phil struggled to a sitting position, dizzy with the pain in his shoulders.

Liz went outside. Phil staggered to his feet. "Trudy?" he said, touching her arm. "Come on, Trudy. Shake it off! I'm no match for her, but with your muscles..." His voice trailed away. He was wasting time. He should have been locking the front door.

Cursing at himself, he hurried toward the door. Liz came back in before he got there. She was carrying an unconscious woman in her arms. The woman had blond hair and was wearing a pair of tight black shorts, a tight pink t-shirt, and sandals. Donna walked in behind Liz.

"Lock the door, Donna," Liz ordered, and Donna did.

"Trudy, Phil," Liz said, holding the unconscious woman as if she weighed no more than a baby, "meet Holly. Holly, meet Trudy and Phil, who are now going to strip naked. Ladies first, Trudy, even if maybe you aren't one."

Trudy obediently removed her bathrobe and stood naked, looking straight ahead, her eyes anguished.

"Oh good Christ in a thicket, what the shit's going on?" Phil said, mostly to himself, very seriously scared.

"Your turn, Phil. Strip."

"No fucking way."

Liz spoke more guttural words. He saw the purple mist emerge from her mouth and head toward him. He cursed and tried to dodge it. Like a heat-seeking missile, it followed and engulfed his head. A frightening coldness spread outward from his solar plexus, freezing his muscles, and an instant later he was horrified to find that the only movements he could make were to move his eyes and to breathe. He tried to speak but could not.

"Strip, Phil," Liz ordered, grinning. "Let's see what you've got."

Against his will, Phil's hands unbuttoned and unzipped his jeans. They dropped around his ankles.

"Mmmm," Liz commented. "No underwear? Well, you're not bad, I guess, though I've seen better. Kick away your jeans, Phil. You won't be needing them for a while."

Phil kicked away his jeans.

"And now, Trudy, since it's your house, lead us all to your playroom," Liz ordered.

Trudy turned around and headed down the hall.

11

Once Upon a Time

"Follow her, Phil," Liz commanded, still effortlessly holding the unconscious woman in her arms.

His body no longer his to control, Phil followed Trudy down the hall, Liz and Donna following him. When Trudy reached her playroom door, she stopped as if awaiting further orders.

"Open it," Liz ordered.

Trudy tried, but as always it was locked. Trudy kept turning the knob, trying again and again to open it.

Liz spoke a guttural phrase. Glowing mist from her mouth drifted to the lock and soaked into the metal. The next time Trudy turned the knob, the door opened.

"Go inside, Trudy. You too, Phil."

Trudy and Phil obeyed.

"Turn on the light, Donna," Liz said when they were inside the playroom too.

Donna found the switch by the door and flipped it on.

"The red light's a nice touch, Trudy," Liz commented. "Crimson's my favorite color. Yours too?"

Liz carried the unconscious woman to Trudy's bondage frame. Phil suddenly wondered how Liz had known about Trudy's playroom in the first place. But then, he reasoned, if she could do what he had seen her do, she could probably read minds too, which made his terror of her grow even worse.

"Come here Phil, and you too, Donna. Strap Holly to the frame. Tightly. Remove her sandals first."

Phil and Donna obeyed.

The young woman soon lay strapped to the slanting

wooden X, forming an X herself. She was about Phil's age and, he noticed, very attractive.

"Okay," Liz said when Holly had been securely strapped to the wooden X. "Stand there by the frame with Donna, Phil. And both of you stay that way."

Liz turned to Trudy. "Sit down on the floor, Trudy," she said, her voice suddenly changing, becoming softer.

Trudy sat down.

Liz sat down facing her, then began speaking a tongue-twisting phrase in the guttural language over and over, chanting it again and again and again. There was no glowing mist emerging this time, but nonetheless Trudy suddenly felt her mind emptying, her concentration narrowing, focusing upon Liz's voice. She fought it, tried to think about something else, *anything* else. But nothing worked. Her world, her universe, soon became the sound of Liz's voice.

Liz stopped chanting. "Once upon a time, Trudy," she said speaking low and slow, "There was a beautiful woman named Erzebet. Like most women, she did not want to grow old and lose her beauty.

"Erzebet lived nearly four hundred years ago, in Hungary. She was an aristocrat, a Countess, and had much worldly power, but she wanted more. She lusted for occult power too, and eternal life, unending youth, beauty.

"She experimented with the occult, but without significant success until she acquired the help of a woman from a place called Sarvar.

"The woman's name was Darvulia. She was a sorceress in league with a demon. She taught Erzebet many things. They became lovers.

"The nobility in Erzebet's day could do almost anything they pleased with their peasant subjects. If a peasant servant in their employ died, no one in power cared too much. And many servants did die in Erzebet's service, hundreds of them, all young women, most of them virgins, because Erzebet killed them, by torture.

"Darvulia taught Erzebet more than just the arcane arts of demonic sorcery. She also taught her new tortures and how pain and fear could be used to enhance the magic in a virgin's blood, because human pain and human fear fed the demon who made the magic work.

"Darvulia's ritual of pain-enriched blood allowed Erzebet to fight her fear of aging with her love of torture. It gave a reason beyond pure pleasure for her killings. It gave new meaning to her life, new purpose.

"Erzebet and Darvulia were together nine years. Then, sadly, Darvulia, who was older than Erzebet, sickened and died. Neither her sorcery nor Erzebet's could save her.

"But almost no one dies forever. Souls are not usually wasted on a one-time-only affair. Most come back, sooner or later, in different bodies. And so it is with Erzebet and with Darvulia. Now, finally, all these years later, in a city and nation that did not even exist when Erzebet and Darvulia last kissed, we have at long last been reunited."

Liz leaned forward, tears suddenly misting her eyes, and gently, lovingly kissed Trudy's lips. "Darvulia, my love," Liz whispered.

She kissed Trudy again, then drew back.

"You don't believe me, of course. But soon you will, after I have helped you remember our life together."

Liz took hold of Trudy's hands. "I know it's not going to be easy for you at first, darling, but I promise to help all I can, starting right now. Just try to relax and trust me a little."

"Do now what I say. Descend into the depths of your mind. Go deeper and deeper until you awaken memories of other places and lives and times. Journey beyond your memories of this life and find the life where you knew me as Erzebet Bathory. *Obey!*"

All the time Liz had been talking, Trudy had been struggling to break her hold, but without success. She couldn't get free, still could not move or speak. Now she felt herself beginning to do what Liz had ordered, sinking deeper and deeper into her memories.

She began to relive moments from her childhood, experiencing them as if they were actually happening again, except in reverse.

Her rememberings accelerated, passed her babyhood, and emerged into the chasm of black nothingness of the time before her birth. But the horrible empty darkness lasted only a moment, then *other* memories began, the thoughts and feelings of an old woman lying alone in a dirty bed, knowing she was dying and terrified of doing so. But somewhere she was also still Trudy McAllen, an observer who had now begun to scream, soundlessly, helplessly, impotently.

The old woman's memories grew younger. And younger. Until suddenly Trudy hurtled into another pre-birth chasm and then began experiencing another life in reverse.

The cycle repeated itself again and again while she kept struggling and screaming in helpless horror. Then her descent into the terror of her former lives slowed, stopped.

She was in bed, naked, with another naked woman. They were making love. Moonlight flooded through tall windows. A small lamp glowed cozily upon the highly polished surface of an ornately carved bedside table.

The scene changed. She and her lover were in a torchlit chamber. There were no windows. She knew the chamber was underground. A place of torture and dark passions fulfilled.

The stone walls were damp and cold. Chained to one of the walls, her arms stretched above her head, was a naked young woman.

Her lover gave her a whip with a metal barb attached to the tip. She raised the whip and lashed the naked captive, making her scream. She whipped her several times more until her flesh was streaked with blood, then she gave the whip to her lover.

They kept whipping the young woman, taking turns, tearing their victim's flesh, slowly killing her, making mocking jokes and laughing at her screams . . .

"Wake up, Darvulia," Liz ordered. "That's enough for now."

The torture scene faded and was gone. Trudy's head was aching and throbbing.

"Open your eyes, darling."

Trudy opened her eyes.

"Now that you have remembered, you will begin to adjust to the truth. But it will be better for you if, for the moment, I do not return your free will.

"I have, however, arranged this evening's entertainment to speed your acceptance of the truth. When you help me torture the young woman strapped to the X, the memories I have raised in you will take root and solidify even as her pain feeds my demon and strengthens me. Then, later, you and I shall make love, our bodies erotically crimsoned by our victim's pain-enriched blood, our souls soaring into realms of blood-passions beyond the ecstasies of the flesh, into the realm of the demon to whom you introduced me so very long ago."

Liz kissed Trudy's lips again. "My love, my love. How my soul has longed for this moment. And soon now, you will discover that yours has too."

12

Mouse Trap Kiss

"Stand up, Darvulia," Liz said, offering Trudy her hand. Trudy got to her feet. "Go to the bondage frame and stand there with Phil and Donna until I get back. I won't be long."

As Trudy walked to stand with Phil and Donna, Liz left the room. Trudy tried and tried to get free of Liz's control. Beside her, Phil was doing the same. Donna stood staring blankly. Holly remained unconscious on the X.

When Liz came back several minutes later, she was carrying some ominous additions to Trudy's toy collection.

On the top shelf of the utility table next to Trudy's clothes pins and spring clips, Liz placed a butcher knife, a meat cleaver, a pin cushion bristling with needles, a pair of pliers, and a mousetrap.

"Just giving us a few *serious* choices," she commented. "Pick up the butcher knife, Darvulia."

Against her will, Trudy's hand reached out and picked up the knife.

"Now, lift the knife."

Sweat streamed from Trudy's face as her arm lifted the knife.

Liz touched the blond-haired woman's forehead.

Holly's eyes opened and slowly focused on the scene. Confusion turned to fear. She pulled on the straps as she looked at the strangers grouped around her in the crimson-lighted room. Her gaze came to rest on the naked giant of a muscled woman holding a butcher knife. The scene suddenly seemed ludicrous. A joke. It *had* to be a joke. Her fear evolved into anger.

"Now, Darvulia, use the knife on her . . . clothing. Make her naked."

Holly looked at the woman in the black jumpsuit who had spoken. Then she looked back at Trudy. "Don't you *dare*. The joke is over. I'm not laughing. Let me go."

"Would you rather she use the blade on your skin?"

"Didn't you hear me? I said the joke was over."

"Proceed, Darvulia. Strip her. Cut off the t-shirt first. After that, the shorts, and any underwear you find."

"Don't you dare hurt my clothes!" Holly protested. "You've all had a good laugh at my expense. Don't push your luck. Let me go right now and I'll buy you all a drink somewhere. Who put you up to this, anyway? Was it Brian's idea? Geoff's? Ray's? Or maybe—"

Trudy's hands shook with her effort to stop what she was doing as she got a fist-full of Holly's pink t-shirt and began slicing with the knife.

"I told you *no!*" Holly shouted angrily.

Trudy kept slicing and Holly kept protesting.

"Goddamn you to hell! Stop it! You've ruined my shirt!"

"So?" Liz commented as Trudy kept cutting. "You won't be needing it, or any shirt, anymore."

"Very funny. But the joke *is* over, folks. So just fucking *stop* and undo these straps. Okay?"

Trudy finished cutting off her t-shirt, then unbuttoned her tight black shorts and started slicing at them.

"Not my shorts too! Please, stop it, *now!*"

Trudy kept cutting.

Soon, despite her continuing protests and ever more angry

curses, Holly wore nothing but a thin white bra and matching bikini panties.

Trudy reached for the bra.

"Please! Don't!" she cried as Trudy cut the bra apart in the
center, baring Holly's breasts, then reached for one of the
straps. Holly's anger was devolving back into fear.

Trudy finished with the bra, tossed it away, and reached
for Holly's panties.

Holly arched against the straps, tried to twist away from
Trudy. "Please!" she pleaded, looking at Liz. "Stop her!"

"Not a chance," Liz replied as Trudy slid the blade beneath the narrow elastic waistband stretched over Holly's left
hip.

"I'll get you money!"

"I don't want money," Liz answered.

Trudy sliced on the left side.

"A natural blond, it seems," Liz noted, leaning closer.

Holly moaned low in her throat and jerked wildly on the
straps. "Please, tell me what I can do to stop you! If this is a
joke, it's going much too far! I'm talking *police* now, understand? I won't have any choice but to tell them about all of
this if you don't let me go right now!"

Trudy finished the job, then tossed the pair of ex-panties
to the floor atop the scrap-pile that had been Holly's clothing.

"Oh God!" Holly sobbed. A shudder ran through her
body. "Damn you all! Damn you! Damn—"

"Take a look," Liz interrupted, stepping aside and motioning to the mirror on the back of the door opposite the
slanting bondage frame. "You're a pretty sight, but rather
immodest, don't you think?"

Holly looked. In the mirror she saw a woman strapped
naked, legs spread wide. She shook her head from side to
side in denial, then lay back and closed her eyes, panting
softly with rising panic. Feelings of nightmarish helplessness
grew steadily stronger, until suddenly they became unendurable.

Mindless panic exploded into violent activity as she began
to frantically jerk on the thick leather straps that held her a
prisoner, her body twisting and arching and straining in its

bonds, her eyes now wide open and filled with a blind, unreasoning desperation, panted groans her only sounds as she struggled in vain to escape the nightmare.

Liz clapped her hands, applauding the show. "Give her a hand!" Liz ordered the others. They began to clap too.

The mocking applause penetrated Holly's panicked mind. She lay back against the frame, panting, sweat glistening on her bare skin. "Someone please help me!" she cried, eyes going from one to the other. "The joke's over!"

"*I'll* help you," Liz promised. "I'll help you feel better *fast*."

Liz touched Holly's breasts, began to play with her nipples.

"Don't do that!"

"You're becoming a broken record, slut," Liz said, ran her hands slowly down over Holly's hips, softly stroked Holly's inner thighs, then reached between Holly's legs.

"Don't you dare touch me there!"

Liz stopped long enough to give Holly's face a stinging slap. "I'll touch you wherever I want," she announced, and did.

"No! Please! Stop!"

Liz again slapped her, then again reached down low. "In a little while you'll be begging me to give you this kind of pleasure, instead of pain."

"Please, just . . . ah! . . . wait a minute. Listen to me. You don't . . . need to hurt me. I'll do . . . whatever you say!"

"You obviously have no conception of what I *need*," Liz noted, "yet." She gave each of Holly's nipples a viciously hard pinch, grinned at Holly's gasps, then stepped back. "Think that hurt? That was nothing. For example, have you ever had a mouse trap snap closed on one of your tits? Hand me the mouse trap, Darvulia."

Trudy handed her the mouse trap. Liz held it up for Holly to examine. "Hold this between your teeth a moment, will you?"

"I'm not going to put that filthy thing in my mouth!"

"Either you do, or I'm going to let it snap shut on your left tit. Your decision."

"You're joking."

"Think so?" Liz set the trap, then tapped it against the side of the frame near Holly's face. The jarring vibration jiggled loose the catch and it snapped loudly closed. Holly gave a small cry and winced.

"Well? What's it going to be?" Liz asked. She set the trap again and then moved it toward Holly's left nipple.

"You crazy bitch! All right? I'll do it," Holly promised, then made herself open her mouth.

Liz tapped the trap to set it off again, then after it had snapped closed she placed it between Holly's teeth.

"Hand me the whip, Darvulia."

Trudy obeyed.

Holly eyed the whip with horror as Liz trailed its triple thongs over her bare breasts.

"Ever been whipped?" Liz asked.

Holly opened her mouth to answer. The mouse trap clattered to the floor. "Don't you *dare* hit me with that whip!"

"You dropped the fucking trap!" Liz exploded. "I did *not* give you permission to let go of the trap." She picked it up. "Stick out your tongue. *Now!* Or your tit gets a mouse trap kiss."

Holly sobbed with frustration, then slowly stuck out her tongue. Liz raised the trap's bar and then let it down, gently, upon the outstretched tongue. "There, now you won't be dropping it again. And don't you look cute, too. But something's missing. What could it be?"

Holly fought the straps. Drool came from the corners of her half-open mouth.

"Hand me two clothes pins, Darvulia, darling."

Liz attached a wooden clothes pin to each of Holly's nipples.

Holly groaned, jerking helplessly on the straps as she craned up her head to see her aching, bizarrely adorned breasts.

"The interesting thing is," Liz noted, removing one of the pins, "that the farther toward the tip of the nipple a clothes pin is placed, the more it hurts. Here, I'll demonstrate the effect for you." She attached the pin to the very tip of Holly's nipple, earning louder, more frantic groans and wilder gyrations, then did the same with the other pin, and stepped back to admire her work. The clothes pins bobbed and swayed as Holly panted with her pain.

"But there's *still* something missing," Liz decided. "Two of the spring clamps, Darvulia, if you please."

Trudy obeyed.

Liz squeezed open one of the clips and bent forward.

Holly mouthed garbled pleadings around the obstructing mouse trap as she fought the straps and tried desperately to close her spread legs.

Liz attached the first clip. Then she attached the other.

"Now, just one more clothes pin, Darvulia, and she'll be properly attired."

Trudy gave her the clothes pin.

"Can you guess where this one's going to go?" she asked Holly. "On your nose?" she suggested, opening and closing the wooden jaws near Holly's face. "No? Well, then," she said stooping low and manipulating the clothes pin into place between the two spring clips, "I guess you must want it *here!*" she finished, emphasizing the point by letting the wooden jaws press closed.

And, finally, Holly threw back her head and screamed.

13

Cleaver

Holly's mouse trap-distorted scream devolved into sobs. She saw her reflection in the mirror, closed her eyes, screamed again.

"You didn't answer my question, slut," Liz noted. "Have you ever been whipped? Better answer. Quickly." She dangled the thong between Holly's spread thighs, then tapped on the lower clothes pin with the whip's handle. "Answer me, or I'll find uses for all those other clothes pins and clips on the table. Have you or have you not ever been whipped?"

Tears streaking her face, Holly tried to answer, but the mouse trap on her tongue turned her speech into humiliating baby talk, so she stopped trying to talk and just shook her head no instead.

"Then how do you know you won't enjoy it?"

Liz removed the spring clips and clothes pins and mouse trap. "There now, that wasn't so bad, was it?"

"Please," Holly sobbed, "you've had your fun. Okay? So, if you let me go, now, I won't go to the police. I won't say anything to *anybody*. I promise!"

"That's very thoughtful of you. I'm *sooo* grateful. Here's a little token of my appreciation," Liz purred huskily, then slashed the whip's triple thongs across Holly's breasts.

Holly screamed and arched upward against the straps, red welts appearing across her breasts. "Don't hurt me anymore, please! I've never done anything to you. Why do you want to hurt me?"

"Because you don't want me to."

"You're sick! You don't realize what you're doing! If you keep making me scream, someone will hear me, and then—"

Lip whipped Holly's breasts again. When a new scream had died away, Liz said, "I'm a sorceress. No one's going to hear anything I don't want them to hear."

Liz lashed Holly's belly. "What's your name, slut?" she asked when another scream had turned into sobbing.

"My name is Holly."

"Don't lie to me. That's not your real name, and everyone here knows it."

"What?"

"You heard me. You must *want* to be punished. Is that why you lied?"

"I didn't!"

"I say you did. Your name is not Holly. I'll prove it to you." She brought the thong down in a stinging slice across Holly's right thigh. Holly gasped and writhed.

"Tell us your real name."

"It's Holly!"

Another slice, this one to the left thigh.

"My name is Holly! I swear!"

This time Liz used an uppercut between Holly's legs. When Holly stopped screaming and jerking on her straps, she turned tear-filled but enraged eyes on Liz. The pain was bringing back her anger. "God damn you! Don't you *ever* do that to me again, or I swear that I'll—"

Liz did it again, harder, twice more, then waited until Holly stopped hollering before she said, "Now, slut, tell us your real name."

"What . . . do you want me to say?"

"Just your name."

"I don't understand!"

Liz whipped Holly's breasts again. "That help your understanding any?"

"Tell me what to say!"

"Your real name," Liz answered, after giving Holly's belly another stroke.

"What do you think my name is?! Whatever it is, tell me and I'll say it! I'll say it!"

"It's not what I *think* it is, is it?" Liz asked, then used another uppercut between Holly's legs.

Holly screamed, struggled, then groaned out, "What *is* my name? Please!"

"Well, well. You're beginning to learn. Okay. Since you asked, your name is Shit. That's right, isn't it?"

"Whatever you . . . say."

"*You* say it. Tell me your name."

"My name is . . . Shit," Holly whispered.

"Louder!" Liz ordered, and gave Holly's belly another slice.

"My name is Shit!"

Liz laughed and laughed.

"What a horrible name. But I guess it kind of suits you. I've seen better bodies at fat farms."

"I'm not fat!"

"Wanna bet?" Liz asked, and raised the whip.

"All right! I'm fat!"

"And ugly?"

"Yes! I'm ugly too."

"There you go, lying to me again. You're neither fat nor ugly. I've seen better. But you're not half bad. At the moment. You won't be much to look at when we finish with you, however, all mutilated and bloody."

"Oh, please, please, no . . ." Holly sobbed, voice breaking. She started to say more, then stopped herself. The woman was insane. Maybe they all were. Images from slasher films her younger brother had rented from a video store began to haunt her. Any remaining anger was swallowed by her returning fear. Her eyes went back to the knife in the naked woman's hand.

"Now, Shit, here's what we're going to do. We're going to let you go."

Holly's expression changed. It *had* been a joke? Relief flooded through her. Liz laughed.

"That's right, Shit. We're going to set you free. But first, we're going to torture you—"

"No, please—"

"We'll whip you some more, especially your breasts and vagina, then introduce you to some megapain. Raw pain, to the max, so to speak, right Darvulia?" Liz asked, glancing at Trudy.

Holly sobbed and jerked on the straps.

"I think we'll start after the whipping by heating needles and sticking them into your tits—"

"Oh, God, *please!*—"

"Then we'll see if you like being burned by hot candle wax and cigarettes outside your body more then being scalded by boiling water outside, and in."

"I'll do *anything*—"

"After that we'll break your fingers and toes, then chop them off with a meat cleaver, use a razor on your pretty face—"

"Oh, God! Someone help me!"

"Then we'll slice and dice your breasts and cook the pieces and make you eat them, before we do some surprise things that you'll like even less, until you beg us to let you die."

"There must be *something* I can do! Please, tell me what it is and I'll do it!"

"And then we'll set you free, after we've drained away what's left of your blood into a bathtub, so that Darvulia and

I can share blood-passions. Of course you'll be dead by
then, but I *will* set you free later on. Free to be my slave,
like Donna there. And like Phil will eventually be, too. You
seem, my demon gives me the power to heal death-wounds
and to bring corpses back to something resembling life.
Sound like fun to you? It does to me. Ready to get started?"

"Please," Holly pleaded, sobbing. "I'll get money for
you."

"But, Shit, dear, all I want is your screams, and then your
blood. Speaking of which, come over here, Darvulia. It's
time you had some fun."

Trudy immediately stepped to the frame.

"I want to taste-test Shit's blood, Darvulia. Make a foun-
tain for me. Bite off Shit's left nipple, then chew it up and
swallow it like you used to enjoy doing. Phil, Donna, help
hold Shit steady for Darvulia. Put the knife down first, Darvulia."

Trudy put the knife back on the utility table while Phil and
Donna held Holly tightly against the frame.

"Go ahead, Darvulia, darling," Liz smiled. "Do it."

Trudy obediently leaned down toward Holly's left breast.

"No!" Holly cried, writhing against the restraining hands
and straps.

"Oh, very well," Liz shrugged. "Shit doesn't want you to
bite off her left nipple, Darvulia. Bite off her right one,
instead."

Holly kept begging as Trudy leaned toward her right
breast.

Trudy fought it, tried with all her strength of will to pull
away. But instead, her mouth opened as she leaned even
nearer.

Her lips touched Holly's warm flesh. Her teeth touched
the nipple, began to clamp shut.

Holly's screams were constant as the pain got worse and
worse.

Trudy's eyes were closed, brows drawn together in a
pained frown as she kept fighting to stop what she was
doing. Then her teeth broke Holly's skin and she tasted
Holly's blood.

As if triggered by the taste of Holly's blood, a flash of

purple light exploded somewhere behind Trudy's eyes, and suddenly there were memories inside her mind, memories that sent a shock of terror through her. And then the memories focused into an invading presence. And the presence took control.

The presence began to form words in Trudy's mind, incantations to counter Liz's power over her. And almost at once, the counter-magic began to work.

The presence made Trudy's jaw muscles release Holly's nipple before doing any more harm. Then, Trudy's head pounding with pain, the presence made her slowly raise her head while repeating the counter-magic chant over and over in her mind.

"Darvulia? What's wrong?" Liz asked with concern.

The presence made Trudy pretend to stagger, then to catch herself on the utility table and pick up the meat cleaver while keeping her back to the frame so Liz wouldn't see. Then Trudy spun around and, uttering a wordless cry, swung the cleaver at Liz's neck.

The cleaver sank with a solid *thunk* into Liz's throat.

Something jerked in Phil's mind, freeing him from Liz's control. A wave of dizziness flooded him. He grabbed the frame to steady himself.

Donna fell unconscious to the floor.

Trudy jerked the cleaver out of Liz's throat. Warm blood sprayed into her face, and onto Holly and Donna and Phil.

Holly screamed.

Sounds gurgled from Liz's mouth instead of words.

Phil cursed weakly, lost his grip on the frame, went onto his knees. Then, vision darkening, he lost his fight to stay conscious and passed out.

The shocked surprise/pain/horror in Liz's eyes sickened Trudy as bubbling blood foamed from Liz's open mouth. But then Liz's fingertips began to glow with purple light. She reached up and held her neck wound closed. And the wound, impossibly, immediately began to heal.

The presence controlling Trudy made her do the unthinkable a second time. Eyes wild, uttering another wordless cry, she again chopped the cleaver into Liz's throat and jerked it out.

Liz staggered back, new blood pumping from her neck, face a mask of pain. But her fingertips were still glowing, and she immediately again started trying to heal herself as she sank to her knees, glaring up at Trudy, eyes now filled with hate, eyes that then began glowing with purple fire.

Trudy's arm raised the cleaver to strike again, but before she could do it a roaring wind smelling of rotting meat erupted from Liz's blood-drooling mouth. Icy fingers of cutting wind tore at Trudy's body. Corpse-cold fists hammered at her nakedness, battered her away from Liz, back one step, two, three.

The possessing presence made Trudy fight back. Teeth gritted, face twisted with effort, her hard-trained leg muscles strained to take her one step back through the roaring wind toward Liz, then another, and another. Aching with the effort, she struggled against the icy force of the death-stench wind, managed to finally reach Liz, to grab a fistful of Liz's blood-drenched hair with one hand, to draw back the cleaver, and to again chop at Liz's neck, then again, and again, and again.

Liz's hands, trying to stop the hammer-blow cuts, began to lose fingers.

Tears streaming down her blood-splattered face, spitting curses in some unknown language from between her clenched teeth, Trudy kept at it and did not stop until Liz's head finally came free.

She flung the head away.

Liz's body flopped to the floor at Trudy's bare feet, jerking and twisting and contorting with violent muscular spasms, blood spraying.

The roaring wind began to subside. The purple fire in Liz's hate-filled eyes, still staring at Trudy from where the head had rolled, began to get fainter, until finally the fire went out, the wind went away, and Liz's headless body stopped spasming.

The presence in Trudy's mind slowly receded, leaving her in control of herself once more.

A horrible moan Trudy only dimly realized was her own came from deep in her throat. The cleaver slipped from her fingers and splashed in the pool of warm blood at her feet.

She buried her face in her crimsoned hands. Ragged sobs shook her body.

Nearby, strapped to the frame, Holly was sobbing too, but suddenly she stopped, afraid even to breathe, because something was suddenly very wrong within her head. *She was no longer alone inside. Something was eating her thoughts. She could feel her memories, her very self, going away.*

In terror she tried to cry out for help. The invader kept her silent. But she could, she discovered, still scream, and so what remained of Holly screamed and screamed. Screamed as the last of her soul was relentlessly devoured. Screamed on, and on, and on.

PART TWO

Aftermath

☐

Evil recognizes Evil, and the recognition is always painful.

Marquis de Sade,
JUSTINE
(Gillette's translation)

14

Hero

Holly's screaming suddenly stopped as she slumped unconscious on the bondage frame. In the blood-splattered butcher shop of a room, Trudy's sobs were now the only sound.

Trudy stood, swaying unsteadily, sobbing raggedly, her blood-smeared face buried in sticky crimson hands, trying and failing to cope with all that had just happened, with what the presence that had come into her mind had just made her do. She teetered on the edge of mindless hysteria, feeling as if she might at any moment start screaming her guts out like Holly had just done.

She saw Donna unconscious on the floor. And Phil. And Holly on the frame.

Trudy knelt beside Phil. He seemed unharmed, but would not respond when she touched his face and called his name.

She forced herself to think about what to do next, about how Holly needed a doctor and about how the police would have to be told all that had happened. About how she had killed Liz.

The thought of telling the police sent new panic racing through her. *I killed in self-defense,* she reminded herself. Phil and Holly would back her up. It would turn out all right . . .

But would it?

No. It would not. She had not simply killed. She had mutilated. Decapitated. And how could she ever justify *that* in court? Tell them she had been possessed by some inner presence? Tell them about Liz's glowing fingertips trying to heal a fatal neck wound? About the supernatural wind that erupted from Liz's mouth? And if she could not tell them about those things, there was no way to justify the way she had killed Liz, or even killing Liz at all. They would see how muscled she was and ask why she didn't just subdue the smaller woman she had decapitated.

The news media and tabloids were going to have a fine old time with what she had done. They would find out about her police record, about her being a runaway who had been a hooker and who'd had drug and alcohol problems, and she would end up looking like a berserking whore needing a new fix. Her last eighteen months, drug free and sober, would be conveniently discounted.

Even if she somehow avoided being locked up in a prison or a mental institution, all her good intentions and hopeful plans were fucked. And beneath it all, always, would be the *memory* of the last few minutes, of what she had done, how it had felt, looked, sounded.

The urge to devolve into panicked hysteria returned. Then something else also returned.

The rotten-flesh stench that had gone away when Liz died had suddenly come back and was rapidly growing stronger.

Trudy whimpered, began backing away from the headless corpse in the black jumpsuit, half-expecting Liz's body to start moving again like a monster at the end of a horror film. And then it did start moving. It began sinking in upon itself like a deflating balloon. The flesh, where visible at neck and hands, was cracking like sun-baked mud, and from out of the widening cracks oozed a viscous pus, foaming at the edges as it evaporated into the air. And the severed head, staring at Trudy with lifeless eyes from where it had rolled near the wall, was also moving, slowly grinning, its rictus smile steadily broadening as its flesh dried and cracked too.

Trudy kept backing away until she touched the wall. Shriveling pieces of dried flesh began to flake off Liz's skull. Her dead hair writhed like snakes as it withered and turned to dust. Her staring eyes sank inward out of sight as the skull emptied, pussified brains evaporating in streamers of rot-scented steam seeping from the fleshless skull-holes at eyes and ears and nose and mouth. Then Trudy noticed that

Liz's corpse was not the only thing decaying and evaporating. Donna's body was rotting away too.

"Phil!" Trudy cried, fearing his flesh would start doing the same.

Gagging on the stench, Trudy made herself go back toward the steaming decay near the frame.

Sloshing barefoot through the evaporating blood-and-pus filth, she reached Phil, bent down, and lifted his blood-stained body into her arms. He moaned with returning consciousness.

She quickly carried him to the door, opened it one-handed, went through, and closed it on the horror in the playroom.

Trudy leaned against the wall, feeling sick. Her stomach was flip-flopping. She clamped her teeth tightly shut against a sudden need to vomit. She could still smell the death-stench because her feet were covered with the filth.

She had a sudden fear that something would knock on the playroom door from the other side. She wanted to scream and run. Phil groaned again in her arms.

She fought down her urge to panic and carried Phil to her bedroom, put him on the rumpled sheets, and turned on a bedside light. Then she remembered Holly. *She was going to have to go back into the playroom for Holly.*

"What..." Phil moaned, "happened...after I blacked out? Is Liz..."

"Dead. I...have to get Holly. Are you okay?"

"No. I feel like shit. My body aches and my head hurts. But I'm okay. Sort of. I guess. What the hell's that fucking awful smell?"

"Oh, Jesus, Phil. Back in the room. What happened..." Her voice broke. "You didn't see. And then I...I was afraid it was going to happen to you."

He reached out and gripped her hand. "What happened?"

She shook her head negatively. "I can't talk about it, yet. I have to keep from coming apart until after I get Holly. I can't leave her in *there*."

"I'll come with you."

"You're in no shape to—"

"Neither are you. How did you break Liz's hold on you? I tried and tried, but—"

"Not now. You stay here. I'll . . . be right back," she said, then shakily forced herself to head for the door.

Phil got to his feet, head pounding with pain. "I'm coming with you. I'm not going to wimp out on you anymore than I already have," he added, walking unsteadily toward her.

"You didn't wimp out on anybody," she responded.

Phil made it across the room to Trudy without falling on his face.

Suddenly Trudy leaned against the doorframe for support. She trembled and closed her eyes against returning hysteria. A sob escaped her throat.

Phil gently put his arms around her. Her body began to shake with sobs. He patted her back, trying to comfort her. "It's okay, Trudy. It's okay—"

"Oh, *sure* it is," she cut him off, pulling back. "It's just fine. I killed a woman! Chopped her fucking head off with a meat cleaver! What a laugh! I'll be the top story on the evening news! I . . . I—"

"Chopped her head off? Shit. So *that's* what happened. Trudy, listen to me. For Christ's sake, it was self-defense of the worst kind. You're a fucking *hero.* If you hadn't—"

"I *know* it was self defense. But the *way* the presence made me kill her, Phil . . . the courts will never—"

"The *presence?*"

"Yeah. I . . . no, not now. Not yet."

"Okay. Let's not think about anything for the moment but getting Holly out of there. Hey, I've got a great idea. You stay the fuck out here. Let me be the hero this time and rescue her all by myself."

Trudy wiped away tears as she stared at Phil. Then she shook her head no. "We'll do it together. But before we go in, I want to warn you about something. After Liz died, her body, it . . . decayed. Like in one of those Dracula films after the vampire's killed at the end."

"You're kidding. Forget I said that. Of course you're not kidding. God. And that explains this awful smell. Just *who,* no, *what* the fuck *was* Liz, anyway?"

"Exactly what she told us she was, I'm afraid. But there's more. Phil, your cousin, she . . . died with Liz."

"You killed her, too? Why?"

"I didn't touch her. But she also started decaying."

"Christ. If Holly has been in there watching—"

"She passed out before it started."

"Then we'd better get her the hell out of there before she wakes up and sees what you saw. She's going to be psycho enough just from going through what she did, without any extras."

Trudy led the way to her playroom door. She hesitantly put her hand on the doorknob. "It stinks even worse in there," she warned. "Try to hold your breath."

Phil took a deep breath. Trudy opened the door.

Donna's clothing lay empty. Like Donna's remains, Liz's had vanished, too. Not bones, not even a hint of corpse-dust remained. But neither did Liz's black jump suit and shoes. Nor the woman Trudy had left strapped to the wooden X.

The straps on the bondage frame were still buckled, but Holly was gone.

15

Erzebet

"Well, if there's a bright side to this royal mess, I guess it's that at least we can stop worrying about your being charged with murder. No evidence. No damned bodies, right?"

Phil was nervously pacing the living room. Trudy was leaning against the doorway leading into the kitchen. They had searched the house for Holly, but neither had expected to find her, and they hadn't.

"Bodies or not, Phil, *I* know what I did. I'll *always* know. I'm exhausted and frightened and just wish to hell none of this had ever happened. But it has, and I might as well get my butt in gear and tell the police," she decided, then made herself pick up the kitchen phone.

"No, wait, Trudy," he said, coming into the kitchen. "Maybe that's not necessary."

"Not necessary? Get serious. Do you think I *want* to call the police? With my record? But we both know I've got to tell them, and after I do we'd better hurry and get ourselves decent and halfway presentable before they arrive. I don't know about you, but I don't intend to go to jail naked and covered in bloodstains and filth."

"What bloodstains? It's vanishing like the bodies in the playroom. We won't even have a mess to clean up in there if we wait awhile. The dead smell's about gone too. There won't be *any* evidence to back up your wild story about how you chopped a woman's head off. They may take you to the psycho ward, but not to jail."

"But—"

"Please, just think about it for a minute. We're both reasonably certain that Holly didn't ever leave the playroom. First of all, she would have had to get loose from the straps, but she couldn't do that when Liz was torturing her, so she damned well couldn't have done it later either. And even if she had, do you think she would have taken the time then to rebuckle them?"

"I guess not. But one thing keeps worrying me. What happened to Liz's clothes? I keep having this crazy notion that Holly put them on before she left."

"My guess is that everything Liz owned decayed. But shit, Trudy. Here we are trying to use logic on something that's not logical. Maybe the decay was random or something. Hell, maybe I would have decayed, too, if you hadn't gotten me out of there."

Trudy didn't answer for a moment. "I still have to tell the police, because we're the only ones who know what happened to Holly. We're the only ones who can tell her family and friends that..." Her voice caught. "That she's never coming home, and why."

"That's very noble of you, but it won't bring Holly back. You've got to think of yourself, and of me, first. We're more important to you than Holly's folks, right? And there's another possibility. What if no one's missing her, anyway? What is she were one of Liz's slaves all along, just playing a role? Another of Liz's tricks? What if she's been missing for a long, long time? It's possible, isn't it?"

"Godammit to hell, Phil, I don't now what to think or do anymore! All I know is that I killed a woman, and—"

"Can we even be certain of that, Trudy? How do you know *you* killed Liz? I mean, after the way you say she decayed, maybe she wasn't alive to start with."

"Phil, stop talking nonsense!"

"What else *can* I talk? What we experienced *was* nonsense, but it sure as hell happened. And maybe Donna was never alive while she was here, either, not like we are alive. Liz *said* she'd brought Donna back from the dead, remember? So your defense, if your nobility makes you tell the police, is like what one of those vampire hunters in a movie tells the police, that he didn't kill the vampire, because the vampire was already dead."

"This isn't a fucking monster movie!"

"Sure acts likes one, though, doesn't it? That's what the cops and head-shrinkers will think, too. And what Liz did to us, possessing our minds or whatever, sure seemed like a nightmare."

"I still have to call—"

"Give me the phone. Let me make a call of my own before you make yours."

"Who to?"

"Donna's folks. It's early in Kansas too, but they can fucking well wake up and talk."

She handed him the phone. He took it, then dialed information. "Make that three calls," he said while he waited for directory assistance to answer. "First two don't count."

Directory assistance answered.

"What's the area code for Salina, Kansas?" he asked. "I'm in a booth and someone's stolen the phone book."

He scribbled 913 down on a note pad Trudy kept near the phone. Then he hung up and dialed long distance information for area code 913, got the number for Donna's folks, and wrote it down too.

"I want to see what Donna's folks will say," he said as he

dialed the number. "I won't tell them who I am. They won't recognize me. I was a kid that last time they heard my voice."

"Phil, they have a right to know what happened to their daughter. You'll have to tell them she's dead."

"Maybe. Maybe not. Not if they already know, which they probably will, if she died somewhere else before she came here."

"Jesus Christ, Phil. You're scaring me more than Liz did."

"I'm scaring myself too. I apologize to us both. It's ringing. Go listen on the bedroom phone."

Trudy headed to the bedroom.

The phone in Salina rang twice, three times, four.

"Wake the fuck up, will you?" Phil grumbled under his breath.

It rang a couple more times before a woman's sleepy voice said hello.

"Uh, hello. I'd like to speak with Donna, please."

There was a long silence, then, "Who's calling?" The woman's voice had changed, weakened. Phil's solar plexus tightened.

"My name's Johnny Jones. Donna said if I was ever back in Kansas to give her a call. I met her in college. I know it's awfully early, but it's kind of important."

There was another long silence, then, "Donna's . . . gone. She was in a . . . car wreck, near Lindsborg, a couple of weeks ago. She . . . died," her mother finished, voice breaking.

Phil had been half-expecting it, even hoping for it, but actually hearing it still shook him. He wasn't faking when he told Donna's mother how sorry he was.

"I . . . I'm really sorry. And I . . . apologize for disturbing you like this. But, could I ask just one more thing? I'm also trying to locate someone else. I think she was a friend of Donna's. Liz Smith."

Another pause, then, "She was . . . with Donna, that night. She . . . was thrown clear. I don't know where she is now. I haven't seen or heard from her since the day of Donna's . . . funeral. And I hope I never do. I . . . told Donna to stay away from her, but she wouldn't listen. And now I'll tell you too, young man. Don't go looking for that woman. She's no good. She's . . ." Her voice broke up.

"Thank you for telling me. I won't bother you any more. I'm . . . just so sorry about Donna." He told her goodbye and hung up. He was staring at the phone, moisture glistening in his eyes, fists clenched on the counter, when Trudy rejoined him.

"You heard?" he asked.

"I heard."

"Still going to call the police?"

"I don't now. I guess not just yet."

"Know what, Trudy? I'm only sorry I didn't get to help you kill her. Car crash my ass. Some how, some way, that thing that called itself Liz fucked over my cousin, turned her into some kind of zombie-slave or something, like she intended to do to us. Or at least to me. Donna's mother wouldn't want you to go to jail for killing Liz. She'd give you a fucking medal."

Trudy didn't respond.

"I think it's time you told me how you got free of Liz's control, don't you? What was that about a . . . presence?"

"It's . . . going to sound crazy."

"What *doesn't* sound crazy about what's been happening to us?" He reached out and took her hands. "Please, Trudy. Go ahead."

"All right. When Liz was making me . . . bite Holly, when my teeth broke her skin and . . . I tasted her blood, I suddenly knew things I shouldn't have known. There were *memories* in my head I knew I shouldn't have had, and then they kind of . . . condensed, or focused, into a presence that began . . . controlling me."

"Christ. Is it still there?"

"Not the presence. But the memories are, though not as clear now. And I have my suspicions about where they came from, and the presence. Or maybe I have more than suspicions. Maybe I *know,* and it really scares me, Phil, because . . ." she hesitated.

"Because?"

She took a deep breath. "Because they make me feel like I

felt when Liz said I was reliving a former life. You were able to watch and hear all that stuff she did with me, right?"

"Yeah."

"Well, the memories feel like the memories of the woman I seemed to become in that former life. It's like they're *her* memories."

"The sorceress Liz said you'd been? Darvulia? Well, it makes as much sense as anything else. I mean, the memories of a sorceress would have known how to counteract Liz's sorcery. Right?"

"Except for one thing," Trudy replied, then hesitated again. She didn't want to say it out loud.

"Come on, Trudy. Don't freeze up now. Get it all out in the open. Maybe telling me about it will help you, and I want to help you all I can. Shit, maybe it will even help me. Please?"

Trudy took another deep breath. "When Liz sent me on that fucking head trip, Phil, I did not become Erzebet Bathory's lover. I . . . I became the Countess Erzebet Bathory, herself."

16

Together

Phil was alarmed by the look that had crept back into Trudy's eyes more than by what she had just said. "Look, Trudy, I hope you're not beginning to believe that you really *were* the Countess Bathory. All that other-lives stuff was just more of Liz's mind-fucking crap."

"Then why do I have Erzebet's memories running around inside my skull? And why did Erzebet's presence take control and make me kill Liz? If you can think of some straws for me to grasp at, to help me fight this fear, I'm listening."

"Okay. They don't have to be a dead woman's memories.

They could just be aftereffects of Liz's tricks, couldn't they? The presence, too?"

"I don't know. It doesn't *feel* that way, Phil."

"The feelings could be aftereffects, too."

"Maybe. But there's something else that I felt when the presence was making me kill Liz. I felt like it had all happened before, fighting to break free of a sorcerous spell, then killing Liz, but in some different way. Or rather, I should say that it felt like Erzebet had killed the woman Liz had been in Erzebet's time."

"Liz said *she* was Erzebet Bathory. You say *you* were. Is this a closed party? Or can I join and be Erzebet too?"

"I'm not laughing, Phil."

"Sorry. Who the fuck do you think Liz was, then?"

"Darvulia. I think. Or rather, Erzebet's memories thought. Think."

"Oh."

She was quiet a moment, trying to reach into the memories. "It's not too clear, but I think that while Erzebet coveted Darvulia's occult power, Darvulia coveted Erzebet's wordly power. Darvulia always wanted to *be* the Countess, not just her lover and teacher. And Erzebet knew that Darvulia was not teaching her all she could, because she did not want Erzebet to become her occult equal. As long as Erzebet's sorcery was inferior to Darvulia's, Darvulia could use Erzebet as an easily controllable pawn."

"Like Liz was doing to us."

"Yeah. I think, or Erzebet does, did, that it was Darvulia's influence that turned Erzebet's occasionally deadly S&M games with her servants into wholesale mass murder and ritual blood baths. By hiding behind the Countess' position and power, Darvulia was able to get away for years with crimes for which she would otherwise have soon been arrested and executed. But eventually, Erzebet learned enough sorcery to fight back, break Darvulia's hold, and kill her."

"Like you did to Liz."

"Right. And it could explain why Darvulia, who was obviously unbalanced, to say the least, might reincarnate thinking she was the woman she *wanted* to be, rather than who she really was in that other life."

"Other life. You *are* starting to accept this reincarnation shit, Trudy. And that kind of scares me more than what happened in the playroom."

"It scares me, too, because if it's true, I was once a monster, a murderess who bathed in human blood, some kind of female Dracula or something, who—"

"Stop it, Trudy." He could see she was headed for the edge again.

"I think we both could use a good dose of normality here," he said. "Let's get cleaned up. It'd do us both good. A shower, nice and hot with plenty of damned soap. I'll scrub your back if you'll scrub mine. Maybe a shower will scour those memories and feelings out of your head. We'll take it one step at a time after that."

"A shower sounds wonderful," she agreed, the impending panic in her eyes receding again.

After they'd showered, Trudy was feeling more stable again. She put on a clean black t-shirt, one Phil had given her. It had "Conan the Destroyer" above a skull printed on the front. "Kind of appropriate, don't you think?" she asked Phil as she tucked the tail into a pair of tight, faded jeans.

"Glad to see you still have a sense of humor."

"Not really," she answered, as she zipped up the jeans and started threading a wide black belt through the loops. "Did you think I was kidding?" She buckled the belt and sat down on the edge of the bed to pull on her high-calf-hugging, buckle-strapped motorcycle boots.

Phil put back on the black Z-ROCK Militia t-shirt and jeans and cowboy boots he'd worn to Trudy's, grateful for his clothes' sake that he'd gone into the playroom naked. "I'm hungry," he said as she finished pulling on his scuffed, pointed-toed cowboy boots. "That dead smell's gone now, and I'm famished. How about you?"

"No thanks. I couldn't eat anything yet. But you go ahead," she said, following him into the kitchen.

"After I've eaten, I'm going back into the playroom," he announced, "but you're not."

"Oh, really?"

"Really. You're going to rest while I get rid of anything that's left to remind us of what happened. Then I'll clean up the living room. Where do you keep your vacuum cleaner? Got to suck up those shards of broken glass from your Ms. Olympia poster."

"I don't think we should separate, Phil. We don't know for certain that the danger's really over."

"Of course it's over."

"I'd like to believe it is. But not yet. So, I'll help in the playroom, and then we can get the living room back in shape together. As for resting, I may collapse later, but right now I'm too keyed-up to have much luck resting."

"I still think I should do the playroom alone. I don't have the unappetizing memories that you do." He opened the refrigerator and looked inside. "Got any frozen waffles?"

"Me? You're kidding, right? There's granola in that plastic sack. Got it at the health food store, so you probably won't like it."

"I'll try it," he decided and reached for it. Trudy got a bowl out of the cabinet for him, and a spoon from a drawer.

"No real milk either?"

"Low-fat milk *is* real milk, Phil, and better for you."

"Right."

He poured some granola and milk into a bowl. "Not bad," he admitted, after his first bite. "Sure you won't join me? Food might do you good."

"Maybe later. You know, I've been thinking about this past-life stuff, and—"

"Trudy, I don't think you should. Not yet."

"Let me finish. It's helping me to deal with it, okay? What if that whole story about Erzebet Bathory was just an invention of Liz's? It'd sure take the punch out of my past life worries, right? I mean, I've just been assuming there really *was* a Countess Bathory, but *I've* never heard of her before, have you?"

"Well, uh . . ."

"Oh, no, Phil. You *have?*"

"Yeah. Sorry."

"Shit."

"Well, you know the kinds of music and movies I like and books I read. There's a Swedish Heavy Metal band that calls itself Bathory, and on one of their albums there's a song about Erzebet called, let's see, I think it's 'Woman of Dark Desires.' I've seen a couple of horror films based on her life, too."

The look of impending panic was returning to Trudy's eyes.

"Just because there *was* a Countess Bathory years ago doesn't mean you were her, Trudy, and you know it. It doesn't prove a thing."

"Sure. Okay. Look, Phil. I'm sorry I'm not dealing with this better, but—"

"Trudy, most people would be a basket case by now. So, don't be down on yourself. I really wish you'd have some food. Just some toast? I promise it'll make you feel better."

She shook her head no. "You have any books on the Countess at your place?"

"No. But I'm sure there are some. Probably in the Dallas Library. But I don't think you should look at them, if that's what you're thinking. At least not so soon after all that happened."

"I can't just pretend it didn't happen. Maybe if I learn as much as I can about Erzebet it would help take the mystery out of it."

"The less you think about her for a while, the better."

"Isn't there some cliché about the fear of the unknown being the greatest fear?"

"That doesn't mean that—"

"And it doesn't mean that it doesn't."

"Trudy, I really think the best thing for both of us to do today is to put some mental and emotional distance between ourselves and what happened, not head to a library to immerse ourselves in Countess Bathory lore. We can talk about it some more, all you want, if you need to, but—"

"Then tell me what *you* know about Erzebet."

"No."

"Dammit, Phil, you just said you'd talk to me about it."

"Not about her. Not yet. Anything else but her."

"But this *is* about her. We can't talk about *it* without talking about *her!*"

Phil finished his granola and took the bowl to the sink.

"Please, Phil?"

He turned around. She looked stubborn. And still very frightened. "Okay," he said. "I think it's a mistake, but okay. You've got enough to deal with without me giving you a hard time. But there's no sense in me telling you about her, because all I know is two movies I don't remember all that well, and that Swedish band's song. So I guess it'll have to be the library."

"Thanks," she said, walking over to him. She embraced him. They kissed. "God, I'm glad this didn't happen to me alone, Phil. If I didn't have you to lean on . . ."

"Yeah. Me too. Tell you what. I'll do the playroom like I said, and you the living room. Then we'll try to rest a little bit, together. I'll call in sick at my job again. The library doesn't open for several hours. And in the meantime, turn on some music while you clean the damned living room. And try to give your mind a rest about all this, at least until we get to the library. Okay?"

"Okay," she agreed, and kissed him once again. "But you are *not* doing the playroom alone."

"Trudy—"

"No. We're staying *together*. And the first thing I'm going to do in the playroom," she added, going to a cabinet, "is to take out that damned red lightbulb and replace it with a very bright white one."

17

Mirror

At first glance the playroom appeared innocently normal. As Phil had predicted, the blood had vanished like the bodies. The death smell was gone too. But there were still plenty of reminders of the nightmare they had survived, such as Holly's sandals and the scraps of her clothing, Donna's clothing, the additions Liz had made to Trudy's toys, and the meat cleaver lying where Trudy had dropped it on the floor.

Even after Trudy installed a 100-watt white bulb in the ceiling fixture, they still saw no traces of the blood and filth that had pooled on the floor and splashed the walls. But Trudy used a mop and disinfectant, anyway, while she tried not to remember why.

One of the first things Phil did was to get the meat cleaver out of Trudy's sight. He had brought along two large black plastic garbage bags. He wrapped the cleaver in one, then put it in the second bag along with the torture toys Liz had added to Trudy's collection. Then he stuffed Holly's and Donna's clothes in on top, double-tied the bag closed, put the bag in the garage for safekeeping until he could dispose of it more permanently later, then hurried back to the playroom to help Trudy.

"If Holly did somehow get away," Trudy said when they were finished in the playroom, "and if she does turn me in, I can kiss my self-defense plea goodbye after scrubbing down the scene of the crime."

"What crime? I don't remember any crime. If someone says there was a crime, I'll say they imagined it, or had a bad dream. And the lack of bloodstains and bodies will back me up."

"I still don't feel right about not calling the police."

"Well, me neither, actually, but then I don't feel right about *anything* that happened here. If there are people, or things like Liz running around loose, and there seem to be, it kind of kicks my entire belief system to hell and gone. It means I've never been standing on solid ground like I thought. Instead, we're all standing on thin ice that's beginning to crack. We're all stranded in some horror-movie jungle with zombie-monsters like Liz lurking in the shadows. We're—"

"I get the point."

"—up shit creek without a paddle. But not to worry. We didn't drown. And now it's over, Trudy. It's really over. I think we've had our share of unexplained tabloid headlines. From here on out things should be wonderfully ordinary. We've got to believe that and get on with our lives, right?"

She didn't answer.

"Right?" he asked again, and gently punched one of her rock-hard biceps.

She nodded her head. "I should get rid of that damned frame, too," she said, frowning at the bondage X where Holly had been strapped. "But I've had enough of this room for now. Probably forever."

"I'll take the frame apart for you sometime," Phil promised. "Maybe we can burn the pieces for firewood next winter."

"You're assuming I'm going to stay in this place. I think I'd better start looking for a new house to rent."

"You're welcome to stay at my place until you find one, if you want," he offered.

"Thanks, Phil. Maybe I'll take you up on that."

Trudy locked the playroom door behind them, then they headed to the living room.

The sun was shining brightly around the edges of Trudy's curtained windows, morning well under way, rush hour traffic rumbling along Plano Road outside. The air conditioner was already fighting hard to keep the muggy summer heat at bay.

When they finished vacuuming and straightening the living room, Phil helped Trudy change the sheets on her bed, then convinced her to lie down with him to rest. He eventually fell asleep, but, though exhausted, she could not.

Her mind kept rerunning what had happened in the playroom. She tried again and again to blank her mind or think about something else, but couldn't. For the first time in eighteen months, she began to think seriously about going off the wagon and getting roaring drunk, even about scoring some drugs and using them to escape. But they were *not* an escape and she knew it. Booze and drugs led to a bottomless pit out of which she might not be able to crawl a second time. And that was when, in desperation, she left Phil sleeping and crept into the living room, alone.

She stripped off her shoes and socks and clean t-shirt and jeans, propped what was left of her Ms. Olympia poster against the wall, then did some warm-up stretches and began to work out with her home weight-set, pushing herself hard, pitting her physical strength against her mental and emotional turmoil, determined to cleanse her mind and spirit by temporarily crowding everything out of her head but her concentration on the exercises. She was dripping sweat, white bikini panties plastered semi-transparent to her hips when Phil appeared an hour later, looking concerned. He'd awakened, found himself alone, and had feared new trouble.

He watched her for a moment, awed as always by her body, then rubbed his eyes and yawned and went to the bathroom. He went from there to the kitchen and rummaged around in Trudy's health-store-stocked fridge and cabinets, found her 8-grain bread, spread it with light corn-oil margarine, dripped some wild mesquite honey atop the margarine, then downed the gooey treat and chased it with some low-fat milk. He found a hardware store catalog on the kitchen counter in a pile of junk mail Trudy had stacked there and began leafing through it, studying the ads, contented to deal for a moment with no more than picture after picture of things he did not want or need.

In the living room, Trudy finished with the weights and plunged into fifteen concentrated minutes of abdominal exercises. Then she did a series of cool-down stretches and headed to the shower, feeling better than she'd dared to hope, beginning to believe she might be able to find her way back to a fairly normal life after all.

She showered, stepped out, and began toweling herself dry. Suddenly movement jerked in the corner of her eye. She flinched back. Then cursed at her jumpy nerves. It had only been her reflection in the steamed-over mirror on the medicine cabinet door above the sink. Or had it? The obscuring condensation didn't look quite right, as if something dark was moving sluggishly beneath it, threatening to break through. . . .

Trudy reached for the doorknob, ready to run. Then she stopped herself, turned back around, took a deep breath, and slowly lifted her towel toward the fogged mirror, telling herself it was only a mirror and she had to prove it to herself right now. Only a mirror. And her imagination.

But what, she suddenly found herself thinking, if I wipe

away the moisture and it's not *my* face underneath looking back? What if it's Liz's?

If the face isn't yours, she answered herself, *then* you can scream and run bawling to Phil, but not before.

Hand trembling, she swiped clear a patch of mirror and saw a frightened woman's face looking back at her. But the haunted face, although pitiful to see, was hers.

She looked at herself critically, disapprovingly. She hadn't seen herself looking so strung out and miserable since struggling to cold-turkey the damned drugs and booze. But at least you're still on your feet and kicking, she told herself, and looked away from the mirror.

As she looked away, out of the corner of her eye her reflection seemed to change. She whipped her eyes back, but the reflection was still her own, except that now the frightened look was even worse.

She opened the medicine cabinet door so that the mirror faced the wall and she couldn't see *any* reflections, real or imagined. Then she finished toweling herself dry, the new self-confidence she'd sweated into herself not entirely gone but definitely badly shaken. The physical danger might be over, but she was mentally and emotionally light years from where she had been twelve hours before, and it looked like it was going to be a long haul before she managed to get herself back into dependable shape inside her head.

Leaving her long dark hair damp and uncombed, she pulled her t-shirt and jeans back on, then headed to the kitchen.

"Good news," she told Phil. He was sitting at the kitchen table, now examining a clothing store catalog from the junk mail stack.

"What?"

"I'm finally hungry, too."

"Glad to hear it. Trudy, I know what I said earlier about the library, but I'm hoping you've maybe changed your mind? I still don't think it's a good idea this soon. How about going to a mindless comedy movie instead?"

"That might not be a bad idea at all," she replied as she poured granola into a bowl. "You don't heal strained muscles by straining them more, and I realize now that my first priority is going to be getting my strained mind and emotions back in shape. So studying up on . . . you know who, I'm not even going to say her name, would just be pouring salt in a wound. You were right and I was wrong. I realize that now," she confessed, thinking about what had just happened to her in the bathroom. "But let's not go to a dark movie theater. Let's go to the Dallas Zoo instead. Deal?"

"Staring at some damned monkeys sounds good to me."

"I wonder what time they open? It's . . ."—she looked at the kitchen clock—"nearly eight now. Seems like it should be later. So much has happened."

"There's probably a zoo phone number with an info recording, " he suggested, getting up and going to the phone book on the shelf. "I'll call it, if there is."

Trudy sat down at the table and started to eat her granola.

18

Cleavage

Trudy and Phil spent most of the afternoon at the Dallas Zoo. Staring at monkeys and other animals did seem to help their spirits, because by the time they were ready to leave they had decided to try continuing to act as if nothing unusual had happened by doing their nightly gig at the Safe Sex Club. Phil had disposed of the garbage bag of bad memories on the way to the zoo by throwing it into a half-full outdoor trash dumpster behind a grocery store miles from Trudy's home.

"I'm starved," Phil said as he drove them away from the zoo. Except for a mid-afternoon snack, neither had eaten since breakfast. "You up for some Tex-Mex?"

"Not exactly what I'm used to."

"Do you good. Won't kill you just this once, will it?"

"I'll have to pay for it in the gym tomorrow, but okay."

"Great. But, uh, you might have to pay for it tonight, too. How much money you got?"

"Enough. But, come on, Phil. You're not broke. You have enough to at least pay for your own, don't you?"

"Yeah. And yours too. I still have that damned credit card. I was just kidding about your paying. You think I was serious?"

"I never know with you. But I'll pay for my own."

"We'll see."

Phil drove them to a small restaurant, where they ordered a traditional gut-stuffing Tex-Mex feast. Trudy had just managed to swallow her last bite when their waitress arrived on another iced tea run.

"More iced tea for you, Ma'am?"

"Please," Trudy nodded. The waitress refilled her glass.

"And you, sir?"

"No, thanks," Phil answered.

"How about some dessert?" the waitress offered.

"No, thanks," Trudy answered. "Even if I could, my jeans couldn't."

"Same here," Phil agreed, patting his full stomach.

The waitress flashed him a smile and walked away.

"She likes you," Trudy noted.

"Naa. Just doing her job."

"She likes you," Trudy repeated, knowingly.

"So? You going to fight her for me?"

"I won't have to. She's not your type."

"I had in mind a mud wrestling match. You both start out fully clothed, in string bikinis, then, as the match proceeds—"

"We grab you and hold your head under."

"Under what?"

"Guess. I'm going to the rest room." She picked up her shoulder bag and slid out of the booth. "Don't let her take my tea," she warned.

"Or your A," he quipped beneath his breath, then laughed at his own cleverness, watching her tightly-jeaned bottom as she walked away from him.

He sipped his tea. The waitress showed up with the check.

She smiled at him again. "How big a tip do you want?" he asked her.

"Excuse me, sir?"

"Do you like mud?"

"Sir?"

"Nothing. Great meal. And service."

"Thank you. Can I get you anything else?"

"No, thanks."

She smiled again, then moved to another table.

He finished his tea. Then he switched Trudy's half-full glass with his empty one.

What the hell's wrong with you? he suddenly asked himself as he put the glasses back the way they belonged. He was playing stupid jokes as if everything were normal. The afternoon and the meal had been good for them, taking their minds off what had happened, but now the night was coming, and . . .

And what? he wondered. What did the night have to do with anything? His years of seeing monster movies and reading horror novels were catching up with him. Night didn't mean shit, because the danger was over. And so, he reasoned, why the hell *shouldn't* he act as if everything were normal and play his damned stupid jokes?

He switched the glasses again. A moment later, catching a glimpse of Trudy out of the corner of his eye, he casually picked up her tea as if about to take a sip. She sat down.

He looked across the table at a pale, frightened woman, her lower lip trembling slightly, her eyes glistening with tears.

"Trudy?" he asked, immediately setting the tea back on her side of the table. He touched her hand. She flinched, then grabbed his hand and held it tightly.

"What happened, Trudy?"

"The mirror. In the rest room . . ." she began, then hesitated, took a deep breath. "I was washing my hands, glanced up, saw the stall door open behind me, and . . . saw Holly, inside—"

"Trudy, no, listen—"

". . . grinning at me, but with Liz's grin—"

"Listen. Stop. Don't."

". . . grinning and grinning, and I . . . whirled around, but the stall door was closed . . ."

"Jesus. Trudy, it's like an aftershock after an earthquake. It's only your subconscious playing tricks on you. It doesn't mean shit. Just some kind of flashback—"

". . . and then, as I was leaving the rest room, I thought I heard the stall door . . . creaking open behind me, and . . ."

"And *nothing*. Listen to me. While you were gone, I found myself tensing up because the night was coming. But then I asked myself so what if the night came? The danger's over, but we're both acting as if Liz were still around. She isn't. *She isn't*. And neither is Holly."

Trudy nodded her head, wiped at her eyes with the back of her hand. "Something happened this morning in my bathroom I didn't tell you. My reflection in the mirror seemed to change."

"*Seemed* to change. That's all."

She didn't answer.

"Still game for the club?"

She hesitated. "Are you?"

"Sure. I'm anxious to see if that meal you just finished pops your costume's thin but vital strap."

She shook her head. "Don't you ever get tired of looking at female parts?"

"Not if they're yours. Jesus, I think I just said something romantic, didn't I?"

"Sounded like it to me, too. You spent too much time watching animals today."

"Yeah."

"Phil, I'm . . . sorry. For getting frightened again, and seeing things."

"For God's sake, Trudy. You don't have any reason to be sorry about anything. Just talk it over with me right away if you have any more . . . experiences. Okay? Promise? Telling someone else will kind of take away its power. Right?"

She squeezed his hand. "Right." She picked up the check and reached for her shoulder bag.

"Trudy, I *was* only kidding about your paying. This one's on me."

"You don't have to do that, Phil."

"I know. But you shouldn't have to buy food that you don't approve of, should you? And I've had several meals at your house for free. So, I'm going to pay and that's that."

She squeezed his hand again. "That's kind of romantic of you, too. Thanks."

Phil made a face, paid with his credit card on their way out, then drove them to the club. Trudy got into her waitress outfit and started waiting tables while Phil sipped beer at the bar. The evening was reassuringly dull and routine, until they were backstage getting ready for their first show.

Phil began filling the prop dagger with prop blood, and Trudy got cold feet.

"Oh, God, Phil. I can't. I'm going to lose it on stage. I just know it. The whip, and the dagger. It's too much like . . . last night."

"It was kind of giving me the jitters too," he agreed. "But I'm going to try doing it, and so should you. I mean, what better way to give all that happened the finger than to go out there and do a pretend version of it without skipping a beat?"

"Look at my hands, Phil. They're shaking like when I was doing cold turkey. I don't think I can even pretend to whip you and cut you."

"Considering our sexual tastes, that's going to make us kind of a dull couple, don't you think?"

"The duller the better. At least for now."

"Trudy, you've gotta try to do it. It's just an act. A fantasy. Come on. Give it a try. If you lose it on stage, just walk off. I'll make some excuse to Marv about your getting sick and we'll call it a night. But at least try it. Please?"

"I really *don't* think I can, Phil."

"Please?"

She hesitated, breathed deeply several times, fighting to calm herself. "Okay, damn you. I'll try. But no promises."

The worst of it proved to be the anticipation. After the music started and they got on stage, reflex took over. It was not Trudy's all-time great performance, and her hands shook when she used the fake dagger to carve R-P-M on Phil's chest with the fake blood. But she got through the act all the way to the end, and the next show later that evening proved easier than the first, the third even easier than the second.

As they were leaving after the last show, Marv called them into his office. "You've got an admirer, Trudy," he grinned while puffing on the cigarette hanging from the side of his mouth.

"Admirer?"

"Yeah. Left you a package after the last show," he replied, then picked up off his desk a gift box wrapped in bright red paper, decorated with a large silver bow. He handed it to her. It was squarish, about a foot on a side, and one or two inches thick. And heavy. There was a note card on top. She didn't recognize the handwriting. It said, "Love your cleavage, Raw." It was not signed.

"No name?" Phil asked, looking at the note. "What'd he look like?"

"Jealous?" Marv laughed. "You should be. I am too, but of Trudy, because it wasn't a guy. It was one hell of a fine-looking woman."

"A woman?" Trudy asked, looking up from the package.

"No need to act surprised," Marv leered. "Bet it's not the first time, right? Say, maybe we could vary the act. Give Phil here the old heave-ho and have you do your number with this got-the-hots chick. I'd like seeing you carve RPM on her chest lots better than Phil's, and I bet lots of our customers would too. What do you say, Trudy?"

"I say *this*, Trudy answered, showing him the extended middle finger of her left hand. She turned to go.

"Hey! Aren't you going to open it?"

"Sure. But not with you around," Trudy replied as she left the room, Phil in her wake.

She opened it in the car. A meat cleaver was inside.

19

Nipple Rings

"After the way she shot me the bird and walked out, I wouldn't give her the time of day," Marv fumed.

"I'm not asking for the time of day," Phil replied, trying to keep the anger out of his voice. "Just a description of the woman who left the package."

"Kiss my ass."

Trudy stood by the door, not saying anything, somehow maintaining an appearance of outer calm, the package, meat cleaver inside, clutched in her arms.

"Marv, please," Phil pleaded. "At least tell me what color her hair was?"

Marv puffed on his cigarette. "Forget it."

"Come on, Phil," Trudy decided. "Let's go."

"Not until he tells us, dammit!"

Marv grinned at Phil and blew smoke.

"Maybe someone else saw what she looked like," Phil suggested.

"If they did," Marv responded, "and if they tell you, they're fired."

"Shit."

"I'm leaving, Phil," Trudy told him. "Please, come with me."

"Time to go, Philly," Marv laughed. "Mommy's calling."

"I ought to kick your—"

"Screw it, Phil," Trudy cut in. "It's not worth it. Let's go."

They left Marv's office. Marv followed, stopped at his door, and called, "How much *is* it worth to you?"

"Not a damned thing," Trudy shot back. "What a prick," she added under her breath.

"Maybe I'll tell you, if you do just one little thing for me."

"Such as?" Trudy asked, turning around.

"Just show me what's inside the box. That's all I wanted in the first place."

"No. It's . . . private."

"Oh? That good, huh? Sure would like to see."

"A set of nipple rings," Phil suddenly said.

"A what?" Marv asked, grin broadening.

"Nipple rings," Phil repeated. "Fourteen-carat gold ones. There, now you know. Tell us what the woman looked like."

"I want to see them."

"They look better when they're being . . . worn," Phil suggested. "Right, Trudy?"

"Uh, right. Sure."

"I didn't know you had pierced nipples, Trudy?" Marv leered.

"Of course," Trudy lied, deciding to follow Phil's lead. "Doesn't everyone?"

"We'll have to make use of them somehow in our next video. The possibilities are—"

"What did the woman look like?" Phil asked.

"Tell me and I'll wear the rings on stage tomorrow," Trudy promised, "just for you, Marv. I'll even give you a private showing first, backstage. How about it?"

"I'd still rather see them now . . . but okay. She had short, kinda spiked, punkish-looking orange-red hair. She was wearing purple jeans, real tight ones, and a skimpy halter top that looked like it was about to break. She was nearly as tall as you are, Trudy. Had muscles like yours, too. Is she someone you met at the gym? What's her name? Phone number? I might be able to find work for her here, too."

"I don't know anyone who looks like that," Trudy replied, confused. She glanced at Phil. He looked confused too. They had assumed it had somehow been Liz, or at least Holly.

"Don't play dumb with me," Marv warned. "Who is she?"

"Are you *sure* that's what she looked like?" Phil asked.

"You calling me a liar?" Marv fumed.

They left. Phil drove away from the club. Trudy sat in the passenger seat, still clutching the package.

"Just some fucking weird coincidence," Phil finally said. "You *do* have a secret admirer who's seen you at the gym, and she had the bad timing to try and get your attention by making a cleavage-cleaver pun."

"Sure, Phil."

"Your nomme de porne, *Raw,* goes with the cleaver too. As in raw meat, right? That's what it has to be. Just some bizarre coincidence."

"I don't think you really believe that."

"Sure I do. Sort of. I want to, anyway."

"Could she be another of Liz's slaves? Maybe she knows what happened, because maybe Liz was in mental communication with lots of slaves, other than just Donna. Maybe this is *the* cleaver I used on Liz, retrieved from the dumpster! It looks the same. Oh God, yes, and now they could be out to get me for what I did to their Mistress!"

"More likely they'd give you a medal."

"We could go back to the dumpster and check the bag."

"Forget it. Absolutely no way am I going to call attention to that bag of evidence, or myself, by going back to peek inside it. And neither are you. It's *not* the same cleaver, I guarantee."

"If we don't check, we may never know whether or not—"

"Trudy, if there were others like Donna and maybe Holly, wouldn't they have decayed away too after you finished Liz off? I'm still going to vote for a coincidence, whether I really believe it or not. And you should too. Tomorrow night your admirer will probably come back to the club, and you can find out if—"

"What makes you think *I'll* be there tomorrow night. I'm not dumb enough to walk into a trap if I can help it."

"Oh, and I *am* dumb enough?"

"I don't know. Are you?"

"I'm not the dumb one. Would she have warned you with a meat cleaver if she intended to spring a trap?"

Silence stretched between them for several blocks.

"Let's not fight, Trudy," Phil said at last. "Neither of us is any dumber than the other, and we're all we've got going for us right now."

Trudy shifted the package in her arms, then nodded her head. "Okay. Sorry my tongue got away from me."

"Mine too. Maybe this surprise package will look different to both of us in the morning."

"*If* nothing bad happens to us before then. And *if* we can get some decent sleep. I think I'm afraid I'm going to have bad dreams."

"Wake me up and tell me about it if you do. Get them out of your system before they can fester. And I'll do the same if I have any. Where do you want to bed down, though? Your place or mine? Maybe mine would be a better bet tonight. Or maybe even some motel."

"You're already headed toward my house. Might as well just keep going."

"Okay."

"No. On second thought, maybe we *should* go to your place."

"Whatever you want, Trudy. The memories at your place are heavier for you than for me. I'll turn the car around right now if you say the word."

"It's not just the memories. If there *are* other slaves out there, they might be waiting at my place, since that's where it all happened."

"But, same question as before—why warn you with the cleaver if they were going to spring a trap?"

She thought about that for a second. "I do need sleep. My mind's not working at all. But let's go to your place, anyway. Just in case. At least for tonight. You got any guns?"

"Sure do. Got a 410 gauge shotgun my dad gave me when I was a kid, a 12 gauge that belonged to my grandpa, my dad's pump-action 22 rifle, and his old Army 45 automatic."

"A small arsenal."

"But I haven't bought shells or bullets since before mom and dad died. So we may have to throw the guns at attackers instead of shoot at them."

"I see. Well, I don't need bullets for the meat cleaver in this box."

He changed directions back toward his place.

"This is such shit," Trudy groaned, running her hands through her hair. "I feel like a fugitive! And if I go to the police for help...Christ. I've changed my mind again. Let's find a motel. I couldn't relax at your place, either. Liz's slaves would know where you live, too. I'll pay for the motel."

Phil shrugged. "The motel's fine with me, but I'll pay. I've got a damned credit card, remember, and you don't."

"Not because I haven't tried. But I'll pay you back sometime."

"Well, you keep track then, because I'm not going to."

Phil drove to a motel on the LBJ Freeway. They shared a shower. Trudy didn't look in the bathroom mirror any more than necessary.

"Too bad you didn't bring any rubbers," she said to Phil as they climbed into bed.

"You're kidding, right?" he asked, then surprised her by pulling a package from the pocket of his jeans. "Always prepared," he said.

"I can't believe it. Do you always carry one of those around with you?"

"More than one, in my car."

"Oh. Why am I surprised?"

They made unspectacular but comforting love and went to sleep in each other's arms. The phone rang, waking them, about an hour later.

"What the shit?" Phil said, groping for the receiver in the semi-dark. He found it and picked it up. "Hello?"

"Phillip?" asked a woman's voice, weak and shaky. "Is that you, Phillip?

"Who?" he asked, stalling, stunned, solar plexus tightening, suddenly cold all over because he recognized the voice, Donna's mother's voice.

"Phillip Hastings? Dorothy's boy?"

"Uh...how did you...get this number?" he stammered, still stalling as he fumbled for the bedside light and flipped it on, halfway expecting there to be strangers waiting in the room, and understandably relieved when there weren't.

"A woman called. Maybe she...gave me a...wrong

number," Donna's mother said, voice breaking. "I'm . . .
sorry to have disturbed . . . you."

"No. Wait. This is Phil. I—"

"Who is it?" Trudy apprehensively asked, sitting up in
bed.

He put a hand over the mouthpiece. "It's Donna's mother.
Some woman called and gave her this number."

"Oh, great. Just fucking great."

"Phillip, did you call me earlier today, this morning, and
ask about Donna?"

"What? Of course not," he lied. "But . . . how is Donna,
anyway?" he bluffed.

"Donna . . . passed away," her mother said. "There was a
car wreck near Lindsborg."

"Oh. That's terrible. I'm so sorry. Maybe I can drive up
for the funeral, or at least send flowers," he suggested, continuing the bluff.

"Oh, no, Phil," Donna's mother said. "It . . . happened a
couple of weeks ago and . . ." Her voice trailed away.

"Well, I'm still really, really, deeply sorry. Is there something I can do, anyway?"

"Well, maybe there is. Would you mind . . . borrowing
Trudy's new cleaver and cutting your balls off for me?" the
voice on the phone asked, changing. Phil recognized the
new voice, too. The color drained from his face.

Phil tried to say something, but no sound came out.

"Or," the voice continued, "would you rather wait for me
to cut them off for you? Give their amputation a personal
touch? Is that what you want? Okay. I'll do it. I promise.
Soon."

Phil tried and failed again to respond.

"And Phil, give that betraying bitch Darvulia a message
for me. Tell her that I don't give second chances, and that
I'm not in any hurry. She's going to have to wait for my
revenge, anticipate it. But when it comes, it'll last a long,
long time, and afterwards, after I let her die, my demon will
take over and show her how Hell tortures souls."

The line went dead. It didn't sound like anyone had hung

up. There was just suddenly a crackling static instead of a voice.

Phil hung up the phone, and somehow managed, eventually, to tell Trudy the bad news that it sure as hell had seemed to be Liz.

20

Oz

"Okay. Fine," Trudy said, pacing naked beside the motel bed. "We're in over our heads. We need help. Where are we going to find it? How the fuck do you fight something like Liz? I chopped her head off and watched her decay!"

"I think, *maybe,* now that the shock's wearing off, that it *might* have been Holly's voice on the phone, but with Liz using it. I know that sounds looney. But, could she have possessed Holly or something, after you killed her other body?"

"The woman Marv described who left the cleaver didn't look like Holly, Phil."

"Well, no. But maybe Liz used some of her magic to trick Marv and make him think she looked different than she did."

"Okay. Maybe she did, and maybe she didn't. But does it really matter? I mean, right now all I know for certain is that we're in a shitload of trouble and need fucking help! Liz could bust in here and take us over again, or worse, any time she wanted. Those memories of Erzebet's are waking up again, Phil, and their terror is feeding my own. I'm going fucking crazy here! What are we going to do?"

"Check the damned memories."

"What?"

"See if those memories you have in your head think Liz

could have possessed Holly or something. I mean, if the memories are still there?"

"They're there. Okay, I'll try," she decided, then hesitantly dipped into the pool of memories.

Scenes and images from Erzebet's life began flashing through her mind as she probed the memories, seeing the faces of people long dead, remembering events long forgotten, delving into the knowledge accumulated in a life not her own. As she went deeper and deeper, the more potent memories aroused waves of emotions, happiness, horror, dark passions. The emotions battered her, bringing tears to her eyes one moment, making her want to laugh out loud the next. She could not concentrate.

She became more cautious, began learning to retreat as if from hot flames when she encountered an emotion-charged memory, strove to confine her search only to the occult knowledge lodged in the strata of deeper memories, until finally she found what she needed. She quickly jerked herself up and out of the dead woman's memories, feeling dirtied.

"Okay. Got it," she said, then paused to take a deep breath, trying to get her own thoughts cleared.

"And?"

"And they seem to think Liz could have done what you thought, possessed Holly. So, it's probably Holly being controlled by Liz we have to watch out for, unless she's making herself look like someone else. Oh, Christ, Phil. Would you just listen to the crap coming out of my mouth?"

"She said you would have to wait," he reminded her. "I'm the one who needs to worry right now. She said she was going to cut my balls off *soon*. So, if you can think of something useful, hurry up and do it. I can't. And at the moment I may want a way out of this mess even *worse* than you do."

Neither said anything for a few moments, Trudy pacing, Phil sitting on the bed, frowning at a cheap seascape painting on the opposite wall.

Trudy went over to the chair where she'd tossed the package. She took out the cleaver and held it in her hand.

"Make you feel better?" Phil asked.

"No. But it's better than nothing."

"Just keep it away from my balls."

"Liz has occult power, right?" Trudy said. "So, it seems obvious we need occult help."

"Occult help. Sure. I'll just look in the Yellow Pages."

"Well, who knows? Try it."

Phil shrugged and dug a phone book out of the bedside table's drawer. He looked under several categories. There were astrologers and palm readers and the like, but neither he nor Trudy thought fortune tellers and spiritual advisors would be much help against Liz.

"Wait a minute," Phil said as he closed the Yellow Pages. "You know I like horror novels and monster movies. Well, there's a local author I heard speak once at the Dallas Fantasy Fair. He was talking about a book he was writing in which Witches were going to be the good guys. He was basing it on some Dallas Witches who had helped a friend of his find her kidnapped sister. His name's Brock. Jim Brock."

"Is his number in the phone book?"

"We'll soon find out," Phil promised, and started looking in the white pages. "No, dammit to hell, it isn't," he said a short time later.

Trudy paced some more. Phil practiced frowning.

"Hey, the guy who puts on the local fantasy fairs should have Brock's number. But I'll probably have to make up a good story of some kind in order to get it from him."

"You could be a reporter wanting an interview," Trudy suggested.

"Okay. I've got the fantasy fair guy's number at home in the flyers he sends out. But maybe it's in the phone book, too. He heads something called Bulldog Productions."

Phil looked through the white business pages. "Here it is. Great."

"You can't call him this time in the morning, Phil. It's still dark outside."

"Sure I can." He dialed the number. The phone rang a couple of times, then an answering machine clicked on.

"Answering machine," Phil told Trudy. "Figured there'd be one."

The recording told Phil he'd reached the number for Bull-dog Productions, told him to leave his name and number after the beep, and so on and so forth.

The beep came. "I'm calling about an interview I want to do with Jim Brock," Phil said in a bored, authoritative voice. "I lost the card he gave me with his unlisted number on it, and thought you might be able to help me."

Trudy listened as Phil left the motel's phone number, then his own and hers.

"Look, Phil, maybe we'll get the number, and maybe we won't. But what we need is help right *now.*"

"I'm open to suggestions."

"I've got one. Let's be moving targets and start by getting the hell out of this room. I feel trapped in here."

Trudy put her black Conan t-shirt and jeans and motorcycle boots back on while Phil got dressed in his black Z-ROCK t-shirt and jeans and cowboy boots. Then they checked out of the motel and started driving the freeways, going first west on LBJ to Interstate 35, a.k.a. Stemmons Freeway, upon which Phil went south, looping toward downtown Dallas. He flipped his radio on. Metal music from Z-ROCK blasted out of his speakers. Trudy groaned.

"You need that to stay awake?" she asked.

"Guess not. Thought you liked Z-ROCK."

"I *love* Z-ROCK. Normally. But my nerves could use something else right now. Maybe that classical station. Okay?"

"My speakers will never forgive me, but okay," Phil complained as he moved the tuner. "You know the frequency?"

"Somewhere on the Z-ROCK side of Q-102."

Phil found it. There was a solo piano playing Chopin. Trudy leaned back, a warm breeze from the open window ruffling her hair. "Thanks, Phil," she said. "Damn if I know what to do. I suppose Liz could even nail us out here, if she wanted to. Look, I don't think we have any choice now, about studying up on Erzebet Bathory. We need all the information we can get about anything remotely related to whatever's going on. Maybe something in a book will help us somehow. So, let's hit the central library downtown as soon as it opens. Okay?"

"Okay."

The piano solo ended on the radio and another number began. Trudy listened for a moment, then cursed, turned the radio off, and cursed again.

"What's wrong now, other than the obvious?"

"I recognized what they started playing."

"So?"

"Let me rephrase that. Fucking Erzebet's memories recognized it. When it began I suddenly kind of went somewhere else, Vienna I think, late 1500's. For a second I could see a damned concert hall, like I was *there* instead of *here*. And on the stage were musicians playing one of *dear* Erzebet's favorites."

"Oh."

"One of Phillipe de Monte's greatest hits, according to the memories, which also tell me that Erzebet knew the guy pretty damned well socially, too. But *I* didn't and don't want to, so *I* turned it the fuck off. Okay?"

Phil took 183 west off 35, kept driving until he'd passed south of D/FW airport, then on toward Fort Worth. Trudy fell asleep and he didn't disturb her. The sky was beginning to grey with the coming dawn when he looped south around Fort Worth and took I-30, once the Dallas-Fort Worth Turnpike, east, back toward Dallas, passing a sleeping Six Flags Over Texas amusement park along the way.

When the sun broke the horizon, Trudy woke up. She squinted into the bright light. "How long did I sleep?"

"Hour or so. Feel better?"

"Not much." She looked out the window. They were on Interstate 20 east of Dallas.

"You hungry?" Phil asked.

"Starved."

"Me, too. I'll stop at some cafe along the Interstate. Then afterwards we can head back toward Dallas."

"Sounds good to me. But . . . I think I should tell you about a dream I just had."

"Okay. Shoot."

"I was in Kansas. That cousin of yours was there, naked, covered in blood. She wanted to show me something she thought would help. I woke up before she showed it to me. But I think it had to do with another fucking mirror."

"Oh. That's it?"

"Yeah. There was more, but it's gone now. It felt really important, though. Also, *Erzebet* feels it's important, and she knows more about this occult crap than I do."

"You starting to decide you *were* Erzebet Bathory, then?"

"No. Shit, no! But these damned memories, whatever they are and wherever they come from, know more about the occult than you or me put together. So I think I'm going to have to start paying closer attention to them. Your cousin wasn't the only one in the dream. There was someone else, in the shadows, and it *felt* like the memories feel, like that presence that controlled me, like Erzebet herself, I mean, wanting to help me, us, too.

"Look, Phil. This other-memory business scares the crap out of me, but not as much as the thought of meeting up with Liz again before I've found a way to give her a decent fight. But if, well, if I start *losing* myself by remembering too much or something, I want you to promise you'll try to pull me back and keep me anchored in who I *really* am. Okay?"

"Jesus, Trudy."

"Please, Phil. Promise."

"Of course I promise. But if you're worried about losing yourself to those memories, going to the library will only—"

"I *know* it'll probably only make matters worse, but what else can I do? Depend upon your Bulldog man to get us in touch with a writer who may or may not help us get in touch with Witches who may or may not know their ass from a broomstick? My life's at stake here. Yours, too. And I'm going to start right now depending first and foremost upon what I *have*, depending upon myself and those damned memories, and upon you."

"Okay. Sounds as good as anything I've been able to come up with over the past few hours, which is next to nothing."

"And Phil, after we raid the library for books on Erzebet Bathory, I'm going to read them while you drive us somewhere I never thought I'd want to go, and still don't, but think we should."

"And that is?"

"Kansas. After the library, I think, *Erzebet's memories think,* we'd better take a hint from that dream I had and go to fucking Oz."

21

Denmark

By 1:00 they had checked an armload of books out of the Dallas Central Library.

Two of the books were studies of Erzebet Bathory's life, one an historical investigation called DRACULA WAS A WOMAN by a Professor Raymond T. McNally, the second an English translation of a French historical novel entitled THE BLOODY COUNTESS by Valentine Penrose.

Most of the other books they dumped in the back seat of the Trans Am had at least one chapter devoted to Erzebet, books with titles such as TRUE VAMPIRES OF HISTORY and IN SEARCH OF DRACULA and THE TRUTH ABOUT DRACULA and LUST FOR BLOOD.

There were also some books that did not involve the Countess but were about magic and Witchcraft, selected because Trudy felt that the intruding memories wanted her to read them.

"It's the damnedest feeling," she said as they drove north on Central Expressway away from downtown Dallas, "the feelings those memories give me, I mean. It's like I normally think up in the top of my skull somewhere. But the *thinking* those memories do comes from down in my gut."

"Gut instincts," Phil suggested.

"Guess so."

"And I've got one too, which says I'm hungry again."

"Very funny."

"Barbecue okay?"

"Last night it was Tex-Mex. This morning it was a plate of preservative-loaded sausages and greasy hash-browns. So, sure. Let's have barbecue. My system's already so polluted that I'll probably never repair the damage anyway."

"Well, lots of people eat it all the time, me included, and it hasn't hurt me yet. But, we don't *have* to eat barbecue if it's against your health food religion."

"Well, excuse me. If it's what *you* want, let's have it. Might be your last meal. Right? To hell with the fact that it might also be mine."

Phil was about to grind out an angry comeback, but stopped himself and took a long, deep breath instead. "Look, I'm sorry if what I said upset you. We can have whatever you want to eat. I don't give a shit. Okay?"

"Barbecue's fine. Sorry I snapped at you. And I shouldn't even joke about Liz beating us. We've got to think only positive thoughts, got to think only about nailing the bitch. Permanently. Somehow."

"Sounds good to me, and to certain body parts I'd hate to lose. Think we could risk a stop at my place? I'd sure like to check my answering machine to see if the Bulldog guy called. And maybe get a gun or two."

"Doesn't your answering machine have one of those functions that lets you call in and check your messages?"

"Oh. Yeah. Now that you mention it, there was something about that in the instruction book. But I didn't pay much attention to it. Didn't think I'd ever need it."

"So you can't use it."

"Not without going home and trying to find the instructions, in which case I could just listen to the messages. Tell you what. Let's go have barbecue at a place I know up on Forest. There's a Lone Star Comics store down a few doors from it. Maybe they know how to get in touch with Brock."

"At a comics store?"

"Sure. When I heard him speak at the Fantasy Fair, he mentioned being a comics reader. And since the shop also carries books, well, maybe he's autographed his novels there or something. If they can help us, we won't need to worry about my answering machine."

"Okay. But let's also call the motel to see if Mr. Bulldog left a message there, since you gave him the motel's number. If he hasn't, let's do the comic store before we eat."

Because of road work on Central Expressway, it took another half hour to reach the Forest Lane exit. Trudy glanced at some of the books while they inched toward their goal. Phil and Trudy both wished the car's air conditioner worked as they broiled in the summer heat, exhaust fumes from other cars wafting through the open windows.

They finally reached Forest. Phil took the exit, went under the overpass, and then drove west to Lone Star Comics and Science Fiction.

He used a pay phone outside a frozen yogurt store to call the motel, but no one had left a message for him. Then he tried Bulldog again and again got the answering machine. So they went into the comics shop.

Trudy glanced at the racks of comics and books while Phil asked the man at the cash register about Jim Brock. She found a novel with Brock's name on the spine. It was called FORBIDDEN TRANSITIONS. The sales blurb on the back cover made the intruding memories start churning in her gut, giving her the strong feeling that she should add the book to her list of books to read. According to the blurb, the book was about *good* Witches fighting evil forces.

"Have you read this?" she asked Phil after she'd carried it over to the register.

"Yeah. It's not bad. Even got Brock to sign one at the fantasy fair."

"I'm going to buy it. I feel I should read it, too, and we might not go by your place to get yours."

"He says Brock usually comes in every Thursday or Friday after the new comics arrive," Phil told her as she paid for the book.

"But he hasn't been in now for several weeks," the register man added, "and I don't have his number or anything. Sorry. Have you tried Larry Lankford at Bulldog?"

"I left a message on his machine," Phil answered.

They left the comics shop and walked to the barbecue

restaurant. Trudy leafed through one of the library books, a copy of Crowley's MAGICK, as she ate a barbecued hot-link sandwich.

"Ozzy did a song about him," Phil mentioned around a mouthful of barbecued beef.

"Who?"

"Ozzy Osbourne."

"I know Ozzy. Who's the song about?"

"Crowley. The guy who wrote that book you're getting barbecue sauce on. You must have heard it since you sometimes listen to Z-ROCK. Song's called *Mr. Crowley.*"

"Oh, yeah."

Trudy went back to reading and Phil to eating.

"There's also Clint's," Phil said as he finished his piece of pecan pie.

"Whose?" Trudy asked, looking up from the book again.

"Clint's Books, up on Campbell. Used to be Fantastic Worlds, then became Nova Books. Another comics and SF shop. Let's check there too, before chancing my answering machine. But I'm not inching up Central all the way. Think I'll take Coit north and hope for better luck."

They reached Clint's Books about ten minutes after leaving the restaurant.

"Brock does shop here," the man working Clint's register said, but I haven't seen him in weeks. I heard my manager talking to a fan about him a week or so ago, though. I think he knows him pretty well. Why don't I call him and see if he can help you? He should be over in our Fort Worth store today. I'll let you talk to him yourself if he's there."

"Thanks. Yeah. Please call him."

When the manager answered, Phil was given the phone and found out that the manager thought Brock was in Denmark, staying with a friend whose sister was in a special clinic there. The manager had Brock's home phone number because Brock had autographed books for him at the store once, but he wouldn't give the private number to Phil.

"Okay," Phil said into the phone, "then call his number for me, will you, please? I really do need to try and talk with him if there's any chance at all he's around."

There was a brief silence on the other end of the line, then the manager agreed to give it a try and promised to call right back, which he soon did, reporting that Brock's phone forwarded the call to a different number, and that a woman named Carla who'd answered had confirmed, after she'd found the manager's name on a list of people Brock had said it was okay to tell, that Brock was indeed in Denmark for an indefinite period of time.

"So much for getting help from Brock," Phil said when they were back in the car. "No need to call the Bulldog man back if Brock's in Denmark. And no need to chance my place, I guess. Probably not worth the risk. Doubt my guns would work against Liz anyway, if a meat cleaver didn't. Sorry. Shouldn't have mentioned that."

"Why not? You see me wince or something?"

"No. But . . . sorry, anyway. Anything else you want to do before we head north to Kansas?"

"I'd like to pick up a few things at the house, but to hell with it."

"We can use my credit card to get whatever we need as we need it," he suggested.

"Then we might as well get started."

"Except for our jobs."

"I'll tell Marv we're both taking a couple of days off," she said, "and he'll probably fire us."

"Yeah, but he'll probably hire us back."

"But what about your clerking job?"

"You kidding? Think I couldn't get another one like it if they can my ass? But they won't. I'll call and tell them my doctor said to get bedrest for . . . how long do you think Kansas will take?"

"I've no idea. Couple of days? A week?"

"I'll tell them three days. You going to give Marv any excuse."

"Suggestions?"

"Tell him we're getting married and taking a honeymoon."

Trudy laughed.

"What's so funny? Maybe we *will* get married, sometime."

The smile left her face. "I think you're serious."

"Anything's possible, isn't it?"

She hesitated, then nodded. "Maybe it is," she answered with a shrug.

Phil called his clerking job. Trudy called Marv, who congratulated her and then said RPM and Slave were fired.

"I'll trade off driving with you," she offered as Phil started back toward the LBJ freeway. "How long do you think it'll take to get to Kansas?"

"Seemed to take forever when I was a kid. But you go ahead and read and don't worry about driving. If I get sleepy or something, I'll let you know."

Phil went west on LBJ until he reached Interstate 35. But instead of taking I-35 south as he had before dawn, he headed north, away from Dallas.

"Next stop, Oz," he said, but Trudy only gave a minimal reaction, already several pages into McNally's DRACULA WAS A WOMAN. "Think it'd bother your reading if I turned Z-ROCK on?" he asked as they left a suburb called Carrollton behind.

"No. Go ahead."

He flipped the radio on then moved the tuner away from the classical station Trudy had earlier requested. When he heard Exodus singing "Brain Dead" he knew he had found Z-ROCK.

Phil glanced at his wrist watch. It was not three o'clock, yet, which meant that Boobie Bondage would still be the DJ. Wild Bill would come on at three. Phil wondered if he'd still be able to pick up the station when Madd Maxx Hammer's show started at six.

Forty-five minutes found them passing Denton, the home of the University of North Texas (until recently called North Texas State University) and Texas Woman's University. Thirty minutes later they reached Gainesville.

"Their transmitter's here," Phil mentioned. He hadn't spoken since they'd left Carrollton, letting Trudy read.

"What?" she looked up.

"Z-ROCK's transmitter's in Gainesville. They beam up to a geo-sync satellite and from there blanket the nation."

"Yeah. I read that article about it you cut out of the *Dallas Morning News* last winter, remember?"

"Oh. Yeah. The one with Boobie's picture. How's the book?"

"Fascinating. But I don't like the way reading about the Countess keeps waking up more memories in me. It's sort of like looking at an old scrapbook and suddenly remembering things you hadn't thought about in years. And the effect is getting stronger the more I read."

"Would you rather I read them or something, then?"

"Sure. But I'm the one who's got to do it."

They were soon beyond Gainesville and shortly thereafter crossed the Red River into Oklahoma.

"I already miss Texas," Phil said, only half-joking.

Trudy glanced up long enough to see the Oklahoma state border sign go by, then she returned her concentration to her book.

PART THREE

Not So Safe Sex

□

The beauty patiently selects the victims for the night. Innocent blood will give eternal beauty eternal life. Woman of Dark Desires. Woman of Eternal Beauty. Woman of Dark Desires. Elizabeth Bathory...

Quorthon,
"Woman of Dark Desires"

22

Pain Eater

Like a fist clenched in darkness, loneliness constricted her soul. Long had it taken her to find her lost love. And now her love was worse than lost. She had betrayed her, utterly.

When she had first seen Donna and sensed a connection with her other-life lover, she had thought at first that Donna herself might be the one. But then she had probed deeper, discovered that Donna was only a link in a synchronistic chain that led, through Donna's cousin, to the one she sought.

She had thought of almost nothing else for more than a week except again tasting her love's kisses, again feeling her embraces, and sharing the blood-passion. But her dream of happiness was now shattered, crushed, totally destroyed. And the disappointment, the betrayal, the loneliness hurt.

But not all of her pain was emotional. Some of it was physical, deep pains from deteriorating organs.

The new body she had been forced to possess was fighting her, trying to die, striving to become a corpse because its rightful soul, the one named Holly, had been displaced. And with the physical pains came great fear, fear that her new flesh *would* die, leaving her fleshless in the vast darkness of Demon Young's Hell.

Demon Young's hunger would be turned upon her. He would amuse himself, for a while, with her soul-screams. The last time that had happened to her she had screamed for half a century before being allowed to reincarnate into new flesh.

Demon Young was a Pain Eater, an ancient being spawned by humanity's oldest emotions, a psychic side-effect of centuries upon centuries of human fear and pain, voracious, fleshless, powerful, a vortex of preternatural consciousness condensed from the psychic effluvia of humanity's darkest passions, existing and evolving in an ever-thickening psychic sewer of spiritual excrement between Life and Death.

Or so Demon Young had told her.

Whether it was completely or even partially true did not matter. What mattered was that Demon Young gave her occult power and physical immortality, of a kind. In return she was only required to have fun, the kind of cruel, sadistic fun with which she had first attracted Demon Young's attention long centuries ago. The kind of fun she intended to soon have with the one who had rejected her love.

Cries of passion and screams of agony were not, after all, so very different, and at least, in the end, she would not be the only one in pain.

But the pleasures of a lingering revenge would have to wait. Escaping to safety and building back a meager amount of energy, in order to monitor the thoughts and activities of her betrayer, had all but exhausted her. And nothing was now more important than feeding and strengthening herself, and Demon Young, upon human fear and pain, upon human blood and screams.

23

Dead Blood

When Marcy Rennal came hurrying out of the north Dallas supermarket, clutching a brown paper sack in her arms, she was worrying about whether or not she would have time to finish her other shopping before picking her kids up at school. She was nearly to her station wagon before she noticed that a woman in a black zippered jumpsuit was leaning against her car. The woman had blond hair and the kind of casual beauty Marcy had always envied.

The woman smiled at her and raised a hand in greeting. Marcy did not recognize her, but that did not mean they hadn't met, because Marcy had never been very good at remembering faces and names. Perhaps they had met at a PTA meeting. Or church.

The woman kept smiling. A small sliver of apprehension pricked Marcy, but she shrugged it off and nodded politely to the woman as she reached her car.

"Hi," Marcy said, brightly. "Beautiful day. Hot," she added, glancing up at the summer sun, "but pretty."

"It certainly is, Marcy," the woman said, holding out her hand. "Do you remember me? Liz Bathory? PTA meeting?"

"Yes. Of course I do," Marcy lied as she shook Liz's hand while juggling her grocery sack in the other arm. The moment their hands touched, Marcy's thoughts blurred. She could not pull her gaze away from Liz's hard, blue eyes.

Liz released her hand. Marcy blinked away her momentary confusion and told herself for the third time that day that she was going to *have* to find some way to slow down, to reduce the stress in her life. But there was always so much to do and not enough time to do it.

"How have you been, Liz?" Marcy asked as she set her sack on the car hood so she could dig in her purse for her car keys.

"Not as well as I'd like, I'm afraid."

"Oh, I'm sorry to hear that."

"I'm feeling kind of rundown," Liz continued as Marcy unlocked and opened the car door. "Dead blood."

"Excuse me?" Marcy asked, turning from the open door to look at Liz, thinking she'd heard wrong.

"You know how it is. You're feeling great, on top of the world. Then someone who loved you in a former life chops your head off and you have to possess a new body, which starts trying to reject you by dying, leaving you trapped inside an almost-corpse with dead blood. And of course only one thing will help after that. *New* blood, spiced by an enriching mixture of fear and pain, right?"

Marcy's polite look of concern had traversed a spectrum of expressions as Liz talked, moving from apprehensive alarm through the uncomfortable embarrassment of confronting the handicapped until finally she decided it was some kind of joke. The woman was smiling, after all.

Marcy returned the smile, thinking it was definitely time to go somewhere, anywhere, else. But she did not want to be too rude.

Marcy made herself laugh. "You had me going for a minute there. That sounds like something my son would say. He loves horror movies. Loves to tell us all the gory details. You must get the same sort of thing from your son, too. And speaking of children," she glanced at her watch, "if I don't hurry I'll never get my other shopping done before I have to pick up my kids after school. But, listen . . . Liz, it's been nice meeting you, again," Marcy said as she picked up the sack of groceries and put them in the back seat. "Thanks for saying hi," she added, turning around and holding out her hand for a goodbye shake.

When their hands touched this time, something jerked deep inside Marcy's guts. Her vision swam, and everything faded to black.

She woke up after what seemed only a few moments, but she was no longer in the north Dallas super market parking lot.

Marcy Rennal was now in some kind of barn. Her beige cotton shirt and brown cotton slacks and white aerobics shoes were gone. So was her underwear. And jewelry. She was lying in dirty, dusty straw, completely naked, her wrists tied behind her back.

Marcy struggled to a sitting position, heart beating wildly. A chain rattled. One end of the chain was padlocked around her left ankle. The other end was padlocked to a thick wooden roof-support post.

She looked frantically around as she tugged and jerked on her bound wrists and chained ankle.

Liz was standing nearby, silhouetted in a sunlit doorway.

"Hi there, Marcy. Have a nice rest?"

"I . . . where—"

"Where are you? How'd you get here? Things like that? You're in a barn on an abandoned farm west of Denton."

"Denton? But that's a long way from—"

"Sure is. But that's where you are. I used sorcery to knock you out in the parking lot, then drove you here."

"Look, I . . ." Marcy began, but hesitated, suddenly blushing with embarrassment as Liz stepped nearer, squatted down, and began to openly study her nakedness. "Please, don't look at me like that."

"Like how, Marcy?"

"You know. Like . . . a man would look."

"Is that what I'm doing?"

"Well, yes, I think so."

"And if I am?"

"It's . . . wrong."

"Is not. Besides, you've got nothing to be ashamed of. Nice breasts. Nice ass. Long legs. Killer thighs. And I love the way your dark brown pussy hair contrasts with your bleached-blond coiffure."

"Look—"

"I *am* looking," Liz grinned. "Want me to touch, too?"

"I . . . just want to know why you've done this to me? Is it," she blushed again, "some kind of . . . sex thing?"

"Might be."

"Did I really meet you at the PTA?"

Liz just laughed.

"Please, you've got to let me go," Marcy pleaded.

"I do?"

Marcy struggled with her wrists again as she asked, "What time is it?"

"Worried about no one being at school to pick up your kids? Hey, if that's it, relax. I took care of it for you. Want to see?"

"What do you mean?" Marcy asked, heart suddenly pounding harder.

"Your kids are outside, in your car. But I fixed it so they

can't roll down the windows or open the doors, and since it's a scorcher of a hot day..."

"You wouldn't," Marcy responded, voice wavering.

"Sure I would," Liz said. "Come and see. Your chain will just barely reach the door."

24

Joke

Liz reached down and easily pulled Marcy to her feet. Marcy winced with the pain of Liz's steely grip on her arms.

"Sorry,'" Liz laughed. "I'm a bit stronger than I look. Making a pact with a demon will do that to you. You know?"

"Demon?"

"Demon. You think I'm joking or just nuts, right? Doesn't matter. Ready to go to the door and see your kids?"

Keeping hold of Marcy's arm, Liz herded her, chain clanking, to the open door. Marcy's station wagon was parked about ten feet away. She saw her children inside.

"Hey! Kids!" Liz called. "Wave to your mother! She can't wave back, but...oh, dear. Looks like they've passed out."

"Oh, God! Let them out! They're not moving! How long have they been in there?"

"Quite a while."

Marcy forgot the chain on her ankle, tried to jerk away and run to the car. Liz released her arm and let her try, then laughed when Marcy's ankle-chain jerked her to a stop. Marcy almost fell. Liz steadied her.

"You've got to let them out!" Marcy cried. "The heat will kill them! Please! Let them out!"

"I'd rather watch you watch them die."

"What? You don't mean that! You can't!"

"Sure I do."

"Okay. Look, I'll do whatever you want. Even . . . you know, have . . . sex with you, if that's what you want."

"Really?"

"But you've got to let my kids out first. And . . . I don't want them to . . . see us."

Liz just laughed. "I'd rather watch you watch them die, first. *Then* have sex."

"Please! Listen to me! My husband and I only have a few thousand dollars in our savings account, but I'll get it for you. You can have our car, too. I won't let the police know about it."

"I don't want money or a car, Marcy. I just want to watch you watch your children die."

"There must be something I can do!"

"I imagine you'll do quite a lot in the next few minutes," Liz answered. "Might as well go ahead and get started. Work up a good sweat. Maybe the chain isn't as strong as it looks. Or maybe you can get your hands free and throw something heavy from the door to break the car's windshield."

"Please!" Marcy sobbed. "Let them out and I'll do whatever you want!"

Liz turned and walked away. "I'll just move over here, out of the way," she said as she leaned back against an empty cattle stall.

Marcy looked at the car, at Liz, at the car, back at Liz.

"Well? What are you waiting for?" Liz asked. "Aren't you going to try saving your kids?"

Marcy jerked on her wrists, pulled on the chain holding her ankle. "Please!" she pleaded, looking back at the car.

"You're not trying very hard, Marcy. Don't you *care* about your kids?"

"If they die, I'll find a way to . . . kill you!"

"You're welcome to try. But in the meantime . . ."

Marcy started jerking harder on her wrists.

"I think there's a rusty nail sticking part of the way out of the wall there by the door," Liz commented. "Maybe you could use it to get your hands free. You're just tied with some old bailing twine I found, so it should shred pretty easily."

Marcy looked at Liz.

"Just trying to help," Liz shrugged.

Marcy found the nail. She turned her back to it and started trying to use it to shred her bonds. Each time she slipped, the nail scratched her wrists and arms, bringing blood.

"Good idea," Liz commented. "Maybe the blood will slicken your wrists and let you slip free."

Marcy kept at it, sobbing and moaning and cursing and sobbing as she worked, sweat streaming. Her hands suddenly came free.

Liz clapped, applauding the partial escape. "Good for you, Marcy! Now, what about the chain?"

Marcy hurried back to the door, looked at the car.

"Car still there?" Liz asked with mock concern.

Marcy started looking frantically around. "Going to take my advice about something heavy to throw?" Liz wanted to know. "Good luck. I think I saw an old crowbar over in that corner," Liz pointed.

Marcy found the crowbar. She took it back to the door to throw it, suddenly cursed her stupidity, ran to the post where the chain was attached and began prying at the padlock. Her muscles ached with the effort, but she kept at it, sobbing and cursing, and suddenly the lock sprang open.

Marcy ran for the car, trailing the chain on her ankle, still holding the crowbar.

"Tommy! Karen!" she cried as she ran. "Mommy's going to get you out!"

Behind her, Liz's laughter filled the barn.

Marcy reached the sun-baked car. Through the window her kids looked already dead.

"Oh, God!" she sobbed and tried to open the door. When it did not open on the first try she did not waste any more time. She swung the crowbar at the side window, again, again, again, while trying to remember exactly how mouth-to-mouth breathing was supposed to be done. When she had a hole large enough to reach through, she unlocked the door and tried to open it again, but it still wouldn't open. She resumed smashing at the window, determined to make the opening wide enough to pull her kids out.

But suddenly she stopped. A dry scream died in her throat. She staggered back from the car. *Her kids had changed. Two dogs sprawled unmoving on the car seat where her children had just been.*

Liz laughed behind her. "Really had you going there, didn't I? But it was never your kids. Just two dead dogs."

Marcy turned, crowbar gripped in her trembling fist, panting, chest heaving, her bare skin glistening with sweat in the afternoon sunlight. "I don't . . . understand."

"I tricked you. A joke. Get it? Ha? Ha? More of my sorcery. Damn, you looked so funny! You should have seen yourself!"

Marcy's expression changed. She lifted the crowbar.

"Oh, dear. You're mad at me now. Damn."

Marcy started walking toward her. Liz didn't move. "Gosh," Liz said, "some people just can't take a joke. Do you intend to kill me with that crowbar just because I put two dead dogs in your car? A law-abiding, church-going, good-suburban-citizen-PTA-mother-of-two like you?"

Marcy stopped. She lowered the crowbar. "Give me back my clothes and my car keys."

"I can't do that."

"You'd better," Marcy warned, raising the crowbar again.

"No, really, Marcy. I can't. I wasn't kidding about having dead blood. And my little trick about your kids was not only fun, but also useful. Your emotions of fear and anger have already psychically fed my demon, and therefore me, new strength, while also pumping occult enrichments into your bloodstream that will make your blood more potent when I absorb it, after your torture."

"You're crazy. Either you've escaped from some mental hospital, or someone needs to put you in one. And maybe that someone should be me."

"Afraid not, Marcy," Liz said. She spoke guttural words in a language Marcy did not recognize. A kind of mist glowing with purple light left Liz's mouth and engulfed Marcy's face, soaking into her skull.

Suddenly Marcy felt a frightening coldness invade her

body, starting in her solar plexus and moving rapidly outward in all directions. Within seconds, in spite of the summer heat, her entire body felt deeply chilled.

Liz walked calmly toward her. Marcy tried to make a warning swing with the crowbar, but to her horror she discovered that her arm would no longer move. Neither would the rest of her. She struggled desperately to make her chilled muscles obey. Liz reached her and touched her forehead.

A shock of pain pounded into Marcy's skull. She dropped the crowbar as she blacked out.

Liz caught her before she hit the ground, then carried her back into the barn and placed her on the floor near one of the thick roof-support posts. Then she used bailing wire to fasten Marcy's wrists tightly together behind the post, bare fingers twisting the wires tight as effortlessly as if she were using pliers. After that, she unpadlocked the chain from around Marcy's ankle, crossed one ankle over the other one behind the post, and then wired the ankles together, too.

Marcy now knelt with her back to the pole, head hanging limply forward, disheveled, sweat-soaked hair plastered against her face.

Liz knelt before her unconscious victim, took Marcy's face between her hands, and gave Marcy's half-parted lips a lingering kiss. "Have a nice nap, darling. I want you well rested for your torture," she whispered as she gave Marcy another kiss.

Liz stood and looked down at her naked captive, feasting her eyes, but only for a moment. Then she left the barn, got into Marcy's car, and drove away toward Denton to hunt two more victims for that night's ritual of torture and blood.

25

Godzilliana

The Trans Am's radio began to lose the Z-ROCK signal after they had crossed the Arbuckles near Turner Falls, Oklahoma. Phil started looking for another hard rock station, but nothing was Z-ROCK except Z-ROCK.

"I hope we're doing the right thing," he mumbled as he disgustedly turned the radio off. "This trip may be nothing but a waste of precious time."

"I'm still open for better suggestions," Trudy replied. She had nearly finishd McNally's DRACULA WAS A WOMAN. Next on her list was the material about Erzebet in Ronay's THE TRUTH ABOUT DRACULA, and after that in Hoyt's LUST FOR BLOOD.

Phil stopped for gas a couple of hours later at a Texaco in an Oklahoma City suburb called Moore. They had a meal at a Dairy Queen nearby, then headed north on Interstate 35 again and, three hours later, near sunset, reached the Kansas border.

"Welcome to the Sunflower State," Phil announced, remembering something he'd heard when visiting there as a kid. "Midway U.S.A. Breadbasket of the Nation. The Wheat State. Home on the Range. The—"

"Land of fucking Oz," Trudy cut in, looking up at the Kansas border sign. She saw two things as it flashed by, that it sported a large sunflower as part of its design, and that there was a blood-stained woman standing naked beside it.

Heart jumping, Trudy jerked around to look back. There was now only the sign, its long shadow stretched thin by the crimson sunset.

"What's wrong?" Phil asked, also trying to look back.

Trudy turned forward in her seat again. "You didn't see her, I suppose?"

"See who?"

"Donna."

"What the fuck are you—"

"She was there, for a second, beside the border sign, covered in blood, just like in that dream I had."

"When she was trying to help you?"

"Yeah."

"Then, maybe your seeing her is a good omen."

"Could also be another of Liz's tricks. Gave me a bad case of chills."

"You're entitled."

Near Wellington they discovered that I-35 became a toll road in Kansas when they had to stop at a Kansas Turnpike booth and take a punched ticket.

When Phil saw a Turnpike rest stop island featuring a restaurant and a service station, he said, "I could use a trip to the john. I wouldn't complain about another meal, either. How about you?"

Trudy had given up reading when it got too dark. She'd been silent ever since, lost in thought. "Good idea."

He parked near the restaurant. They went into their separate rest rooms. Trudy's was empty. She went into a stall, closed the door, and slid the lock home. Just as she was about to flush, she heard a woman begin whimpering and whispering outside the stall door. But she had not heard anyone else come in.

Fear tightened her solar plexus. Anger followed an instant later.

"Who's there?" Trudy asked, not certain that she wanted to know. Her voice had only wavered slightly.

The whimpering-whispering got louder, but Trudy could still not sort out any words. She got even angrier.

"Either speak up, or shut up."

The whispering stopped and the whimpering began getting softer and softer until soon Trudy could no longer hear it.

Something splattered wetly upon the floor beyond the closed stall. A thin trickle of red began sluggishly snaking beneath the door toward Trudy's motorcycle-booted feet.

Trudy cursed and pulled back her feet, breath catching in her throat. A second scarlet trickle joined the first, then a third, a fourth.

She felt the intruding memories stir deep in her mind, felt them pushing toward the surface of her consciousness, began feeling the presence of she who had taken control in the playroom, which frightened her as much as the crimson trickles pooling at her feet. But the presence did not take control of her this time. Instead, Trudy suddenly sensed words forming in her mind and realized that the presence was trying to communicate with her, and the message was clear. *She must touch the blood-like ooze upon the floor.*

She recoiled from the thought, then reminded herself that she had decided to follow the memories' guidance. She reached down, groaned and pulled back her hand, then made herself reach down again, hand trembling, and extended her index finger, until, finally . . .

She touched it. A sliver of ice jabbed into her finger, chewed up the nerves in her arm, shot into her brain. She felt dizzy, sick. She shivered. Then she heard a woman's voice beyond the stall door.

"Promise . . . you'll try to . . . help . . . me," the weak, insubstantial voice haltingly said, "and I . . . will try . . . to . . . help you."

Silence. The memories urged a reply.

"Okay. Sure. I . . . promise," Trudy managed. "Uh, who are you?"

No reply.

"Are you Donna?"

"I . . . was . . ."

Trudy took a deep breath. "Do you know how to stop Liz?"

No reply.

"Tell me how to stop Liz, and I'll do anything I can to help you."

"Liz . . ."

"Yes. I'll stop Liz, if you'll tell me how."

"Forget . . . Liz. Must stop . . . Demon . . . Young."

"Stop who? Liz's demon?"

No reply.

Trudy *felt* the presence beyond the door going away, a sense of heavy oppression lifting.

"Donna? Don't go . . ." Trudy began, but then she saw that the blood on the floor was steaming away. Within moments it was gone.

Trudy sat where she was. Breathing heavily. Feeling even sicker. And feeling silly, too. Talking to a ghost in a john. Ridiculous. But what her brain thought didn't matter, because her heart was still pounding heavily in her chest, and her skin was still damp with the cold sweat of her lingering fear.

She was still sitting on the commode a few minutes later when she heard the rest room door open. Two women came in, talking loudly about how stiff they were from sitting so long in a car.

Trudy flushed the commode, stood, zipped up her jeans, tucked in her Conan the Destroyer t-shirt's tail, buckled her belt, took her shoulder bag, meat cleaver inside, off the hook on the stall door where she had hung it, then unlocked the door. She ignored the two women's stares as she washed her hands and then bent over the sink to splash cold water on her face.

The two women whispered together for a moment, then one of them tapped Trudy on her arm. "Excuse me," the woman said, "but haven't we seen you on TV?"

Trudy straightened, face dripping water onto her t-shirt. She turned and looked down at the short, heavy-set woman in the flower-print dress and suddenly felt like a giant alien visiting a foreign planet. It was not the first time she had felt like that in her life.

"Aren't you one of those women wrestlers?" the other woman, a near-twin of the first, asked.

Trudy could only stare at them, still trying to regain a firm emotional footing after what had just happened to her. "No," she finally managed to say. "Sorry." She turned to look for a paper towel dispenser. There were only hot-air blowers.

"Sure you are," the first woman insisted. "You're Godzilliana!"

"Won't you please give us your autograph?" the other one asked, fumbling in her purse for pen and paper.

"I'm not a wrestler," Trudy replied. "Excuse me, but I'm not feeling very well right now," she added, then turned to leave. One of the women grabbed her arm. Trudy stiffened.

"Come on. Level with us. We're fans! You wear a lizard skin bikini and bite the heads off white mice at ringside before each bout. See? We *are* fans! Come feel her arm, Joanna! It's hard as a rock!"

Trudy jerked her arm free. "Watch my lips, ladies. I am *not* a fucking wrestler, and I do *not* like having my arm grabbed by strange women in a fucking strange toilet. Okay?"

"How *dare* you speak to us in such a vulgar manner?"

"If it wasn't for your fans," the other one joined in, "you'd be nothing but a muscle-bound female freak!"

Trudy spun and walked away.

"We'll never cheer for you again, freak!" one of them promised.

Trudy gave them the finger behind her back without turning around and went out the door.

Phil was leaning against a cigarette machine waiting for her. "Took you long enough," he commented. "Hey, you don't look too good. Kinda pale. And your face is wet."

"Couple of women in the john thought they'd seen me bite the heads off mice on TV," she answered, wiping at her wet face with her hands.

"What?"

"Thought I was a wrestler. Called me a freak."

"They really upset you."

"Not as much as what happened earlier. Before the *fans* showed up, I had a visit from Donna."

He was silent a moment, then said, "Oh."

"Oh? Your fucking cousin's fucking ghost haunts me in the fucking john and all you can say is *oh*?"

"Sorry."

Trudy ran a hand through her hair. "I didn't see her this time, but I . . . heard her voice. To make a long story short, she said she'd help me if I'd help her, and I said okay. But when I asked her how to stop Liz, she said to forget Liz and told me to stop . . . I thought she said *Demon Young*. I guess she meant Liz's demon. Then she went away. So for all I know it might have been *another* of Liz's tricks."

The two women came out of the rest room and gave Trudy a dirty look, their noses in the air.

"Excuse me, ladies," Phil said to them as they walked by. "I'm her manager," he hooked a thumb at Trudy. "I would appreciate it if you'd apologize for upsetting her."

The women stopped. "You should teach her how to treat her fans, Young Man," one of them indignantly said.

"All we wanted was her autograph," the other bristled.

"Oh, God! She didn't tell me you asked for autographs. She *hates* to give autographs. Didn't you know? Just pray she doesn't turn nice and smile at you, because that means she's about to attack. If I were you," he lowered his voice conspiratorially and stepped nearer, "I'd get out of here *fast*. The last time I tried to pull her off an autograph hound, she broke my arm. And I can't afford to bail her out of jail again this week. So please, for my sake and for your own good, leave while you can. And if you don't take my advice, I just hope to hell your Blue Cross is paid up."

The women's expressions' had slowly changed from snooty superiority to mild concern. They glanced at Trudy. She had decided she might as well play along, so she smiled her sweetest smile and took a step toward them.

Phil stepped in front of her as if to try holding her back. "Hurry!" he urged the women.

Trudy pushed him out of the way and took another step forward, still smiling.

The women finally gave ground, turned and hurried away, glancing apprehensively back.

Trudy suppressed a laugh. "Thanks, monkey," she said, punching him lightly on the arm.

"I'd say that seeing you smile again was reward enough, but instead I think I'll demand a more substantial reward, later."

She resisted an impulse to tossle his hair. "Come on. Let's get some food and get back on the road before my fans decide to call the cops."

26

Bathory's Barn

Marcy awoke to find Liz kneeling in front of her. Her body hurt, muscles cramping, feet and hands numb. She tried to move, discovered how she was bound. She tried to groan but no sound came out. Liz had given her back the power to move but not the ability to make sounds.

Marcy again tried to ease her strained position without success. Her knees hurt the worst, because she had been kneeling, unconscious, with most of her weight upon them for several hours. Her head ached too, her temples throbbing with pain.

"Have a nice nap?" Liz asked her brightly.

The barn door was open. It was nearly dark outside. Crickets chirped beyond the door. An old-fashioned kerosene lantern Liz had set on the floor illuminated the shadowy interior of the barn with soft yellow light.

Marcy and Liz were not alone in the barn. A slender young woman with short-cut dark hair was tied naked to a roof-support post on Marcy's left. A young man with curly brown hair was tied to a post on her right. He was also naked, his trim body athletically muscled. Both the man and the woman were kneeling with their wrists and ankles bound with bailing wire behind their respective posts, the same as Marcy, but unlike her both were still unconscious.

Liz smoothed back Marcy's disheveled bleach-blond hair. "I'll let you make sounds again soon," Liz promised. "It would be cruel of me not to let you beg and scream all you want when I start to torture you. But don't worry about someone hearing and spoiling our fun. There's no one except you and me and these two others for miles. Even if there were, my sorcery would not allow anyone to hear anything I didn't want them to hear. The same goes for anyone seeing the light from this lantern."

Marcy pulled on her numb hands.

"I know how anxious you must be to get started, Marcy, darling. It's kind of like being at a dentist's office, don't you think? Waiting for the pain to begin gives you butterflies, right? But first, I want to introduce you to Kathy and Charles."

Liz stood up and spoke more words in the guttural language Marcy had heard her use before. Glowing mist left Liz's mouth and settled around the unconscious woman's head. She stirred. Liz repeated the words and the same thing happened to the man.

Both grimaced, tried to groan and could not, slowly realized that they were bound. Both pulled on their wired wrists behind the poles, looked in confusion around them, saw Liz and Marcy and each other, tried to speak but could not.

"Marcy, this is Kathy," Liz said, presenting the dark-haired woman. "And Marcy, Kathy, this is Charles," she added, motioning to the man. "I found Chuck bicycling near Denton. I had the car hood up. Chuck thought I needed help. Is he hung like a stud, or what, girls? Yum. Oh, look! How cute! We've made him blush!" she laughed. "Do you suppose we could make him get hard, too?" She walked over to him, reached down, began stroking and manipulating his penis and testicles as Charles struggled and struggled without luck to get free.

"Well!" Liz laughed a few moments later. "Just look at that, girls! Wow! Either of you want to go for a ride? But I'm forgetting why you're here. None of you will have time for fucking tonight. I have too much planned to do to you."

Liz turned from Charles and went over to Marcy. "To continue the introductions, Kathy and Chuck, Marcy comes from north Dallas. She's a good little homemaker, a wholesome, church-going, PTA-ing mother of two. I found her in a supermarket, looking delicious. Don't her tits just make your mouth water?

"And Kathy," Liz said, smiling at the dark-haired prisoner, "was jogging not too far from where Chuck was bicycling. Aren't her legs awesome? I just bet she's really proud of them. We'll have to test how strong they are before the night's through.

"Now that you've all been introduced, we can get on with the business at hand." Her gaze found each pair of eyes in turn.

"I am going to torture the three of you this evening," Liz told them matter-of-factly. "I've been doing this sort of thing for centuries. I do it not only because I enjoy it, but because it's vital to my continued health and strength.

"I made a pact with a demon centuries ago. He calls himself Demon Young. He exists in the realm between Life and Death. Of course you'll get to meet him, too, but not until after I let you die.

"Demon Young is a Pain Eater. The occult vibrations generated by human fear and pain gave birth to him, and others like him, long, long ago. Your fear and pain tonight will therefore strengthen and delight Demon Young, and thereby also strengthen and delight me.

"Unfortunately for you three, Demon Young and I need *lots* of energy tonight. My body was recently destroyed and I was forced to possess this new one, which is now trying to die because I'm not its rightful soul. Am I boring you, Marcy?" she asked, giving Marcy's head a pat. "Marcy already heard some of this earlier today," she explained to the others.

"Anyway, I guess all you really need to know is that I'm first going to absorb pain-energy from you, and then, later on, obtain more strength for my new flesh by draining and absorbing your blood. But please, don't worry too much about dying when your blood is gone, because I intend to bring you back to life afterwards. I'll even heal the wounds I'm about to give you. Then you'll become my helpers.

"There. That takes care of the preliminary pleasantries. I'd offer you the chance to ask questions, but you'd just waste time asking silly ones. So, we might as well get started. Okay?

"Because I acquired Marcy first this afternoon, and because she's therefore been waiting the longest, it's only fair that I start with her. And with that in mind, I have a question for you, Marcy."

Liz turned and picked up a metal fishing tackle box she had placed on the floor near the lantern. Its surface was dull and rusty. Liz knelt on the floor between Marcy's spread knees.

"Here's the question, Marcy. Do you like to fish?"

Marcy looked down at the fishing box then back up at Liz. She pulled hopelessly on her bound hands.

"Well, I *love* to fish," Liz continued, "when I can catch the right kind of things, like naked women, and men.

"I found this in what's left of the garage," she said, hefting the fishing tackle box. "It looks a lot like my grandpa's did when I was a little girl. This farm is a lot like the one he had in Kansas, too, and so's this barn. But let's continue talking about fishing, shall we?

"Grandpa was always so proud of me because I wasn't squeamish about putting worms on the hook like some girls, and boys. He never guessed that I used to imagine I could hear the worms screaming as I pushed the hook into them.

"He never guessed I used to torture things in his barn, either. The first was a kitten that I beat to death with a stick. That was when I was eight. I'd been inspired by reading a library book about the Countess Erzebet Bathory, the woman I slowly began to realize I'd been in a former life, and whose name I now use. I used to secretly call grandpa's barn Bathory's Barn of Horror. Sounds kind of corny to my adult ears, but who knows? Maybe you'll call this barn that too before the night is over!"

Liz opened the lid of the fishing box. The rusted hinges squealed in protest. "Now, let's see what we have here. Oh, goody! Look, Marcy! Fishhooks! You can do the most interesting things with fishhooks. Certain parts of the human body were just *made* for fishhooks. Or maybe it's the other way around."

She picked a large, rusted fishhook off the top tray. She brought the hook near Marcy's face. "Ever had a fishhook stuck through your lips, Marcy?" she asked, bringing the barbed point slowly toward Marcy's mouth. Marcy's terrified eyes followed its approach. She turned her head to one side. The hook followed. Marcy whipped her head to the other side. The hook followed again as Liz's grin grew wider and wider.

"Come on, Marcy. Pucker up like a fish and I'll ram the hook through. Then I'll tie a line on it and jerk, so that you'll learn how a fish feels when it takes the bait. Won't that be fun?"

Marcy drew in her lips and bit them tightly shut.

"What's wrong, Marcy? You want a worm on it, first?"

Liz touched the rounded bottom of the hook to the sensitive flesh directly below Marcy's nose. Marcy flinched and turned her head away again.

"Rather have it through your nose?" Liz asked, touching the tip of Marcy's nose.

Marcy kept moving her head, evading the hook. The other prisoners could only watch, both worrying if Liz intended to use fishhooks on them too when their turn came.

"I think it's time for you to start making sounds, Marcy, since your torture is about to get started."

Liz spoke more glowing-breath words. "Now, Marcy, tell me, do you want the hook in your nose, or in your lips?" she inquired, moving the hook toward Marcy's mouth again.

Marcy cleared her throat and said, "Leave me alone!"

"Oh, I see. You don't want your face marred. Well, I'm easy to get along with. How would you feel about me sticking it through a nipple?" Liz asked, gesturing with the hook toward Marcy's left breast.

"Liz," Marcy said, taking a deep breath and making an effort to calm herself, "it is time to let us go home." Marcy remembered once reading somewhere that the best way to treat crazy people was to talk to them authoritatively in a calm and reasonable voice. "My husband and children will be worried sick about me, and I'm certain that Kathy and Charles have people worrying about them, too. All we want is to go home. And to help you. We *will* get help for you. We will help you get better. I know that's what you *really* want, Liz. Untie me now, please, so I can help you."

"I'm so glad you want to help me," Liz grinned.

"Of course we do. Now, release me," Marcy ordered, using her mother-knows-best voice, "and I will—"

"Does that little speech mean you don't want the hook through a nipple, *either*?" Liz asked.

Marcy fought to remain calm. She took another deep breath. "What I want, Liz, is for you to release me. Then I'll get help for you. I promise."

"You sure are hard to please, Marcy. Damn if I can think of anyplace *else* to hook, except . . . oh, Marcy! Of course! How stupid of me! I understand, now. You *do* want it through your lips, just not the ones on your face!" she exclaimed as she suggestively lowered the hook toward Marcy's genitals. Marcy squirmed against the post.

"Untie me, Liz. *Un-tie me*."

The hungry gleam in Liz's eyes told Marcy that nothing she had said had gotten through. Liz still intended to torture her. *To torture her!*

Marcy gave in to the panic that been building. She wrenched violently on her wired wrists. "Help! Someone!" she cried, then screamed as loud as she could.

"Nice scream," Liz murmured. "I look forward to hearing more. Makes me tingly all over. I can tell Demon Young liked it, too. And remember, now, you can scream all you want. No one will hear you except those of us lucky enough to be in Bathory's Barn of Horror."

Marcy fought tears. "Please, let me go home! I'll do—"

"Anything?" Liz supplied.

"Yes!"

"Oh, Marcy, I've heard that so many times over the centuries. It's one of the clichés tortured people, or those who are about to be tortured, like you, almost always say, along with things like 'No!' and 'Mercy!' and 'Please don't!' and my personal favorite, 'I can't stand any more pain!' But of course none of those words ever stopped me, or any torturer worth their salt.

"Now hold still, Marcy," Liz said as she brought the hook back to Marcy's face. "I really think it's best to start with your mouth. Oh, don't look so disappointed. Maybe we can try other places later, but for now . . . pucker up, darling, because here it comes!"

"God damn you!" Marcy exploded, jerking her head to one side, anger mixing with her fear. "Leave me alone!"

"You're not holding still, Marcy, or puckering," Liz laughed, then tried again. Marcy turned her head away again. Liz kept laughing and trying.

"Damn you!" Marcy cried, continuing to evade the hook, "Oh damn you damn you damn you! *Stop it!*"

"No, *you* stop it," Liz responded, then spoke an ominous sequence of sorcerous words.

"Oh, no! No!" Marcy had time to cry as the purple glow sank into her skull and she felt the coldness spread outward from her solar plexus again. And again, within seconds, she could no longer speak or move, except to breathe and move her eyes, watching helplessly as Liz reached up, squeezed her lips together, and then slowly, teasingly, brought the fishhook nearer, nearer, positioned the point, and began pushing it into Marcy's captive flesh.

27

Psycho City

Trudy and Phil ordered carry-out in the turnpike island restaurant and got back in the Trans Am. Trudy started on her hamburger while Phil gassed up the car at the nearby service station, then they headed north once more.

"Next stop, Wichita," Phil announced, seeing a mileage sign. "Should be there in a half-hour or so. Want to stop for the night? Get a motel?"

"Sounds good to me."

"When you gonna tell me about what you read today?" Phil asked around a mouthful of hamburger. "Want to wait until we're in the motel?" Steering one-handed, he fumbled with his french fries then stuffed several in his mouth.

Trudy swallowed her last bite of hamburger and said, "Might as well tell you now. No reason to wait. Actually, after reading several of those books, the basics are pretty much what you heard Liz tell me in the playroom. The Countess tortured young women and bathed in their blood. Well, to be fair, McNally's book points out that there's no actual evidence for the blood bathing. It is not mentioned in the trial records.

"But what Liz didn't tell me was how Erzebet died. After Darvulia's death, another supposed's sorceress advised her to switch from peasant blood to noble blood, and evidently Erzebet was so strung out by then that she did. The authorities had to do something when the complaints about missing daughters began coming from aristocrats instead of peasants, and eventually Erzebet was imprisoned in her own bedroom, the door and the windows bricked up except for slits at the tops of the windows for air and a food hole in the door. She survived that way, all alone in that room, nearly four years, then died."

"Oh. Not a nice way to go."

"She was never actually sentenced," Trudy continued. "Her family was too powerful, so to avoid an open scandal, her sentencing never happened. She was just left in her bricked-up room to slowly die. The servants who helped her torture and murder the other servants, however, were sentenced. They were publicly tortured and executed."

"Poetic justice."

"What I'd really like to talk about more than the gory details right now, what I really think may be more important to us, is the way reading about Erzebet made me *feel*, or rather how those memories I've been trying to listen to made me feel."

She wadded up the paper in which her hamburger had been wrapped and put it in the carry-out sack. "Sometimes what I read woke up other memories, and other times what I was reading seemed like things I already knew. But usually, it just made me angry." She took a sip of Diet Dr. Pepper.

"Angry? Well, I guess Erzebet wasn't someone who makes you feel proud of your species."

"No, you misunderstand. It's not what the Countess did that angers the memories. It repulses them, and me, but it doesn't really anger us."

"It repulses the memories?"

"Yeah. That surprised me too, since they seem to be Erze-bet's memories. Notice I said seem. I'm still not ready to accept that they really *are* a dead woman's memories. I hope I never am. But on the other hand, even if the memories really *are* Erzebet's, would feelings of repulsion be so sur-prising? If *you* had murdered hundreds of innocent young women in the heat of some sado-sexual passion, then looked back with the distance of centuries detaching you from your crimes, repulsion might be the *least* of what you'd feel."

"I'd hope so, anyway," he answered. "But does reading about the tortures maybe also . . . excite you? Just a little?"

"Does it you?"

"I didn't read the stuff, and I don't have those memories complicating things. But given my tastes in sexual fantasies, I wouldn't be surprised if Erzebet's exploits didn't make certain parts of me stand up and take notice. The movies I've seen that were supposedly based on her story had some pretty exciting sado-scenes, as I recall. Besides, Erzebet was sort of a real-life version of your fantasy domitrix creation, Raw Pain Max, wasn't she? And you know how I feel about Raw."

Trudy didn't answer for a moment, then she said, very quietly, "But Raw would never *really* do what Erzebet did, Phil. That makes a difference, doesn't it? I . . . hope?"

"Of course it does, Trudy. Jesus. I'm sorry if you thought I meant that you, or rather Raw, would really—"

"Do I excite you more when I'm playing Raw, than when I'm just, you know, myself?"

"*Both* of you excite me. Just differently."

"When we're in bed, making love, would you rather be chained up having Raw get you off with her whip?"

"Trudy, speaking of getting off, we're getting off the track here. I mean, asking whether I like Raw better than I like you! You're both the same person! Can't I enjoy having Raw sexually torment me sometimes, and enjoy having straight sex with Trudy other times?"

"It just suddenly seemed kind of . . . important, to me. Maybe I'm just trying to reassure myself that I'm not really like Erzebet. Even if reading about how she tortured young women did excite me some, I've *got* to believe I'm different from her, because these fucking memories running around in my head make me feel like I *was* her once long ago. Oh, shit. Listen to me. Psycho city. Tell me when I start to look like Norman Bates, will you, please?"

He reached over and gave her leg a squeeze. "You're not a psycho, Trudy."

She put her hand atop his where it rested on her leg. "I hope you're right."

"I am. Now, you said reading the books made you feel angry?"

"Makes the memories angry," she corrected, "and for a couple of reasons I've been able to kind of identify. First of all, it makes them angry to see the stories reduce Erzebet's entire life to little more than a tabloid headline in a supermarket checkout line. You know, *Lesbian Countess Tortures Nude Girls to Bathe in Their Blood*, right next to some new Ghost of Elvis story."

"Lesbian, huh?"

"What's *that* supposed to mean?"

"What's what supposed to mean?"

"The way you said lesbian."

"The *way* I said lesbian?"

"Like it explained everything."

"Hey, I didn't mean anything like that. You think with *my* off-center sexual tastes I'm going to throw stones or take cheap shots at women who simply like other women better than men? Why are you jumping on me, Trudy? Have you had women lovers yourself?"

"What if I had? Would it matter to you?"

"I don't know. I don't think so. Should it? Have you?"

"No. But I've had offers and been tempted to give it a try a couple of times when they were already good friends, good people who really had their shit together, compared to me, anyway, and I talked to them about it and, well, this whole business with Liz and Erzebet and all is just ripe for lesbian stereotype trashing, you know? Guess that's why I jumped on you, and why books that reduce Erzebet's life to an exploitation tabloid-headline make me so angry."

"But if Erzebet was lesbian, she just was, right? I mean,

facts are facts, and history's history, and that's *my* sage statement for the day."

"Actually, I think Erzebet would have been called bisexual, today. She was attracted to men, because she had an illegitimate child by a peasant boy who worked at her father's castle when she was a young girl. And there's a story about her once running off with a handsome nobleman.

"But an aunt supposedly introduced her to lesbianism, too, at an early age, and she seemed to prefer being with women later on. Her favorite torture objects were young women, at any rate. Or maybe that was just because they were easiest to lure to the castle with offers of work, and because even back then the fates of vanished girls were probably cared about less than the fates of vanished boys.

"Another thing that makes me mad about reducing her life to her worst traits is that it tends to make her seem something *other* than one of us, I mean, a *real* person who had the same cares and concerns as anyone. For example, she was married and had children, and letters she wrote to her husband when he was away fighting wars, which was most of the time, by the way, could have been written just as easily by any modern woman left lonely at home, worried about her kids' health, wishing her husband could be with her more.

"But there's something else that makes the memories angry, something that may be more important to us. The memories make me feel the most anger when I read about Erzebet's blood baths, because the stories say she did it to try and keep her beauty. They say she was extremely vain and sat in front of her bedroom mirror for hours sometimes, staring at herself, worrying about getting old. And that she bathed in the blood of young girls to try and hold off old age. The stories in effect reduce her monstrous acts to little more than a vain woman giving herself beauty treatments! And the memories know differently. They know there was more to it than that. Much, much more.

"When I was reading about it, I could almost see her face sometimes in my mind, like a reflection in a mirror, but she was not watching for signs of old age in her face. She was watching for something else. I don't know what. Maybe I could force the memories to let me see it, maybe I'll even have to, eventually, but I don't want to, because the thought of seeing what she was watching for terrifies the shit out of me, Phil, and it did her, too. Whatever she was afraid of seeing in the mirror was why she took the blood baths, *to keep it from appearing.* Understand? No, of course you don't. Can't. I'm not even sure I do myself, saying it out loud to you now."

Phil thought about what she'd said as he finished his hamburger and french fries and Coke, and Trudy was content to sit silently watching the road for a few miles, arms crossed over her solar plexus. Talking about the memories to Phil had made her feel chilled inside, even though the summer night air coming through the car's open windows was still hot enough to keep a sheen of sweat glistening on her forehead.

"I wish I could help you more than I am in all this," Phil said.

Trudy looked over at him. "You've stuck with me, Phil, and that alone is a lot."

"Not really. We're in this mess together."

"But you *could* have given me the slip, left me to sink or swim on my own. *You* didn't kill a woman, or whatever I did to whatever Liz was. You could have taken the easy way out, even gone to the police, but you never even considered it, did you?"

"Don't make me sound like such a dummy," he joked, but his subdued tone of voice told her all she needed to know. She leaned over and kissed his cheek.

"I did think of something, though," he said a moment later. "You've had trouble with mirrors a couple of times since Liz gave you those memories, right?"

"So?"

"Well, couldn't it be somehow related to how the memories feel about Erzebet and her fear of mirrors? You could have been picking up those feelings before you'd read the books, before you'd *consciously* discovered the mirror-fear."

"You're right. I should have thought of that myself."

"Sometimes it's hard to see things from too close up."

"Yeah."

"Our exit's coming up," Phil said, motioning to the South Wichita exit sign. "Notice the lightning?" he asked, hooking a thumb behind them. Trudy looked around. In the southwest, low on the horizon, lightning from a summer storm was flickering. "Probably rain later. Maybe a Kansas tornado will even take us to Oz."

"You can spot thunderheads even in the dark, monkey."

He slowed and took the exit. At the exit toll booth he paid a dollar and twenty cents to the uniformed attendant. Then they started looking for a motel.

28

Taste Test

Outside the barn, crickets had stopped chirping when screams began disturbing the night. But an hour had passed since then, and the crickets, now used to hearing scream after anguished scream, were chirping happily away once more.

Liz licked fresh blood from her fingers. "Not spicy enough, yet," she said like a cook testing a recipe. "Your blood needs more pain, I'm afraid, Marcy, darling."

She walked away from Marcy and stopped in front of Charles. She touched her fingers to a trickle of his blood, smiled at him as she raised her fingers to her mouth, then slowly licked away the crimson smear. "Yours too," she told him, then she went to Kathy. "And yours," she decided after another taste test.

Marcy, Kathy, and Charles were no longer tied to the poles. They now stood in the center of the barn. Their only bonds were the punishing strands of tightly twisted bailing wire that kept their hands behind their backs, and their fishhooks.

Marcy wore a fishhook through her lips. Charles' and

Kathy's lips were also held closed by the rusted metal of a piercing fishhook. All three mouths were badly swollen around the invading hooks.

Marcy and Charles and Kathy were all standing beneath an overhead beam. That was because of the fishing lines that Liz had attached to their fishhooks, lines she had then stretched across the overhead beam and tied to rusted harness hooks on the opposite wall, after pulling them tight, and tighter, and tighter. Which explained why all three were straining as high as they could on their bare tiptoes, standing flat-footed being out of the question if they did not want to find out how much their flesh could take before it started to tear.

Their bodies glistened with sweat and streaks of blood. Liz had used a fishing knife and a pair of old pliers on all three after inserting their hooks but before releasing them from the poles. They had now been straining on their toes for nearly ten minutes. Marcy's calves had started to visibly tremble as she took tiny staggering steps, trying desperately to maintain the awkward, tiptoed, hands-behind-her position without falling.

"Poor little muscles," Liz said, noticing Marcy's trembling legs. She squatted down and ran her hands up and down Marcy's strain-hardened calves. "This should teach you that it's always a good idea to stay in shape, Marcy," Liz lectured, "like Bicycling Chuck there, and Jogging Kathy. What are you going to do in ten *more* minutes, if your muscles are already trembling like this now? Have you tried resting one leg?" she asked. "Like this?"

She grasped Marcy's left ankle and pulled up and back. Marcy squealed a fishhook-muffled scream and hopped frantically on her right leg, fighting to get her balance back.

"Does that help, any?" Liz wanted to know. "Maybe we should try resting *both* legs," she suggested, taking hold of Marcy's right ankle too.

Marcy desperately begged as best she could through her sealed mouth.

"Don't you think your lips could hold you on their own, Marcy, dear?" Liz asked. "They look pretty strong to me.

And don't worry about the fishing line breaking. I did some special fishing-line-strengthening sorcery before I pulled it tight. So, want to try hanging from your lips?" Liz inquired, increasing the pull on Marcy's support leg.

Marcy's sounds became even more frantic.

"Hmm. Well, okay," Liz said with a laugh. "Perhaps we'll try the total suspension later. But for now. . ."

She let Marcy's left foot rejoin her right one on the hay-strewn floor. Then she stood up and plucked Marcy's line like a guitar string.

Marcy screamed.

Liz plucked again.

And again.

Liz gave the line a final pluck, then retrieved the pliers from the floor near one of the posts, came back to Marcy, and positioned the metal jaws around the tip of Marcy's left nipple. Marcy's nipples were already swollen, having felt the bite of the pliers while she'd been tied to the post. Without another word, Liz began to squeeze and Marcy began to scream.

"By the way," Liz said a few squeezes later, "don't worry about fainting and hanging from your hook. My sorcery won't let you faint, I promise." She eyed Marcy's other swollen nipple. "Is that one sore, too?" she asked with mock concern as she moved the pliers and started squeezing again. "Guess it was," she laughed several screams later.

Liz put the pliers in one of her jumpsuit's pockets.

Marcy groaned and sobbed and panted, tears streaming from her eyes as she continued stagger-stepping to keep her balance.

Liz walked to Charles and plucked his line.

He screamed.

She laughed, plucked the line again, then took the pliers out of her pocket and reached down between his legs.

Like Marcy, he begged as best he could through his sealed mouth as he felt the cold kiss of the metal jaws Liz was positioning upon his testicles. Then she squeezed, savored his scream, repositioned the jaws, squeezed again, then repeated the procedure another time. And another. And another.

When Liz felt Charles had had his proper ration of pain, she moved to Kathy.

"And how's the tuning on your string, Kathy?" she asked, plucking Kathy's line. She listened to Kathy's scream, then said, "Sounds a bit flat. Maybe I can sharpen it a bit with these," she suggested, holding up the pliers. She moved them to Kathy's left nipple. And squeezed.

Kathy screamed and screamed as she strained to maintain her tiptoed position.

Liz kept working upon Kathy's breasts several minutes more, then patted Kathy's sweating buttocks and said, "You're really in good shape, darling." She leaned forward and gave Kathy's cheek a kiss, then put the pliers back in her pocket, stepped back, and surveyed her three victims.

"Well, you'll all be happy to know that Demon Young and I both feel much stronger and more healthy already, in spite of the fact that so far you've only been in very mild pain. Mild, that is, compared to what I have planned for later on."

Liz began to undress. "Right now, however, I need to siphon off some pain-energy a little more directly. I hope you won't mind my being naked, too. It's not a sign of disrespect, I assure you. Being naked simply makes my absorption of your pain easier. You do understand, don't you?"

When Liz was completely naked, she sat down on the floor near her three sweating, straining victims, then stretched out on her back, spreading her arms and legs until her body formed an X. She closed her eyes and began speaking harsh, guttural words in her spell-language.

Liz's breasts and vagina began sparkling with flashes of purple light. Then tendrils of glowing, purple mist emerged from her and began stretching toward the captives.

Each of the two tendrils of glowing mist from Liz's nipples split into three streamers of serpentine violet light, then attached themselves to Marcy's and Kathy's and Charles' nipples. The tendril from Liz's vagina split into three streamers, one attaching itself between Marcy's legs, one between Kathy's, and one between Charles'.

Marcy's and Kathy's and Charles' pain suddenly intensified, doubled, tripled, kept getting worse and worse as the streamers thickened and glowed brighter, the brightness flowing back along the streamers and tendrils toward Liz, flooding her with the building energy of her victims' growing pain.

Liz moaned and cried out with the pleasure of the sado-sexual pain-energy flooding her body.

She felt Demon Young near the surface of her consciousness, also basking in her victims' agony as Marcy and Kathy and Charles kept screaming and screaming and screaming in the grip of the pain-intensification spell.

Liz gasped and groaned and writhed with pain-passion nearly one full minute more, then began revoking the spell.

The tendrils of glowing mist slowly dimmed and vanished. The screams of the three victims changed to broken sobbing.

Liz sighed contentedly and stretched. Then she laid unmoving for nearly five minutes, eyes closed, hands over her solar plexus, taking deep, measured breaths. Finally, satisfied that the new energy was properly synchronized with Holly's body, she opened her eyes and sat up.

She looked at her three captives. Marcy's calves had begun to cramp during the intensification spell. She now stood nearly flat-footed, blood streaming from her horribly stretched mouth.

Charles' and Kathy's swollen lips were bleeding worse too, their calf muscles trembling and threatening to begin cramping.

Liz beamed at them all. "You were wonderful!" she told them. "Demon Young and I are so very, very pleased!" Then she went from one to the other, taste-testing their blood once more. When she had finished, she was silent a moment, then gave them her verdict.

"As wonderful as you all three were, however, well, I don't know quite how to tell you this," she said with mock sadness, "but my experienced palate tells me that your blood, Marcy, and yours, Chuck, and yes, yours too, Kathy, all still needs more pain."

29

Ally

Trudy and Phil stopped at a 24-hour convenience store and bought some toothbrushes and toothpaste and various other toiletries. Then they found a motel near the Wichita airport.

"I thought he was going to ask for your autograph too," Phil remarked, referring to the motel registration clerk. He flopped down on the bed. "He really looked you over."

"I'm used to it. People have been staring at me like that ever since I grew taller than most of them. The muscles only make them stare harder. Now, if I were a man, no one would blink."

"I disagree. You'd turn heads either way."

"But for different reasons," she said, stretching out on the bed next to him.

"Tired?" he asked, turning over on his side to look at her.

"Of course. But you must be exhausted. You should have let me drive part of the way. Eight hours is a long time to sit behind that wheel."

"It wasn't so bad until after Z-ROCK faded."

"Which was early on." She reached over and pulled him on top of her. He put his arms around her as they kissed.

"Uh, just how exhausted are you, Trudy?" he asked, kissing her again as he slipped a hand beneath her t-shirt.

"Why do you ask?" she responded as she reached around with both hands and slid them beneath the waistband of his jeans. She pushed them deeper.

"I ever tell you that you have an incredibly sexy ass?" she asked as she gave his buns a hard squeeze.

"Ouch!" he complained, laughing. "I ever tell you that you have one too? Among other parts?" He gently squeezed her left breast while teasing the nipple with his index finger.

"Mmmm," she moaned, then nibbled his ear lobe. "Have another rubber in your pocket?"

"Sure."

"Too tired to make love to me?"

"Yeah, I am. Sorry," he apologized, then wiggled off her and sat on the edge of the bed. He began to pull his cowboy boots off. Trudy got a fistful of his t-shirt and wrenched him onto his back. He was already grinning, but when he saw her half-angry expression he laughed out loud.

He whipped his arms around her neck, jerked her down, kissed her.

"Have you decided what reward you want for helping me with those fans?" she asked, several kisses and two t-shirt removals later.

"Yeah. I have," he answered as he unbuckled her belt.

"And?"

"I want you to make me taller." He unzipped her jeans.

"You're tall enough already, for me."

"I didn't mean all of me."

"Oh," she laughed, arching upward so he could slide her jeans down to her knees. Then he pulled her black bikini panties down too and sat astride her, reaching down to her breasts as she reached up and began undoing his jeans. "Which part isn't tall enough?" she innocently asked after unzipping him.

"Gosh," he said as if surprised, looking down at himself. "I guess none of me is anymore, thanks to you. But there's just one more thing," he added as he changed positions so she could pull his pants farther down. "Can we take our boots off first?"

"What for? Lay down. You've been in the driver's seat all day. It's my turn, now. Which pocket is that rubber in?"

Phil got to remove his boots about a half-hour later. Trudy took hers off too, then they showered together and tried out the toiletries from the supermarket.

After the shower, Phil turned on the bolted-down motel television while Trudy finished up in the bathroom. He began flipping channels. On KTVH Channel 12, the local CBS affiliate, they were superimposing a weather message over the network programming, scrolling the message from left to right across the bottom of the screen. Phil only saw the end of it, but then they started repeating it.

"Maybe we *will* get to see Oz," he remarked when Trudy came out of the bathroom.

"Pardon?"

"They just had a severe thunderstorm warning on TV," he explained. "Possible damaging hail. Possible isolated tornadoes," he added, pulling back a corner of the curtain to peek out the window. The window faced west. He saw a flash of lightning in the distance, then he let the curtain fall back into place. "Hope it doesn't hail on my Trans Am."

"How could you tell new dents from the ones it already has?"

"Very funny."

He turned the TV off and they got into bed. Trudy snuggled into the crook of his arm.

"Phil?"

"Yeah?"

"I'm tired as hell, but I'm kind of afraid to sleep. I'm afraid that on top of what happened in Dallas, that the stuff with Donna today, and the books I read, and the memories I stirred up will, you know, give me bad dreams. It's silly to be scared of bad dreams, I know. But I am. *Terrified*, to be honest, now that I'm admitting it to myself."

He stroked her hair. It was still damp from the shower. "I'll make a deal with you, Trudy. If you have a rough time, wake me up and I'll help you talk it out of your system, but you have to promise to do the same for me if I'm the one who wakes up scared. Okay?"

She was quiet a moment, then reached up and kissed his cheek. "Okay, monkey. I really like you, Phil. I'm beginning to think I might even, you know, love you, in fact."

He pulled her closer. "Me too, about you. I guess I might even love you too. It'd be funny if that story you told Marv about our getting married turned out to be true, sometime."

"Marv. The club. It all seems like another world, tonight. I wish I was back in last week, you know? I'd give a lot to be thinking about nothing more than another dull night at Marv's club. Do you really think he'll hire us back, again?"

"Sure. He can't resist us. Or at least you. Don't forget

how bad he wanted to see you modeling those nipple rings," he laughed.

"He did seem pretty interested," Trudy laughed too. "But damned if I'm going to get my nipples pierced just to get our job back."

"But Trudy, didn't you know? *That's* where I wanted you to wear your engagement rings."

"Ring-zz?"

"I was going to buy two."

She slid her hand down his body until she held his penis, which immediately started to stiffen. He inhaled sharply at her touch. "And I wanted you to wear yours around *him*," she said, squeezing. "Does this mean the engagement's off?"

"I didn't know it was officially on."

"Well, I can't believe I'm saying this, but I guess I'm game for it, if you are. Uh . . . are you? Do you think?"

He turned sideways, nestling into her arms and pressing himself against her. "Trudy, I can't believe I'm saying this either, but . . . yeah. Sure. Okay. Shit, yes. Let's be totally crazy and get fucking officially engaged! And maybe, if we get out of this mess alive, and still like or love each other afterward, we'll even do what comes next. Get married, I mean. It might be kind of damn neat being married to you."

"Me too, to you," she whispered, kissing him.

"Well then, I'll officially ask. Will you marry me, Trudy?"

"Yes, I guess I just might."

"Wait a minute. I didn't ask you from on my knees. What would Raw say about that?"

"Raw's back in Dallas, and *I* don't require that kind of silly shit."

They kissed, several times, in various places. Then Phil put on another condom and positioned himself between Trudy's muscular thighs. They made slow, official-engagement love, then went to sleep.

A crash of thunder woke Phil. It was raining heavily outside. Trudy wasn't in bed.

Lightning flashed through the thin curtains. In the sudden flicker of light he saw Trudy. She was sitting with her back to him, facing the mirror that hung above the cheap motel writing desk beyond the foot of the bed.

"Trudy?" he called. She did not turn around. With the next flash of lightning, he saw her reflection in the mirror. Her eyes were closed. "Trudy?" he called again as he got out of bed. She still did not respond. "Oh, shit," he said under his breath, knowing now that unless it was normal for Trudy to walk in her sleep, and as far as he knew it was not, something was definitely wrong. He remembered her talking about how the Countess had stared into mirrors.

Thunder boomed. Scattered chunks of hail began to clatter against the motel roof and the cars parked outside.

He had nearly reached Trudy and was about to touch her shoulder when there was another flicker of lightning. He saw her reflection for only half a heartbeat, but that was long enough for him to see that Trudy's face was no longer alone in the mirror. Superimposed over her sleeping face was the face of a gray-haired woman, her mouth open wide as if frozen in mid-scream, her eyes staring with horror.

Phil wanted to scream and turn and run and almost did. But instead he told himself he hadn't really seen what he'd seen, that it had just been his imagination combined with his thinking about the Countess. He touched Trudy's bare shoulder. Her flesh was cold.

"Trudy?" he called, louder, gripping her shoulder harder. Thunder rumbled. "Trudy! Snap out of it! You're having a bad . . ."

He never finished the sentence because just then the lightning flashed again, and in the mirror he saw neither Trudy nor the screaming woman. He saw a human-shaped sack of flesh sitting where Trudy should have been, the skin transparent, the inside filled with a dark mass of writhing red-tipped tentacles.

This time he did scream, and run. But he stopped himself after a few steps and turned, sobbing like a frightened child, his bladder threatening to give way, and made himself walk one step, two, three, back toward Trudy.

He reached her. He kept his eyes on her, not the mirror. He took hold of her arms. He began trying to make her stand up, to get away from the mirror.

He was thrown back, stumbled into the bed, fell back onto it. Trudy was still sitting in front of the mirror. She had not moved. Something else had thrown him back. Something he had not seen.

Heart hammering in his ears, he tried to sit up. A weight pressed down on him, pushed him into the mattress, plastered itself over his face, chest, all the way down to his feet. He could no longer move. He could no longer breathe. The thing was cold against his nakedness, horribly cold, and moved against him like a wet sack filled with wriggling snakes. Then one of the snakes wrapped itself around his penis and began to move like a lover's hand. Suddenly a woman laughed inside his head.

Hello, Phil, she said, the words winding themselves around his panicked thoughts. *I'm Trudy's ally. My name's RPM. That stands for Raw Pain Max. But you can call me Raw. Tell Trudy I said hi.*

The weight left him. He gasped for air.

In the chair in front of the mirror, Trudy screamed.

30

Window

Trudy jerked to her feet and spun away from the mirror as her scream died away. The sudden violence of her movements knocked the chair over onto its side.

From the bed Phil saw Trudy's face in a flicker of strobe-light lighting. Her eyes were still closed, but her face was now twisted with terror, her mouth open as if still screaming, *like the gray-haired woman he'd seen in the mirror.*

Struggling to get his breath back, Phil scrambled to his feet and started to grab Trudy's arms, to shake her awake. But then in another lightning strobe he saw her eyes were now open. "Trudy?" he called. He cautiously put his hands on her arms. Her flesh was still cold.

"What's . . . wrong, Phil?" she asked, her voice unfocused, unsteady, the nightmare she'd just escaped still fresh in her mind. "Your . . . hands are cold, and you're shaking."

"No fucking wonder! You don't remember any of it?"

"I . . . remember a dream. A very bad . . . dream. Just like I was afraid of having." She took a deep breath, trying to calm herself. "Sorry if I woke you."

"Don't you even remember screaming and knocking over that chair?"

"I *dreamed* I screamed. Uh, when did I get out of bed?"

Phil slid his arms around her. "You're cold too," he told her, "and shaking too. Let's either get back into bed or get some clothes on or do both."

Thunder exploded outside. Trudy jerked in his arms at the sound. More lightning flashed, and again a second later. The hail began beating down harder, and the wind was working itself into a howling frenzy.

"Or maybe I've got a better idea than clothes or bed," he said, pulling Trudy's hand.

"What?"

"Bathroom."

She let him lead her into the bathroom. He turned on the light, shut the door, turned on the heat lamp, and then turned the shower on hot. "Instant sauna," he explained, "and instant soundproofing. That storm was getting on my nerves, and they've got enough on them already. Have a seat," he offered, putting down the lid on the commode. He leaned back against the sink, arms crossed on his chest, shivering. Trudy sat down.

"I promised to talk bad dreams out of your system, Trudy. So, tell me about it. Then I'll tell you what nearly scared the piss out of me. Literally."

"You had a bad dream, too?"

"I wish. Go ahead. You first."

"It can . . . wait till morning. You tell me what you—"

"No, Trudy. It fucking well can't wait until morning."

"Phil, I don't want to talk about it now," she responded, getting angry. "Okay?"

"No. You have to remember as much of it as you can, right now."

"Not if I don't want to. I'm trying to get over it, and I do not want to bring it back right now. *And I won't!* Understand?"

He didn't say anything, just ran his hands through his hair and took a deep breath, then reached down and touched her shoulder. Her flesh was warmer now, he was glad to discover. "That bad, huh?" he asked.

"I'll tell you in the morning."

"Maybe after I tell you what happened to me, you'll see why I'm so hot to hear about your dream. And speaking of hot," he added, eyeing the steam that was pouring out of the shower. He reached into the shower and turned the hot water down but not off.

"Thunder woke me," he told her. "I saw you sitting in the chair, facing the mirror."

"Oh, God," Trudy whispered. "Just like in my dream?"

"Your eyes were closed. I got up and called your name. You didn't respond. I started to touch you, then I saw an old woman's reflection in the mirror along with yours."

"Oh, God," her voice wavered, "oh, God, God . . ."

"In your dream too?"

She just nodded, tears glistening. He pulled a tissue from the wall dispenser and handed it to her. She wiped at her eyes.

"The old woman seemed to be screaming about something she was seeing in the mirror," he continued. "Then in the next lightning flash, I saw it too. It was—"

"I . . . know," she said, interrupting, "some kind of . . . tentacles, tipped with red, like blood . . ."

"Yeah. And they were inside some sort of flesh I could see through. When I saw *that* shit, I . . . ran. But only a few steps, then I came back and something, not you, because you didn't move, threw me onto the bed, laid on top of me, and started suffocating me. It also started fucking with my dick. It was cold, and it . . . *wriggled* against me, like snakes, or—"

"Tentacles."

"Or tentacles."

"Oh, God, Phil," she moaned. "It happened to me too, a cold wetness suffocating me, just before I woke up."

"And did it speak to you, too?"

"*Speak* to me?"

"Well, it spoke to *me* and said to tell you hi."

She just looked at him.

"It, or rather *she*, because it was a woman's voice inside my head, said hello and called me Phil, then mimicked what you say in our act, said her name was RPM, Raw Pain Max, but I could call her Raw. She also said to tell Trudy hi. Oh, and one more little thing. She claimed she was your *ally*. Then the thing pressing down on me went away, and you screamed. There's my little bedtime story. Now it's your turn."

"*My* ally?"

"That's what she said."

"In my dream, it was *Erzebet's* ally. Oh, God. Those memories in my head must *really be* Erzebet's, Phil. And that must mean that I *was* her, long ago. And that the thing she was so frightened of . . . in the dream, her Ally, it never went away, and it still . . . owns me!"

"It doesn't have to mean that at all, Trudy," he said, alarmed at the direction her conclusions were leaping. He had to get her back on level ground fast. "There must be lots of other explantions. I'll help you think of some, if you'll give me more to go on by telling me about your dream."

She nodded. "Okay. Sorry I was so bitchy about telling you. I didn't know what you'd been through." She took a calming breath and dabbed at her eyes with the tissue.

"I was lying in bed. I heard someone calling my name. I looked up, and—"

"You *really* looked? Or was this in the dream?"

"In the dream. I thought. Think. Maybe it really happened?"

"Sorry I interrupted. Go on."

"I looked up and saw Donna. She was in the mirror, beckoning to me, calling my name. I got up and went to the mirror. I sat down in the chair. But when I looked into the mirror, I didn't see Donna any more, or myself.

"The mirror had become a window, looking into a shadowy, high-ceilinged room. The windows had been bricked over, but small slits had been left up high, too high to see out of. The only light the room had came through these slits.

"Then I saw a dark shape in the room, someone moving around, pacing, and suddenly I was *in* that room, and I wasn't me. I was Erzebet Bathory, imprisoned in her castle, walled up alive. And I was insane with terror, pacing, pacing, heart hammering and jerking unsteadily every few beats, threatening to stop with every breath.

"God, Phil. I've never been so afraid, not even through all we've had happen, as I, or rather Erzebet, was. Because it was thundering outside the castle."

"Erzebet Bathory was afraid of thunder?"

"No. But she'd been having a nightmare with thunder in it, and she was convinced that the dream was about to come true. Each time lightning flashed through the slits, she whimpered. It was pitiful to hear. Even worse to hear it coming out of your own mouth.

"It had been a week or more since she'd slept much. She had been waking up from the same nightmare shortly after falling asleep, a dream in which her Ally came through her bedroom mirror for her soul.

"She had been imprisoned nearly four years, and had not been able to *feed* her Ally in all that time. So she knew that the Ally would eventually come to feed on her. Come to feed upon her soul."

31

Soul

Trudy was quiet a moment, fighting a silent battle with herself to continue telling Phil about her dream. She breathed deeply several times. "Don't be impatient, Phil," she said, looking up at him. "I'm trying."

"I know," he said, smoothing back a stray lock of her hair from her face. "Take all the time you want. Okay?"

She nodded, took another deep breath, then said, "In the dream, I—Erzebet—had been fearing the Ally would come for her soul ever since she'd been imprisoned. Then she'd started having the recurring nightmare, and knew the time was near.

"In the thunderstorm from her nightmare, the lightning flashes flickering through the slits of her windows would show the Ally coming nearer and nearer in her bedroom mirror, until the Ally's reflection replaced hers, ate her reflection as it ate her soul.

"Now the actual storm was coming nearer and nearer. I stopped pacing and huddled in a corner, as far from the place the mirror had once hung as I—Erzebet—could get."

"Where the mirror *had* hung?" Phil interrupted.

"Before they sealed me—her—in, they'd taken the mirror away, telling her she wouldn't be needing it anymore. It was intended as part of her punishment, a cruel joke. Everyone knew how she used to stare into that mirror for hours on end, and they all assumed it was because of her vanity. It had been, too, when she'd been younger. But for a long time she'd done it because the mirror was a way to focus her occult powers, a way to contact her Ally."

"And you knew all of this in the dream, because you *were* her, in the dream."

"The memories that have been intruding in my head since that night in the playroom were the *only* memories I, she, had, and there were more of them, of course. Her whole life's worth."

"Are they all still there now?"

"I don't know," she frowned. "I hope not," she added, then after a moment of introspection, she said, "but yes, oh God, yes. They are. And they make me feel so . . . *dirty*. All the horrible things she did . . . to all those young women, and . . . even though I'm repulsed, I can also feel the excitement, the dark passions. Oh, God, Phil! How am I going to deal with this? Live with this? Like this? If the memories stay with me, I don't—"

"Remember our deal?" he cut in, squatting down so he

could look at her eye to eye. He took her hands in his. "I'll help you if you'll help me? It goes for more than just bad dreams. Okay? You are *not* Erzebet Bathory, no matter what memories you have. And even if you once *were* her, it does not, I repeat, does *not* matter now."

"But it does matter!"

"Not to me. That counts for something, doesn't it?"

She nodded, gripping his hands.

"Can you finish telling me about the dream?"

"I'll try. The thunderstorm got . . . closer. Lightning flashed through the slits high up on the windows. I kept—"

"Erzebet," he reminded her.

"Erzebet . . . kept huddling in the far corner, not wanting to look at where the mirror had been, but looking at nothing else. Each lightning flash she expected to see the mirror hanging there again, and her Ally coming closer within it.

"And that's exactly what happened," Trudy said, staring into Phil's eyes. "*The mirror came back,* and her Ally *was* in it. Then the Ally made her walk across the room to the mirror and made her sit in the chair in front of it.

"She started screaming. Couldn't stop. Watching. Screaming and watching her nightmare come true as the Ally slowly devoured her reflection, her soul.

"When her reflection was gone, so was all light. I could still hear the thunder, but no longer saw the lightning. In the darkness I felt something cold pressing down all over me, choking me, suffocating me, burying me in tentacled ice. I had no breath for more screams. I jerked up and spun away from the mirror. Pain hit me. In my chest. My heart stopped beating. And . . . I died, inside that . . ."

"Not you, Trudy," he gently reminded her, squeezing her hands. "*You* didn't die."

"*Erzebet* died," she corrected herself. "And then *I* woke up."

"Christ," he said, standing up. The upper fourth of the bathroom was now filled with steam. He reached into the shower and turned the water off. "Warmer, now?" he asked. She nodded. He leaned back against the sink once more.

"So, it all began with Donna," he noted. "She said she'd help you, but if this is her way of doing it—"

"It *is*, Phil. It was horrible. But I think . . . I *know* that it's something I had to do, to face. And Donna knew it too, I guess. And I *will* find a way to help you back, Donna," Trudy promised.

"How?" Phil asked.

"I . . . don't know, yet."

"Trudy, remember your saying Donna mentioned in the john about stopping Demon Young? Could Demon Young be the thing in Erzebet's mirror? The thing that told me it was our Ally?"

"I don't . . . Just a second," she said, reluctantly delving into the memories. "No," she said a moment later. "Erzebet's Ally was *not* Demon Young. In Erzebet's memories . . ." she hesitated, delving deeper, "*she had to fight Demon Young, too!* Phil! That's it! Darvulia had the power to control Erzebet because Darvulia had made a pact with a demon who called himself Demon Young! And in order to fight back, Erzebet made a pact with a different demon, a demoness, called . . . no, there's no name. Just the Ally."

"She fought a demon with a demoness? The match of the century. Shit. This just gets better and better. And to top it all off, I'm supposed to believe Erzebet's demoness came here tonight calling herself Raw Pain Max?"

"That can't be her real name. I think . . . Erzebet thought . . . that the Ally was ancient. Pre-human. Maybe even pre-Earth."

"Yeah. Fucking Lovecraftian."

"What?"

"Lovecraft, a horror writer who did stories about pre-human monsters trying to reconquer Earth."

"Oh."

"They usually had tentacles, too, come to think of it. Wonder what kind of a mirror Lovecraft had?"

Trudy didn't respond.

"Well," Phil continued, "maybe Erzebet's Ally used your fantasy domitrix name just to get our attention. Or maybe it—*she*—has a sense of fucking humor."

"I don't know."

"If she wanted my attention, she got it. But what kind of demon-name is Demon Young, either, for that matter?"

"Maybe demons don't care what they're called."

"Sure. Call them whatever you want. Just call them."

"But . . ." she faltered, remembering Erzebet's terror, "once you call them, that's it. They *never* leave, never let your soul go. It's *forever*. Even if they sometimes let you come back, reincarnate or something, they're never far away. They're always watching and . . . waiting. And . . . that's what has happened, I think . . . to me."

"No, Trudy. Remember you're not Erzebet. You're—"

"Then why did that thing come *here?*" she shouted at him. "*I* haven't made any pacts with any fucking demons! But Erzebet did! And it came to *my* motel room, calling itself *my* Ally! Don't you see, Phil? The only possible explanation is that Erzebet and I, we must share, no, *be* the same soul!"

"I won't accept that, Trudy. And you're not going to start believing it either."

"I think maybe it's too late for that, Phil," she answered after a moment, voice gone flat, tears streaming, "because if I'm honest with myself, and I've got to start being if we're going to get out of this alive, I'm afraid I've already started believing that it's true."

"Trudy, look, we haven't even talked about the most obvious answer. More of Liz's tricks! Your dream, the mirror—"

"No, Phil. Not this time. You can believe that's a possibility if you want. But the memories know, *I* know, that what happened tonight was not Liz's doing. And I know something else too," she said, standing up. She took hold of Phil's hands.

"Erzebet became a kind of monster, Phil. But Darvulia had a lot to do with that. And now Darvulia, Liz, wants to do it to me again. Well, if I keep . . . whining around, about whether or not I once was or wasn't Erzebet Bathory, she just might succeed. So I'd better get my act together, and fast."

Phil pulled a fresh tissue out of the wall dispenser. "Okay, Trudy," he said, handing her the tissue. "Whatever you want to do, or believe, I'll stick with you. You know that. What else can I do? We're officially engaged now, right?"

She managed a weak smile for him as she dabbed at her eyes with the tissue.

"We came here to find a way to fight Liz, Phil. Well, let's look on what bright side there is. Maybe we've already found it."

"Or it found us," Phil suggested.

"Whatever," Trudy responded. "Because in the end the only thing that should matter to us is stopping Liz. And remember this while you're at it, and I'll try to keep remembering it too.

"I'm convinced that Erzebet and her Ally beat Darvulia and Demon Young once before, so we sure as Hell can beat their asses too."

32

Fresh Horror

The sky was graying with the coming dawn outside the barn. Inside, Marcy and Kathy and Charles hung upside-down by their ankles from the overhead beam. They hung in a single cluster, a length of bailing wire that tightly cinched their waists together holding them so that each faced outward.

The beam overhead creaked as they swung back and forth, a pendulum of blood-streaked bare flesh, their heads approximately three feet above the dirty hay on the floor, hands still wired behind them. All three had passed beyond screaming, their voices torn raw by all they had suffered throughout the night. But all three could still whimper and moan, and were doing so.

Liz was standing nearby. She had not bothered to put her clothes back on. Her nakedness was smeared with her victims' blood. In one hand she now held a length of rusted barbed wire about three feet long.

"Well, it's finale time, ladies and gentleman," she announced. "All that's left now is to move the blood left in your bodies from the inside to the outside, so that I can absorb it. So, let's get it over with, all right?"

"Please . . . don't . . . kill me," Marcy sobbed. "My child . . . ren . . ."

Liz leaned down, grabbed Marcy's hair, pulled her head up, and gave her a lingering kiss on her swollen, blood-stained lips. "Don't worry, Marcy. Your kids will be fine without you. They'll only miss you for a little while."

She released Marcy's hair. Marcy sobbed brokenly as her head hung down again. "No," she whimpered. "Please!"

Liz gave the cluster of bodies a shove, let them swing back and forth several times, then swung the length of barbed wire. The first stroke thudded solidly into Marcy's belly. She gagged and coughed raggedly, the closest she could now come to a scream. Blood from several deep gouges in her belly streamed down her torso.

Liz lashed Charles' thighs. Then Kathy's breasts. Then Marcy's. Then Charles' chest. Kathy's neck.

Blood began spurting in a thin stream from a pierced artery in Kathy's throat.

Liz kept at it, varying her targets, ripping at her victims' bodies without pause, on and on and on until blood was streaming freely into their faces and dripping in a crimson shower onto the floor beneath their heads.

Then the whipping stopped.

Liz quickly stretched out on the floor underneath her torn and fatally bleeding victims. She began intoning incantations, her eyes closed as she started rubbing the blood that was dripping onto her into her skin like a cosmetic.

The blood began vanishing into Liz's flesh.

Liz's appearance began to change.

Liz became a writhing, rotting corpse. Then that changed too until she had become a heaving, semi-transparent, vaguely human-shaped flesh-sack filled with madly wriggling black and purple tentacles, the sucking scarlet tip of each struggling frantically to get as near the surface as possible, attracted to the dripping blood like piranha's to raw flesh.

Eventually, long minutes later, weakened by loss of

blood, all three of the captives hung unconcious, their blood flow slowing.

Liz resumed her human shape. By the time she got them down to the floor and unbound them, Kathy and Charles were no longer breathing. But Marcy was, just barely.

She spoke an incantation and made a beckoning gesture. "Mar-cee," she called sweetly. "Wake up, Marcy."

Marcy half-opened her eyes and half-saw, her vision blurred, Liz leaning over her. Marcy whimpered weakly, feeling terrifyingly weak, chilled, suffocating, fighting for each new breath.

"Well, Marcy, we're just about finished. I feel so much better now, thanks to your blood, and Kathy's and Chuck's. They're already dead, by the way. I guess you had the strongest will to live. Probably because of your kids. But whatever the reason, you have my congratulations. I know it hasn't been easy for you, these last few hours. Anyway, since you lasted the longest, I'm going to reward you by making you the first I bring back to life."

Marcy whimpered some more as a shudder passed through her.

"I'm . . . dy . . . ing . . ." Marcy panted, gasping for air.

"Is that a question?"

"Plea . . . zze . . . don't . . . let . . . me . . ."

Marcy's vision was dimming, a ringing in her ears getting louder and louder, every breath harder to take.

"I . . . I . . ." Marcy wheezed, vision darkening, thoughts unfocusing. She desperately wanted to sit up, but she could no longer even lift her head.

"You know, Marcy, we're going to have lots of fun together, you and I and Kathy and Chuck. And one of the first things we're going to do once you're all three back among the living, is to get a welcome-home party ready for someone who has badly wronged me, someone I used to love, and who used to love me. Won't that be fun?"

"She's in Kansas right now, but when she comes back, probably thinking she's discovered a way to fight me, we'll spring a trap and show her there's nothing in her future but horror and pain. She owes me lots and lots of screams."

Marcy fought to get just one more breath, her cooling

flesh shuddering with the effort. Her eyes filled with a new terror as death's blackness came closer in her mind. Then her terror increased as she sensed something vast and hungry moving within that blackness.

"H . . . helll . . . p . . . meee . . ."

"By the way, you'll be meeting Demon Young when you're dead. Be polite to him and maybe he won't make you scream too much before I bring you back."

The hungry thing was reaching for Marcy's soul. She could feel it, sucking her away, a bloated, intensely evil presence, lapping wetly at the corners of her consciousness.

"No . . ." she gasped, "nooo . . . no—"

Marcy's breathing stopped. Her staring eyes began to glaze.

"You're going to make a beautiful corpse-slave, darling," Liz said to the dead woman as she gently closed her eyelids. "I'm sure you'll be pleased. Of course, most of it will be an illusion, but what isn't?"

She stroked Marcy's gouged and bloodstained breasts. She kissed Marcy's cold lips. "The power of sex unlocks many occult doors, Marcy. And necromancy is no exception. When I use sex in a certain way, in conjunction with certain powers Demon Young has given me, I can reanimate any corpse I choose. Like you."

Liz stretched out atop Marcy's cooling flesh, reached down between Marcy's legs with her left hand to cup Marcy's genitals, then used her right hand to hold Marcy's left hand against her own vagina.

"Ready, darling?" Liz asked, her voice tightening with a growing desire. "Good," she breathed, then began using her hand on Marcy's sex as she placed her lips against Marcy's mouth and started chanting a guttural necromantic incantation.

As Liz's excitement grew, she began to visualize her sexual energy as a serpent coiled around the base of her spine. She willed the serpent to awaken, to uncoil, to move slowly upward along her spinal column, higher and higher. Holding the image firmly in her mind, she also began visualizing a serpent coiled about Marcy's spine, also awakening, also moving upward.

Liz's left hand began glowing with purple light, and each word she now spoke emerged from her mouth as a breath of glowing lavender mist. Beneath her half-closed eyelids, her eyes blazed with purple fire.

The glow from her left hand began to infect Marcy's flesh, slowly spreading from Marcy's genitals down Marcy's legs and up Marcy's torso as Liz's sexual excitement burned ever hotter, her chanting growing louder, the words coming faster, her glowing hand moving faster and faster between Marcy's legs as she edged nearer and nearer to the orgasm whose explosion of sexual energy she would use to reanimate Marcy's corpse.

In Liz's mind, her spine-serpent and Marcy's had both nearly reached the base of their skulls, were rearing back their glowing heads, preparing to strike.

Marcy's body was now glowing from head to toe, vibrating with building energy. Her torture-wounds were beginning to heal.

Liz screamed a harsh command and visualized the spine-serpents striking upward into her brain and Marcy's, their glowing fangs sinking into the occult power-zone mystics called the Third Eye.

As Liz's scream of command died away, Marcy's cold, glowing hand moved against Liz's sex.

Liz began chanting different phrases, concentrating and focusing the energy her sexual excitement had raised, willing Marcy's hand to move like a lover's. Marcy's hand glowed brighter and became warmer as it responded. Liz gasped and cried out with nearing ecstasy.

She held the climax off for a few heartbeats longer, then screamed the final words of the necromantic ritual. Her scream devolved into wordless cries of passion. And suddenly hers was not the only voice. Marcy was now crying out her passion too, faintly at first, then louder and louder as she arched up against Liz's body, her lips seeking Liz's, her still-chilled tongue invading Liz's mouth as orgasm after orgasm ripped through them both, their glowing bodies emitting pulse-synchronized strobe-light bursts of violet energy until Death had been chased from the last corner of Marcy's flesh and she lay panting and moaning, eyes still closed, beneath the sorceress who had just healed her death-wounds and raised her from the Dead.

Liz eased herself off Marcy's body, knelt beside the moaning corpse-slave, and stretched. Her breasts and genitals, and Marcy's, were still glowing faintly, pulsing in time with their magically-linked and synchronized heartbeats.

"Wake up, Marcy, darling," Liz called. "Time to rise and shine."

Marcy obediently opened her eyes, eyes filled with fresh horror, and cold tears.

PART FOUR

Kansas

□

Despair has its own calms.

Bram Stoker,
DRACULA

33

Little Sweden

The Kansas dawn threatened more rain.

Shortly after seven o'clock, Phil and Trudy checked out of the motel and drove to a small café nearby for breakfast. The Wichita newspaper Phil bought at the café told him that several tornadoes had been sighted around the area during the night. Severe thunderstorms were possible again later that afternoon and evening.

When they had come out of the bathroom after talking the night before, the storm had still been raging. Phil had draped a spare blanket from the closet over the mirror, then they'd left the lights on, turned the TV on too, and, praying the storm wouldn't cut off the electricity, they'd crawled into bed, pulled the bedclothes up to their necks, and held hands most of the rest of the night, one of them staying awake, watching TV, and watching for any new signs of trouble, while the other tried to sleep.

At one point, though he hadn't told Trudy, Phil had grasped at religious straws by digging the standard-issue motel *Bible* out of the bedside drawer. But when thumbing through it started to make him feel sleepier, he put it back in the drawer and concentrated upon an old Laurel and Hardy movie being shown on TV instead.

In the end, neither he nor Trudy got much sleep, but at least they met no more nightmares during their short naps.

While they ate breakfast, they talked about what they should do next. Maybe they had found a way to fight Liz, but maybe they had not. Even if they had found a weapon in Erzebet's Ally, they did not know how to use it—her. Erzebet's memories remembered using the Ally to fight Demon Young, but there was a frustrating gap in the memories con-

cerning exactly how that had been done. And neither Phil
nor Trudy was anxious to confront Liz and her demon until
more certain they at least had a fighting chance.

"So?" Phil asked as he sopped up sticky maple syrup with
his last bite of buttermilk pancake. "What do you think our
next move should be?"

"What do *you* think."

"Well, we could drive up to see Donna's parents in Salina,
though I hope we can do this without disturbing them, you
know? But after last night, as far as I'm concerned, you're
in charge of this hunting expedition. What do the memories
make you feel like we should do next?"

She was silent a moment, then said, "I first want to go
where Donna died. Where did her mother tell you it happened?"

"Somewhere near Lindsborg."

"Is that farther away than her parents?"

"No. It's closer. I remember going through there when I
visited Donna as a kid. We were going to Coronado Heights
for a picnic. That's on a hill west of Lindsborg. The story
goes that Coronado went up there on his expedition through
Kansas because it was the highest spot around. Kind of a
local legend, I guess. Don't know if it's true or not."

"Then let's go to Lindsborg," Trudy decided.

Phil used his credit card to pay for breakfast. The sun was
breaking through outside.

"I want to stop at a service station and buy a map," Phil
said as they got into the Trans Am. The hail the night before
had not been large enough to give the car any new dents, as
far as he could tell.

After he had his map, he discovered that I-35, upon which
they had traveled from Dallas, branched in Wichita, one
branch continuing northeast as the Kansas Turnpike, the
other branch heading north as I-135, which led near Lindsborg.

They headed north on I-135.

Half an hour of flat Kansas farm-and-pasture scenery
later, a bright sun now rapidly warming the summer day,
they passed Newton. Another half hour and they were passing McPherson. Fifteen minutes north of McPherson they

saw a billboard advertising Lindsborg as Little Sweden, U.S.A.

"It's an ethnic-theme town," Phil explained. "Got any Swedish blood in you, Trudy?"

"Not that I know of. You?"

"Ya, sure. Maybe. I've got blond hair anyway, right?"

The Lindsborg exit sign appeared a few minutes later. Phil got off I-135 and went west, then north again, following signs.

Just south of the small town was a large wooden Dala Horse painted bright-orange, advertising the Old Mill Museum and Park. They crossed a bridge over the Smokey Hill River. At the city limits, a sign with a Dala Horse painted on it greeted them.

"Welcome to Lindsborg, Little Sweden, U.S.A.," Phil said, reading the sign with a badly executed Swedish accent. "Woops," he said a moment later. "Missed it."

"What?"

"There was a sign saying downtown was to the left, but I wasn't paying attention and didn't see it in time to turn."

"I imagine *any* street will do, don't you?"

"Might be tricky, Trudy, but I'll try."

"Monkey," she said, giving his arm a soft punch.

The Viking Motel appeared on their right. Then a sign indicated that turning left would take them to Bethany College.

Phil turned left down Swensson. After a couple of blocks, they crossed a Missouri-Pacific railroad track. The Bethany College campus went by a block or two after that. A couple more blocks brought them to Main. He turned left.

"This is incredible," Trudy said as she watched the old-style wooden houses go by. "They're really beautiful."

"Lots of community pride, I guess. Or ethnic pride, huh? Notice that most of them have a Dala Horse with the family's name on it out front?"

"I wonder how old some of them are? The houses, I mean."

Phil shrugged. "Houses like these in Dallas would probably have been bulldozed by now," he commented, "like they did the Commerce Street Newsstand downtown."

"You still mourning that newsstand?"

"I'll *always* mourn that newsstand."

They reached downtown Lindsborg a few blocks later. The lampposts were decorated with Dala Horses and other Swedish designs. Phil angled the Trans Am into a parking slot in front of the Swedish Crown Restaurant. He glanced at his watch. It was not yet nine o'clock. Most of the shops looked closed. But people were going into a doorway down the street.

Phil and Trudy got out and walked to the door. A sign above it said it was the entrance to The Courtyard. Through the door and down an enclosed and inclined brick walkway, passing shops on their right along the way, they reached a small skylighted courtyard where people were sitting at tables drinking coffee and eating cinnamon rolls from the Courtyard Bakery. Phil ordered two coffees while Trudy headed toward a table near a group of young people she assumed were college students. She felt them watching her as she sat down, and for once attracting stares was exactly what she wanted.

They needed to find out exactly where Donna's car wreck had taken place, and, if possible, without asking Donna's parents. On the drive from Wichita, they had discussed the possibilities—back issues of the Lindsborg newspaper or contacting local law enforcement authorities might work. But just asking local people might be the easiest and fastest.

As she sat her shoulder bag on the table, Trudy glanced over at one of the college boys who was still watching her. She smiled at him. "Hi," she said. He grinned and nodded. Several of the others turned to look at her again, too.

"We noticed a restaurant down the street," she said to him, improvising.

"Swedish Crown?"

"Yes. Is it a good place to eat lunch? We're from out of town, if you hadn't guessed," she added, smiling again, "and are here to see the sights, and shop."

"It's a real good place to eat," he told her. "Where are you from?"

"Dallas."

"We went there once. Saw Southfork Ranch. Are you an athlete?"

"Kind of."

Phil showed up with their coffee. He said hi, too.

"Didn't you say you had a cousin that lived up here somewhere?" Trudy casually asked Phil as she took her coffee from him.

"Yeah," he nodded as he sat down. "But she died." He looked at the college kids. "Had a car wreck near here recently. Any of you hear about it? Her name was Donna, and—"

"I heard about it," one of the other boys said.

"Me, too," said a young woman. "It was horrible."

"I never got straight exactly where it happened," Phil mentioned, taking a sip of coffee. "Was it out on the main highway? Or . . ."

"No. It was out west of town," one said.

"It was near where the backroad up to Coronado Heights crosses Highway 4," added another.

"Well, thanks," Phil said. "I might like to, you know, see the place, since she was my cousin and all. How do I get to Highway 4?"

"Stay on Main, going south. It deadends into 4. Then just follow it around the curve and out of town."

They drank their coffee and steered the conversation elsewhere, then left, found Highway 4, and drove out of town. They hadn't gone far beyond the city limits when Trudy moaned down low in her throat.

"Trudy?" Phil asked, glancing over at her. She was looking out the window, northward at a castle-like structure sitting atop a distant hill.

"Do . . . you see it . . . too?" she asked, voice unsteady.

"What? Coronado Heights?"

She closed her eyes. "Thank God," she sighed, then laughed weakly and looked over at him. "I thought I was slipping into more weird shit. I thought for a second that it was Erzebet's castle. Why the hell didn't you tell me there was a fucking castle up there?"

Phil shrugged. "Sorry. I didn't think about it upsetting you. Besides, it's not *really* a castle. Donna's folks told us it was built during the Depression by one of those work gangs the government organized. WPA? To make jobs for out-of-work people, you know?"

Trudy looked at the structure again and kept watching it as they drove west on Highway 4.

"This must be it," Phil said as they came to an unpaved road that seemed to lead straight north toward Coronado Heights.

He pulled onto the backroad and stopped the car. He started to get out.

"No," Trudy said. "Don't get out."

Her fists were clenched atop her legs. A tear was trickling out of one eye.

"Don't ask me how I know, Phil, but your cousin was already . . . dying, when the car wrecked. Liz engineered the crash to cover up what she'd earlier done. Then later she stole Donna's body from the cemetery and . . . brought her back to life."

Phil didn't respond.

"There's nothing for us here. We have to go up there," Trudy said, looking at the miniature castle atop the distant hill. "Your cousin was taken up there, first, the night she died. And she's waiting for me there now."

34

Coronado Heights

The unpaved road ran straight toward Coronado Heights for several miles, angling up a steady incline as it tunneled between rows of windbreak hedge trees. Pastures and fields lay beyond the thorny-branched barriers. In the Trans Am's wake dust billowed from the unpaved country road. As they passed a farmhouse, a black and white dog ran out of a driveway and chased their car, barking furiously.

The nearer they drew to the Heights, the harder Trudy had to fight to stop herself from asking Phil to turn the car around. She could feel Donna waiting for her atop the hill. By the time Phil left the straight road and started negotiating the curves that actually led to the top, Trudy's fingernails were digging painfully into sweaty palms.

The miniature fortress atop the hill came into view close-up as Phil rounded the last turn, reaching the summit.

Trudy's fear suddenly mutated into a crushing grief. Tears blurred her vision. She felt what Donna had felt in the moment she knew she was going to die. First disbelief. Then blazing anger. Extinguished by an inescapable acceptance that drained her of all her dreams and hopes, leaving her empty, leaving her nothing. Except horror. Because later, when she died in the crash, into her nothingness oozed Demon Young.

Trudy inhaled sharply, biting her lower lip to keep from crying out as she sensed Donna's terror of the dark presence suddenly lashing her soul with tentacles of razor-sharp ice, slicing at her consciousness, relishing her terror, absorbing her fear, eating her pain. . . .

Phil stopped the car near the fortress. He looked at Trudy and didn't like what he saw. "Trudy?" he asked, gently putting his hand atop her clenched fists. "You okay?"

She wrenched her car door open and got out. Phil got out too.

Trudy stood with her arms crossed tightly over her solar plexus, staring out over the flat Kansas farmlands that stretched to the horizon to the east. Puffy white cumulus clouds drifted through the blue sky overhead, their dark shadows racing across the checkerboard squares of pastures and fields below.

"She . . . Donna, loved it up here," Trudy said, wiping at her eyes as Phil came around the car to stand with her.

"Yeah. How'd you know? More of those feelings?"

Trudy nodded, then continued, her voice tightening with anger. "Liz knew how much Donna loved this place, too. That's why she brought her here, to contrast childhood happiness with adult horror, mocking her, trying to crush the last spark of resistance from Donna's soul. But it didn't quite work, Phil.

"Donna resisted to the last. In punishment, Liz left her dead in Demon Young's realm of pain until after she'd been buried, instead of bringing her back to life right away. But even that did not entirely destroy Donna's *self*. There was enough of *Donna* left, once I freed her from Liz's spell in Dallas, to defy Liz's brainwashing. If there hadn't been, she would have never tried to help us like she has.

"And now," Trudy wiped at her eyes again, "it's my turn to try and help her."

"How?"

Trudy was silent a moment, then told him, speaking very softly, "I have to try and set free the part of Donna that's unable to let go of the Earth, Phil. The part of her that's up here with us and is afraid to leave. She's afraid she'll drift back into Demon Young's Hell.

"I feel her, nearby. In there," she motioned to the fortress.

"You mean, uh, her ghost?"

"Let's go try to find out."

Trudy started walking toward the building.

"Uh, wait a minute, please?" Phil said, pacing her.

She stopped.

"Look, I don't like the way you seem to *know* things today. Is is because of what happened last night? Getting back all of Erzebet's memories? Or because of . . . the Ally?"

"All of the above, I guess."

"It's made you more psychic or something?"

"Evidently."

"I . . . don't think it's a good idea."

"You think I do?"

"That's not what I meant. I meant, are you sure it's safe? It *could* still be Liz tricking you."

"I told you last night. I know it isn't. Now come on. I promised Donna I'd help her, and I'm going to try to do just that. Right now. In there. Whether you come with me or not."

"I'm coming," he promised. "Hey, are you going to leave your shoulder bag in the car? We might need the cleaver."

"What for?"

"Oh. Yeah. Well, okay. Forget it. Let's go the fuck in."

The miniature castle was built of reddish-brown rocks native to the region. As they entered the shadowy interior through the only door the bottom floor had, the temperature dropped.

"Night air," Phil whispered, "insulated from the sun by the stone walls."

"What?" she whispered back.

"I was explaining to myself why it got colder when we stepped over the threshold. Night air."

"Oh? I don't remember it being cold enough last night to make our breath frosty like this," she mentioned, still whispering. "Do you?"

"I was trying not to notice that. Do you, uh, know where the ghost . . . is?"

"Not yet."

They slowly walked deeper into the small fortress. Small windows high up on the walls let shafts of light pierce the gloom. Erzebet's memories began swirling wildly in Trudy's head, the stone walls stirring thoughts of the castle in Hungary where she had committed her monstrous crimes.

Trudy struggled to keep her own thoughts clear and Erzebet's memories under control.

In the large single room on the bottom floor, there was a fire-blackened fireplace and stone picnic tables and benches. Kids had scrawled graffiti on the walls. Names and dates and messages were carved into the soft sandstone rocks here and there.

"Where . . . is she?" Phil quietly asked.

Trudy turned toward a narrow flight of stairs. "She's up there," she pointed. "In the sunlight. Waiting for me to set her soul free."

"And you . . . know how to do that?"

"Of course not," Trudy shrugged, "but I think Erzebet does. Coming?"

"Wouldn't miss it," Phil said under his breath as he followed Trudy to the stairs. He shivered.

They mounted the stairs and emerged onto the roof. Trudy stopped. "Can you see her?" she asked.

"Where?"

"Right over there," Trudy pointed. "She's standing by the railing, looking out over the land. Her hair's blowing in the wind."

"Uh, Trudy, there isn't any wind."

"There is for her. You don't see her?"

"No."

"You stay here. I have to go closer."

Phil watched Trudy approach the far corner of the roof. Even in the sunlight, his breath was frosted and he kept shivering.

Trudy stopped. She saw Donna look over at her. Donna's eyes caught the sunlight like melting ice.

"You helped me last night," Trudy said.

Donna nodded.

"You showed me the Ally. The Ally can stop Demon Young?"

Another nod.

"I, the memories in me, can't remember how to use the Ally. Do you know how?"

The semi-transparent image of Phil's cousin slowly shook her head negatively.

"Can you not speak with me as you did in the bathroom on the Turnpike?"

Another slow, negative head shake. Donna's ghost turned her face away and looked back out over the land. Trudy felt a deep yearning to spread wings and fly, and she suddenly knew it was Donna's desire she felt, knew Donna had fantasized about flying into space from up there as a kid.

"What must I do to help you fly free?" Trudy asked. The answer came not from Donna, but from Erzebet's memories.

Trudy took a deep breath and closed her eyes. She slowly spoke foreign words the memories told her to speak. With her eyes closed, she did not see the glowing purple mist that began to emerge from her mouth and drift toward Donna's ghost.

Keeping her eyes closed, Trudy raised her arms like a preacher giving a benediction. She kept speaking a phrase over and over in words she understood only because Erzebet did.

When she felt it had been long enough, she opened her eyes. Donna's ghost was gone.

Trudy wiped tears from her eyes and turned back to Phil. There was moisture glistening in his eyes too.

"She's . . . gone?" he asked, no longer whispering.

Trudy nodded. He walked over to her and pulled her close.

"I guessed she had," he quietly said, "when it got warmer. What was that purple glow I saw for a moment? It looked kind of like Liz's breath did in Dallas, before we were paralyzed. But I think it was coming from *your* mouth, Trudy. And I didn't like the idea of that very much."

"I didn't see it. My eyes were closed. But I don't like the thought of it, either. I had to help Donna, though, and I'm convinced that now I have. Maybe all sorcery glows purple or something."

Trudy ran a hand through her hair. "I can tell you something else, too. Sorcery hurts. I got cramps in my solar plexus. Thought for a moment I was having a fucking heart attack."

"You feeling okay, now?"

"I won't feel okay until we've stopped the monster who killed your cousin."

"And who also wants to kill us. Was Donna able to tell you any more about using the Ally?"

"No. She'd helped me all she could. So I—Erzebet—said the needed words and set her free. Erzebet used a kind of Hungarian spell with Gypsy origins, the memories say. And occult powers granted by the Ally made it work."

"So, Donna's . . . free, now? In heaven or something?"

"I don't know where she is, Phil. But at least I know where she *isn't*. She's not with Demon Young. Her soul was never supposed to escape him, no matter what happened to her physical body or to Liz, but somehow she did escape. Was she religious, do you know?"

"No. I don't. Could have been, though."

"Whatever, she was a strong young woman, Phil. Be proud of her."

"I am."

"Good. Me too. Let's get out of here, okay?"

"You don't have to ask twice," he answered, as he took her hand and led the way back down.

35

Earth-Anchor

The college student had been correct about the food at the Swedish Crown. It was delicious. But Phil enjoyed it more than Trudy. Trudy was preoccupied with thoughts she had not yet shared with Phil. She had said very little since leaving Coronado Heights, and Phil hadn't pressed her.

He finished the last bite of a Swedish dessert he couldn't pronounce, a type of cheesecake garnished with Lingonberries, then took a sip out of his cup of King Oscar coffee. Trudy had already finished her meal, sans dessert.

"How you doin'?" he asked her as he glanced at the bill the waitress had left on the table.

"I'll make it. Sorry I've been such bad company."

"Yeah. If you're not careful, I'll never bring you to Kansas again."

She gave him a small smile that didn't last long. "You mind if I go ahead to the car?" she asked. "I want to look up something in one of the books. Just give me the car keys and you can finish your coffee."

"Okay. I want to use their restroom too before we take off." He gave her the car keys and she left. He took a couple more sips of the rich coffee, then took the bill to the cash register.

"Everything all right, sir?" the checker asked as she took his credit card.

"With the food, yes. Great. Wonderful. Could you tell me where your restrooms are?"

"Down this hallway," she pointed, "on the right."

"Thanks."

He finished paying, went to the bathroom, then headed

outside. He picked up a tourist-info newspaper on his way through the entrance/exit alcove.

He stopped. Trudy was not in the car. He looked up and down the street. He did not see her. He began to feel nervous. "We should never have separated," he mumbled under his breath. "Shit." Anything could have happened. Liz might have followed them from Texas for all he knew. He might never see Trudy again. She might be—

"Here I am," Trudy said, coming up behind him.

He spun around. "Where the hell were you? I was kind of, you know, worried."

"Sorry. I doubled back and went to the restroom too. Didn't you see me? You were still drinking coffee."

"No. I didn't see you. I don't need extra scares like that. Let's not separate again, okay?"

"Phil, I'd better level with you. I sort of staged an experiment, and it seems to have worked, because you didn't see me."

"What are you talking about?"

"I tried out a kind of a spell, from Erzebet's memories. It hurt too, by the way. I think maybe it hurts because the Ally draws energy from the pain, then gives it back as occult powers."

"Oh, wonderful. Fucking fantastic. Trudy, you shouldn't be messing with that crap. If you—"

"And how am I going to fight Liz if I don't mess with that crap?"

"I—"

"I came over to the table, watched you finish your coffee, then stood in the hall as you went by to the bathroom, and you never knew it."

"And did you come into the fucking john to watch me take a piss, too?"

"Don't get angry with me, Phil. Please. Because I've got problems enough as it is without you getting on my case. I have to try using the spells Erzebet says I should be able to use, and—"

"Erzebet *says*. Look, Trudy—"

"Godammit! Don't fuck with me on this, Phil. We've

got got to work together. I need your fucking help! Okay?"

Passersby were giving them looks. "Uh, I don't think they're used to hearing street language on the street here, Trudy. Maybe we should get in the car if we're going to—"

"I want to know if you're going to help me or not? Because if you're not—"

"Okay! *Yes!* I'll help, dammit! Satisfied? Now give me back my car keys, if you haven't turned them into a frog or something."

"That's not funny, Phil."

"You're telling me?"

She gave him back the car keys and he unlocked the doors. Oven-temperature heat poured out of the black car. They got in. Phil cursed as the sun-baked seatcovers tried to burn the backs of his legs through his jeans.

When the windows were down, Phil started the engine and backed out. Trudy reached into the back seat and started searching through the library books. She found the one she wanted and leafed through it as Phil drove down Main.

"You really did want to look up something?" he asked.

"I didn't *lie* to you, Phil. I just didn't go *straight* to the car."

He turned left off main and headed out of town. He glanced at his gas gauge. "Where you want to go next?" he asked. "Salina?"

"Remember that motel we saw on our way in? I want to go there."

"What? You want to stay here in Lindsborg? It's hardly noon, Trudy. We could drive to—"

"We don't need to go anywhere else, Phil. I've helped Donna. Now I've got to help myself, and you. And everything I need to do that is there," she hooked a thumb at the books in the back seat, "and here," she pointed at her own head, "and wherever Erzebet's Ally calls home. I've got some *inner* work to do. And before you say anything, I don't *want* to do it, okay? But I don't see any other way for us to have a fighting chance against Liz. Do you?"

Phil glanced at her, saw the strained look on her face. He shook his head negatively. "I don't have any other suggestions. No. But for God's sake, Trudy. Be careful messing with that occult shit. Promise?"

"I'll have to do whatever I have to do, Phil. But I'll try not to get you involved in it any more than necessary. Just be my earth-anchor, you know? So I'll have a reason to hold onto *Trudy*."

"Earth-anchor. Yeah. I'll sure as hell try."

He drove to the Viking Motel and checked them in.

After he helped Trudy carry the books into the room, she sat down cross-legged on the bed and arranged the books around her. "Okay," she said. "I'm not going to waste time before getting started, so don't talk to me for a while. And, I hate to ask this, Phil, but I'm going to need it to be as quiet as possible, so, could you leave the TV off?"

"Sure. I've got this tourist newspaper to read anyway," he answered, waving the newspaper he'd picked up in the restaurant. "Want me to get you a Coke or something?"

"Maybe later," she said, opening a book.

Phil settled down in a chair by the window and started looking through the newspaper. He glanced up at Trudy from time to time. She was so engrossed in the books, first looking at one, then another, comparing the two, then reaching for a third, that Phil felt he might as well have been in the room alone.

He finished looking through the newspaper. "Uh, excuse me, Trudy. But, are there any of those books you aren't going to need?"

"You can read one of them if you want, but the less you know about the occult the better earth-anchor you'll be, according to Erzebet's memories. Look. I know this is going to be boring for you. Why don't you go exploring? Or shopping downtown? Buy some Swedish stuff. Ogle some college girls."

"I'm not leaving you. We shouldn't be separated. Liz might try to—"

"Liz is in Texas."

"We can't be sure of that."

"Liz *is* in Texas. Go on, Phil. I'm not going to do anything but read and think this afternoon. I won't do any occult experimenting while you're gone. If you hang around here, being bored, your mental . . . vibrations . . . are going to make it harder for me to concentrate."

"I'm not leaving you alone."

Before she could stop herself, a flare of irritation with Phil made her push at him, mentally.

"But if you say it's okay," he said, standing up, "I'm gone. See you later."

He was outside the room and walking toward the car when it struck him that something felt wrong about the way he'd suddenly changed his mind. He almost went back into the room, but a reluctance to do so rose up before him like an invisible wall. With a curse he turned and unlocked the car.

Trudy heard him drive away. "I shouldn't have done that to him," Trudy angrily said, talking to herself. "Damn."

You didn't do it, came a reply inside her head. *I did.*

"Oh, shit," Trudy cursed. "Not voices in my head. Oh, God. No . . ."

I'll do whatever is necessary to whomever I please, said Erzebet, or the Ally, or both. Trudy couldn't tell which. *You will now stop whining and continue our work.*

And, a few moments later, Trudy obediently did.

36

Other Demons

Phil drove back to Lindsborg's Main Street and parked in front of an old blacksmith shop. He was still angry with Trudy for asking him to leave and himself for going. He got out of the car and wandered down the street into a shop called Prairie Woods, where he found himself surrounded by imported blond furniture made of Swedish Pine, which, he was told, was much harder than American Pine because of the shorter growing seasons in northern Sweden.

He browsed through Prairie Woods then went across the

street to a place with a giant Dala Horse out front. The shop was called Hemslöjd. It included a Dala Horse factory where custom-personalized Dala horses were made.

He finished looking around the Hemslöjd shop and went to the Swedish crafts shop, then to other shops, still angry every time he thought about Trudy back at the motel doing God knew what alone. He decided to go back and check on her, several times, but each time he immediately felt a mental push that changed his mind, making him suspect she was pulling more occult tricks on him, which made him even angrier. And more worried, about what it might be doing to her.

But eventually, by the time he'd been into and out of all the shops along Main and had consumed two cinnamon rolls and a cup of coffee in The Courtyard, his anger was fading and his spirits lifting.

He went back to one of the shops and bought a surprise for Trudy. Then he drove a block east to the Swedish Timber Cottage, a gift shop the tourist newspaper had said was housed in a timber cottage that had been dismantled in Sweden and reassembled in Lindsborg.

He bought several more things in the timber cottage, including a jar of imported cloudberry jam. Then he went next door to Fantastisk to see the Gnomes Home in the basement, about which he'd also read in the newspaper.

While in the basement, he heard Trudy speak his name close to his ear. He jumped and nearly broke a gnome. But Trudy wasn't there. What was there, however, inside him now, was a strong urge to return to the motel.

He hurriedly drove back to the motel. The door to their room was standing open. He rushed inside. He did not see Trudy. Panic grabbed him. Then he heard Trudy start to laugh, in the bathroom.

He looked around the corner into the bathroom and saw Trudy staring at herself in the mirror, smiling. She looked up at him with glassy eyes.

He started to speak, but she interrupted before he could, asking, "What is it, Phil? Need to use the bathroom?" He had the feeling she was about to laugh again. "Have I upset you, little boy?"

"Trudy, just what the hell—"

"You think I'm Trudy?" she asked. The words chilled him, and the kind of smile she was smiling didn't help. It looked too much like Liz's grin.

"You *are* Trudy, Trudy. Now stop scaring me and—"

More unpleasant laughter came from Trudy's mouth. Then suddenly her smile became a grimace of pain as her eyes closed and she put her hands to her head. "My fucking head hurts like shit," she groaned, rubbing her temples.

"Trudy?"

"Yeah."

"What the hell was that all about?" he demanded.

"The Ally. Or Erzebet. Or both. I can't . . . control her, or them. But it's okay, because—"

"It is damned well *not* okay, Trudy!"

"Well, it'll have to be, until this is over, one way or the other."

"Trudy, you were fucking possessed!"

"You think I don't know that? Just like in the playroom. Let's talk about it on the road."

"Road? Aren't we staying here tonight?"

"We have to leave. Help me get the books back into the car, okay?"

"But we'll have to pay for a whole night!"

"It's important we move, before we're . . . found. And we may have to *keep* moving, now that Erzebet and the Ally are active, because while Liz may be in Texas, Demon Young is not bound by flesh or distances." Her head pounded as she stood up and walked out of the bathroom. She cursed at the pain. "I need some aspirins, bad."

They checked out of the Viking Motel.

Phil filled the car's gas tank with gasoline. The filling station didn't have any aspirins for Trudy. Phil stopped at a convenience store and got some, along with a six pack of Classic Cokes, several Slim Jim beefsticks, and a bag of Fritos. Trudy took three aspirins, put the bottle in her shoulder bag, then washed the aspirins down with a Coke as Phil drove back to I-135.

"North or south?" he asked. "Salina's north."

"The other way."

He went south, back the way they had come that morning.

"You're tense," Trudy said. "You're gripping that steering wheel like—"

"For God's sake, Trudy, of course I'm tense!"

"The Ally won't hurt you, Phil, or me."

"Sure. There's nothing to fear from a Lovecraftian *thing* that has occult powers and possesses people. Nothing to worry about at all. That's why Erzebet was not afraid of the Ally when it came to eat her soul," he sarcastically added.

"Maybe if I explain more—"

"Hey, don't bother. The less I know, the better idiot-anchor I'll make, remember?"

"The Ally, and Erzebet too, I guess, wanted to be alone with me. That's why she, or they, made me say that. It's okay now if I tell you more about—"

"What a load of shit."

"Phil. Come on. Just listen, will you? All your bitching isn't helping matters much."

He didn't answer.

"Phil?"

"Okay. Talk. I'll shut up."

"I don't want you to just shut up."

"I'll shut up and *listen*, okay? Jesus."

Trudy paused a moment, trying to bypass the anger that had been building. Then she said, "Erzebet did not know enough about her Ally before they fought Demon Young. Darvulia found out what Erzebet was planning before she'd had time to fully prepare. Darvulia herself was preparing to take over Erzebet's body so that she could become the Countess she wanted to be. So when the psychic battle broke, Erzebet had to give the Ally more or less free reign to fight Demon Young.

"Demon Young eats human fear and pain," she continued, "and so does Erzebet's Ally. They, and others like them, were spawned by human fear and pain, somehow, ages ago, and so that's what they eat, the occult vibrations associated with human fear and human pain."

"Wonderful. Haven't I seen something like that in *several* horror movies?"

"But they eat something else, too, if they get the chance. Other demons."

"Yum."

"Phil, *please* don't be flippant right now. You're angering the Ally, and—"

"I thought you said she wouldn't hurt me."

"As long as you don't anger her too much, she won't."

"Oh, hell, Trudy. I'm just pissed in general. Go on with your story. I'll try to be a good boy."

"I hope so. Where was I?"

"The demons were eating each other."

"Yeah. That's how the Ally defeated Demon Young. Only trouble was, you can't really *destroy* demons. So Demon Young was just kind of . . . engulfed, see? And he never stopped fighting to get *out*, which he obviously eventually did, sometime after Erzebet's death."

"Obviously."

"But because Erzebet's soul was linked to the fight, as the years after Daravulia's defeat went by and the struggle went on and on with Demon Young inside the Ally, Erzebet was driven into the darkest, most violently sadistic depths of madness, which made her careless, which eventually got her imprisoned."

"Well, I feel lots better now, knowing that the price of using the Ally against Liz is for you to be driven insane."

"There's another way to use the Ally, the way Erzebet had originally intended, if she'd had time to prepare."

"And you know what that way is?"

"No."

"Do Erzebet's memories?"

"No. I think that's why she made me use the cleaver in the playroom instead of calling the Ally, which would have meant more of the same kinds of problems she had in Hungary after defeating Darvulia.

"Erzebet knew, you see, that the cleaver would not really destroy Liz. But it *would* destroy Liz's flesh and drain her energy levels, slow her down, giving Erzebet time to prepare with the Ally, and with me, like she did not have time to prepare in Hungary long ago.

"Erzebet knew of course that Liz would try to possess a

new body. She could have tried stopping Liz by killing everyone else alive in the room, meaning Holly and you and then me too. But Liz might still have possessed someone farther away, if she'd had the strength. So, Erzebet sort of *gave* her Holly, see? Hoping that you and I would be left alone for awhile. And we kind of were."

"Kind of? I don't recall being left alone."

"She wasn't strong enough to attack us directly, which was better than nothing."

"Only barely. But, Trudy, if there's another way to use the Ally and Erzebet doesn't know what it is, the Ally must know the way herself then, right?"

"The Ally claims not to know either."

"And you believe her?"

"I . . . yes. I have to trust her."

"Well, I don't. How was Erzebet going to learn the other way if *no one* knew what it was?"

"By experimenting. Which she didn't have time to do much of, before Darvulia attacked. So that's why we're going to keep moving, to try and buy me the time I need. They say they'll help me do experiments inside my head while you drive us around to keep Demon Young from pinpointing our location. All I need is their instructions and the use of your rearview mirror."

"More mirrors again, huh? But what if it's a lie, Trudy? I've always heard that demons, or demonesses, or their Master, Satan, aren't necessarily known for telling the truth. Maybe there *isn't* any other way to use the Ally."

"The Ally and Demon Young and other Pain Eaters like them have no Master, although more than one of them have amused themselves by calling themselves Satan from time to time."

"And the Devil didn't mind, I suppose?"

"There is no Devil. And no God, according to the Ally. Just Pain Eaters playing games of pain and death. But sometimes special humans come along who strive to ease the suffering Pain Eaters cause, to defuse the fears and hatreds Pain Eaters propagate, and to release the tortured souls Pain Eaters have captured. That's what Jesus was doing on the Cross. And Buddha with his—"

"Occult bullshit is bad enough, Trudy, but don't let them feed you religious bullshit too!"

"You're wrong to make a distinction between religion and the occult."

"Really? Okay. I'll play along for a moment. If Jesus had the answer you're looking for, why not get a Bible and a Crucifix and maybe a fucking priest while you're at it, then just—"

"The Ally says that Jesus wasn't allied with a Pain Eater like Erzebet and I are. So, we don't have the options Jesus had, not to mention the occult knowledge and skills Jesus learned after years of study in Egypt and Tibet. And the religion we know today as Christianity is more the product of Pain Eater tricks than what Jesus actually taught. Pain Eaters have feasted on fear and death for hundreds of years under the sign of the cross and other religions. Remember the Crusades? The Inquisition? The Holy Wars of the past in the Middle East and the Jihads of today and—"

"The Ally has twisted answers for everything, I see. How wonderfully fucking convenient."

"Uh, Phil, you're . . . angering her. I think that maybe you should . . . apologize."

"Not fucking likely. Apologize to a *demoness*? Sure."

"I mean it, Phil. Apologize. Quick! *Please*."

"Okay! I fucking apologize!"

Trudy let out a sigh of relief. "That was close, Phil."

"What would she have done if I hadn't apologized?"

"Oh, you *would* have apologized, eventually."

Phil started to say something, then stopped himself. A mile went by in silence as he kept his thoughts to himself, not that, he supposed, the Ally couldn't read them.

"Trudy, about Erzebet's blood-baths," he said a little while later. "Was that because of the Ally, too?"

"Indirectly. The blood is needed to maintain a physical body that has died and been reanimated. Darvulia was already that way when Erzebet met her. So she needed to absorb blood, through her skin, at least once each month. She didn't tell Erzebet the real reason for it, though. She said it was to maintain beauty. Erzebet's vanity and worries about getting older were no secret, so Darvulia used them against her."

"Darvulia took the famous blood-baths *with* Erzebet, then?"

"Yeah."

"Cozy."

"They were lovers, remember? Liz called it sharing blood-passion. But after Darvulia was dead, Erzebet—"

"Did Erzebet kill Darvulia, then?"

"Darvulia was kept alive by Demon Young's power. So, when the Ally engulfed Demon Young—"

"It was goodbye Darvulia."

"And hello pain, for Darvulia. Because Demon Young took Darvulia's soul with him when he was engulfed."

"Good for him."

"But not for Erzebet. Linked to the Ally and the ongoing struggle as she was, Darvulia's addictions to pain-energy fixes and blood-baths intensified the ones Erzebet had already developed on her own."

"All of which meant it was not a good time to be a peasant girl working for the Countess."

"And Liz has those needs now, because she's Darvulia reincarnated," Trudy continued. "When she makes corpse-slaves of people, like she did Donna, she absorbs their blood to kill them off after torture. Donna would have died even if Liz hadn't staged that car crash, because Liz had already drained off most of her blood."

Phil saw McPherson up ahead on the right. "You want to keep going back to Wichita?" he asked.

"No. I think . . . I want to go . . . more to the west. Let me look at that map," she said, opening the glove box. She got the Kansas map out, looked at it for a moment, then said, "On the other side of McPherson, take the exit for Hutchinson."

37

Circles

They drove into Hutchinson less than a half-hour later, the largest city they had seen since leaving Wichita. A Holiday Inn with a Holidome appeared on their right. A mall sprawled on their left. A jumble of grain elevators rose in the distance.

Trudy had turned the rearview mirror toward her and had been trying to concentrate on her experiments. She looked away from the mirror and rubbed her neck. "When we're through with this mess, I don't ever want to look in a mirror again. I always felt mirrors were creepy. Now I'm beginning to learn why."

"What's been happening in there?"

"Can't talk about it. Rules of the game. Sorry."

Phil shrugged. "I don't suppose we're going to stop here?" he asked. "That Holiday Inn maybe?"

"No. Turn right at that stoplight."

"Where are we going?"

"It's better if I don't think it out in advance. I'll decide as we go, so that Demon Young can't anticipate our moves."

"Do you really believe Demon Young is *looking* for us?"

"*I* don't know what to believe, Phil. But I'm not in charge of this horror show. All that matters at the moment is that *Erzebet* believes it. And the Ally *knows* it."

"Sorry I asked."

Trudy ordered several more turns as they zigzagged through Hutchinson, past the Kansas Cosmosphere and Discovery Center, past the Kansas State Fairgrounds, circling back through the towering grain elevators, then cutting into the downtown section where they saw an elegant 30s-style Fox movie theater that was no longer open for business.

"I'm beginning to feel like a rat in a maze," Phil complained fifteen minutes later. "Is this kind of random driving really necessary?"

"Same answer as before. It's not my idea."

"Yeah, but—"

"I'm just following feelings, letting the Ally guide us. Okay?"

"No. But I'll try to shut up about it."

They eventually left Hutchinson and headed west, went through Nickerson, angled northwest into Sterling and Lyons, went east on K56 for eleven miles, took K46 north one mile for a side trip through a small town that had Little River painted on its water tower, drove an unpaved backroad further east to an even smaller town with Windom on its water tower while Trudy kept experimenting, only looking away from the mirror when she wanted to give Phil new directions. He noticed that each time she pulled away from the mirror, her expression was more anxious and worried and fearful than before.

South of Windom, they got back on K56 and headed east. Before long they saw a roadsign announcing the mileage to McPherson.

"We're driving in circles!" Phil exclaimed.

"Not . . . really," Trudy answered, pulling her eyes away from the mirror. "I'm beginning to feel that . . . yes, the Ally *is* taking us someplace."

"No idea where, I suppose?"

"It's just a feeling of anticipation I have, and it's getting steadily stronger. Also, I'm . . . getting scared. I think she's going to make me do . . . bad things. Not to you, or anyone . . . alive, though. And before you tell me you don't think it's a good idea, I'm still open for better suggestions. I've asked before and you've never had any. And neither have I. So I'm going to grit my teeth and do whatever I need to do to get through this mess, as if Erzebet and the Ally would let me do otherwise, anyway. Just watch my back for me, okay?"

"I just wish I could do more than that to help you."

"Me too. But you can't."

A few miles later, she had him turn off K56 again, then

directed a series of turns on backroads, some sanded, some graveled, some rutted dirt, driving between fenced fields and pastures and thorny-branched hedgerows and farms, many of the farmhouses standing abandoned, slain by the hard times that were killing farms everywhere.

Phil was driving down a narrow, deeply rutted dirt road, the setting sun in his eyes, when Trudy said, "Slow down. There's a turnoff up ahead."

"I don't see anything but hedge trees and weeds," he replied as he slowed the Trans Am. It had been over two miles since they'd even seen an abandoned farmhouse.

A narrow break appeared in the hedgerow to their right. Across it stretched a rickety, wood-framed barbed wire gate with a buckshot-scarred NO TRESSPASSING sign dangling from it. On the other side of the gate stretched an expanse of rolling hills covered with tall weeds and sunflowers and native prairie buffalo grass. A rutted, weed-choked path that might once have a been a road led away from the gate across the pasture and down into a shallow, treeless hollow that was already filled with evening shadows.

"We have to go into the hollow," Trudy told him. "Think your car can squeeze through that opening?"

"It can try."

"I'll open the gate," she said, and got out. The gate was held closed by only a loop of rusted bailing wire. She removed the restraining loop and pulled open the gate. The stiff-stalked sunflowers and weeds fought her as, muscles straining, she pulled it farther and farther open until at last it stood at a right angle to the hedge row.

Phil carefully steered through the narrow gate. Trudy pushed the gate closed, put the loop back in place, and got back in the car.

"Why'd you close it?" he asked. "We might want to leave in a hurry, for all we know."

"We're not supposed to be trespassing, remember? With it closed, maybe no one will notice we are."

"As if anyone's near enough to see. I think we're the first to torture a vehicle on that road out there for a very long time. But you're the boss. Why do we have to go down into the hollow, anyway?"

"There's . . . someone there, someone the Ally wants to see."

Phil looked across the treeless, grass covered expanse. "I don't think there's anyone there, Trudy. Not for miles."

"Just drive. Okay? Now? I already mentioned it might have to do with someone that wasn't alive, remember?"

"Vividly."

Phil started slowly driving down the rutted path, cursing under his breath as the Trans Am endured the jarring, punishing ruts and holes, wincing at the sound of the tall weeds and sunflowers scraping against the underside of the car. A startled jack rabbit in their path leaped up and bounded away.

Phil kept following the ruts down into the hollow, turning left and right and left again, passing from the fading sunlight into the twilight shadows. At the bottom, the ruts skirted a small pond covered with a layer of green algae. Frogs leaped from the bank into the pond as the Trans Am bumped past. On the other side of the pond, the ruts led up out of the hollow.

Phil was halfway to the top, almost back in sunlight, when he suddenly slammed on his brakes. The car jerked to a stop. He had nearly run into a twilight-shadowed barrier hidden among the tall weeds. It was a stone fence. They climbed out of the car.

The fence was crudely made of badly weathered, unworked stones of various kinds and sizes piled atop each other. Many had toppled to the ground over the years and lay scattered about. The fence was, however, still two to three feet high.

There was a break where there had once been a gate, but it was not wide enough for the Trans Am. The fence ran for about twenty feet to each side of the gate before making right angles and disappearing among the grass and weeds.

"Do we go around it, or what?" Phil asked.

In answer, Trudy pressed forward through a thick patch of waist-high sunflowers and went through the gate. Phil followed.

There were other weathered stones hidden by tall grass and sunflowers and weeds on the other side of the gate.

Headstones. The Ally had brought them to a graveyard.

"There . . . was once a . . . church, up there," Trudy said, looking at the crest of the slope, her voice gone flat, her staring eyes glassy. "You . . . must wait here."

"I don't think so, Trudy."

"Do not . . . speak," she ordered. "I must . . . search."

She slowly walked away, moving stiffly. Phil decided that no matter what she said, he was going to stay near her. Then he discovered he could not move his feet forward. He could, however, move back toward the car. But he didn't. He stood as close as he could to the invisible barrier and sweated in the summer heat as he watched Trudy searching among forgotten graves in the deepening twilight, remembering what she'd said about there being someone in the hollow the Ally had wanted to see.

She moved farther and farther away from him. When she squatted down from time to time to examine a weather-eaten headstone, the weeds hid her from view. Phil wondered how she could see well enough to read in the thickening shadows. He got his answer a few minutes later when she momentarily turned her face in his direction.

Trudy's eyes were now flickering with purple fire.

38

Whispers

Trudy continued searching among the weed-hidden graves, purple fire flickering in her eyes, until finally she squatted down out of sight to examine a headstone and did not stand up again.

Worrying because he could no longer see her, Phil tried moving forward again but still could not. After several minutes more, he tried calling Trudy's name, just to be sure she was all right. But then he discovered that whatever was keeping him from moving forward was now also keeping him from making a sound, and, he learned a moment later, keeping him from moving back toward the car.

Night falling, Phil stood rooted in the Kansas pasture, unable to move or talk, worrying about Trudy, tension and fear growing. He thought about the meat cleaver in Trudy's shoulder bag in the car, wishing he had it with him, even if he didn't really believe it would do any good against the kinds of danger he was afraid might appear.

Crickets chirped around him. Frogs croaked by the small pond. The grass rustled in a warm evening breeze. Stars began to appear in the darkening sky overhead. In the southwest, towering thunderheads caught the gold-edged scarlet blaze of the setting sun and Phil remembered the Wichita newspaper's prediction of more severe storms that night.

When it was darker still, Phil saw lightning flickering beneath and among the billowing thunderheads while overhead the stars burned with a fierce brightness in the rural night sky.

Suddenly the crickets and frogs fell silent. The breeze died. Faintly in the distance Phil heard the lazy rumbling of thunder. And then, from the direction in which he'd last seen Trudy, he heard her begin to whisper.

Phil could only stand and listen and wait and fight his growing fear. He tried to hear what she was whispering, but she was too far away. He could tell, however, that it sounded repetitive, like a chant.

The line of thunderheads slowly drew nearer, marching across the flat Kansas plains toward the place Phil stood listening to Trudy whisper among the graves. He tried to stop worrying about Trudy and what she was doing by worrying about more practical things, such as whether or not he would be able to drive the Trans Am out of the pasture and down the rutted dirt road beyond without getting stuck in the mud if it rained too much, and wishing again he had replaced his worn out windshield wipers with new ones.

The thunder grew steadily louder, the lightning now flickering brightly enough to strobe-light the motionless grass and weeds.

Then, in the darkness between lightning flashes, twin

specks of purple fire rose into view from the direction of
Trudy's whispering. A gust of storm-cooled wind rustled the
grass. And when the next strobe-light flicker came from the
rumbling sky, Phil caught a glimpse of Trudy.

She had taken off her clothing and was standing naked in
the weeds. But she was no longer alone. Something faced
her, the back of its head featureless and white. *Skull white*.

Mouth dry, fighting terror, Phil kept looking, waiting for
more lightning.

Lightning snaked across the sky. The ghostly figure facing
Trudy wore scraps of dark clothing that did little to conceal
the stark white bones beneath, a stoop-shouldered Hallow-
een skeleton whose head was slowly nodding as it listened to
her whispers. Then it reached out skeletal hands and touched
her bare shoulders.

Trudy's whispering stopped. In reply, after a long pause in
which thunder rumbled, there came a thin, hollow voice,
wheezing words too softly for Phil to make them out. Trudy
whispered something else. The voice weakly answered.
Trudy whispered again. A long roll of thunder kept Phil
from hearing any reply.

The thunder got louder, the lightning brighter. The wind
grew stronger as a chilling thunder-squall swept the pasture,
heralding the nearing storm.

Then in the darkness between flashes Phil saw Trudy's
purple-fire eyes move. The next burst of lightning revealed
she was again alone, and that she was now gliding toward
him, arms outstretched, mouth open as if screaming, eyes
blazing with purple fire, her bare feet several inches above
the tops of the tall grass and weeds.

The enforced silence killed Phil's cry of terror in his
throat. A moment later, the purple fire in Trudy's eyes began
to dim. New lightning showed her nearing the ground, then
touching it and crumpling to her knees.

Kneeling among the graves, Trudy closed her eyes and
screamed. But she screamed only once, then gasped several
sobs, as if trying to get her breath, and called, "Phil? Help
me . . . please, if you . . . can?"

He felt something jerk inside him. Whatever had rooted

him to the earth no longer did. Reflex urged him to run to the car. But he made himself hurry forward to help Trudy.

He squatted down and slipped a supporting arm around her bare shoulders. She shivered against him.

"Can you make it to the car?" he asked, again able to talk. A smell of Death clung to her.

"If you'll . . . help me. I'm . . . so cold . . ."

Phil took off his Z-ROCK t-shirt and helped her slip it on, then he started helping her back to the car. Twice they stumbled over headstones in the dark. But finally they found the gate and went through.

A drop of wind-driven rain splattered against Phil's face as they reached the car. He helped Trudy into the passenger seat. She was shivering violently now. He closed her door.

He thought about trying to find her clothing for her, but the rain was starting to fall harder. He had to get the car out of the pasture at once. There wasn't time to search for her clothing in the dark.

He slid behind the wheel and slammed the door and started the engine. He flipped on the headlights, backed up, wheeled the car around, and headed out of the pasture as fast as the rutted pathway allowed, grass and weeds scraping loudly beneath the car, worn out windshield wipers fighting the thickening rain while he struggled to see out of the clear swath the wipers were managing to make.

He rounded the pond and headed up the slope toward the pasture's gate. He jerked a glance at Trudy and by the glow of the dashboard's lights saw that she was still shivering, staring straight ahead, eyes glassy.

They reached the gate. He opened the car door. A gust of rain-saturated wind wrenched it out of his hands. He jumped out and fought the wind and rain and thick weeds until he had opened the gate, then he got dripping-wet back into the car and drove through the narrow opening, scraping the left side of the car on the barbed wire-wrapped gatepost as he emerged from the pasture and onto the narrow, rutted, dirt-turning-to-mud road.

He gunned the engine, fishtailing slightly in the deepening mud, determined to keep the car moving forward until he reached a gravel road he remembered crossing a mile or two away.

As he peered through his clear swath of windshield, his headlights and the flashing of the lightning revealed the branches of the road-bordering hedge trees whipping violently in the gusting wind.

The rain was hitting the car in wind-driven sheets now, the visibility down to less than a car-length beyond the Trans Am's phoenix-painted hood. He nearly slipped off the narrow road into the deep ditch that ran along the right side. Cursing, he somehow got the car back where he wanted it and kept going.

It began to hail, the chunks of ice banging noisily against the car's roof and hood.

The rain fell even harder, effectively cutting Phil's already limited visibility to zero. But stopping meant getting stuck in the deepening mud, so he kept going, steering all but blindly, nearly sliding into the ditch again and again.

Then suddenly something was looking in at him through the clear swath of windshield, crouching low upon the hood, something made of swirling rain and wind, except for the eyes, which were of purple fire.

The fiery eyes burned into his brain. His mind emptied. His grip on the wheel began to relax. The Trans Am headed for the ditch.

Trudy screamed a guttural phrase.

The numbness left Phil's mind. He jerked the steering wheel. The car fishtailed wildly. He fought to get it back under control.

Trudy screamed more syllable-twisting words. Her body began to pulse with a purple glow, the words emerging from her mouth wreathed in purple light, shooting laser-straight through the windshield, piercing the thing crouching on the hood.

It threw back its wind-and-rain head as if in agony and vanished. The glow left Trudy's flesh. Phil regained control of the car, his hands shaking so badly that only by gripping the steering wheel with all his strength could he maintain a semblance of control.

"What in fucking hell was that!" Phil shouted, voice breaking with terror.

"For a moment," Trudy answered, "Demon Young... found us, but we are...hidden...again, and now...I will try to help...more..."

She closed her eyes. Her lips moved soundlessly. The hail and rain and wind slackened. A pocket of calmer weather now surrounded them, keeping the worst of the storm at bay, and Trudy kept concentrating to keep it that way as she directed Phil back onto Highway K56, around McPherson, and then south on I-135, back toward Wichita.

39

Reverend Johnson

They were nearly to Wichita before running out of the storm. Trudy stopped concentrating on the weather spell. She slumped groaning in the bucket seat, rubbing at her strain-stiffened neck.

Phil had not interrupted her concentration by asking questions, but now that the storm was behind them, he wanted answers.

"Trudy, just what the hell happened in that graveyard? I saw something that looked like a—"

"Phil. Please. I...can't talk about it. Not yet."

He started to complain, but stopped himself and said instead, "Well, thanks, for the help with the storm and that ...other thing."

"And thank you for getting me out of there."

The storm flickered and flashed behind them in the north. The first scattered street lights on the outskirts of Wichita loomed ahead.

"I wonder if there's any place I could get clothes this time of night," Trudy said, self-consciously pulling down on the tail of Phil's t-shirt. "Being naked in one of Marv's videos is one thing, but riding around half-naked in Wichita, Kansas is something else."

"If I wasn't so strung out from all that's happened," Phil said, "I'd probably find your predicament exciting as hell."

She smiled weakly. "I probably would too. You could tie my hands behind me, buckle me down with the seat belt, then pull the shirt up a little bit higher at each stoplight, until..." Her voice trailed away. "What the hell's wrong with me, thinking things like that at a time like this? It's probably the Ally's doing. Or Erzebet's. Lots of my twisted urges may *always* have been their doing, but I guess in Erzebet's case anyway that means they're mine as much as hers, since we're the same. And don't tell me we're not, because I know better, now. I think. Okay?"

A block passed in silence, then she said, "Damn it to hell, Phil. Those were my favorite boots."

"I thought about trying to find your clothes for you," he responded, "but the storm was closing in, and—"

"You did the right thing."

"Why did you take them off?"

"*I* didn't. The Ally was in control. And both Erzebet and the Ally believed it was necessary to be naked to make the spell work."

"Oh. Well, now that we seem to be kind of safe again, I'd like for you to give me back my t-shirt, and—"

"Do *what?*"

"Let me finish. Give me back my t-shirt, and put on your new one before we reach too many lights."

"New one?"

"I bought you a t-shirt in the Swedish Timber Cottage. It's in one of those sacks on the backseat. Hope it fits. I got a large. Maybe the tail will be longer than that one of mine. And there are some other things back there I was going to surprise you with too. Thought maybe they'd cheer you up some. No jeans or boots, though, I'm afraid."

Trudy leaned over and kissed his cheek. "Thank you, Phil," she said, touched that he'd thought of her.

She reached into the backseat and started rattling paper sacks as she looked for the shirt. She found it, slipped Phil's shirt off and the new one on. The white t-shirt showed three burly Vikings, armed to the teeth, standing on the deck of a Viking dragon ship. The caption said, *Take a Liking to a Viking*. And the tail *was* longer.

"Wonder if they'd have clothing in there?" he said, looking at a 24-hour supermarket that was coming up on their right. "Wouldn't hurt to check," he decided, and pulled into the parking lot. He put his Z-ROCK t-shirt back on then went into the grocery store.

Trudy reached into her shoulder bag and got out the aspirins Phil had bought in Lindsborg. Then, anxious to dull the throbbing of the headache caused by the painful occult work she had recently been forced to do, she got one of the warm Cokes that was still left, popped its top and used it to chase down three aspirins.

Without warning, her mind started replaying what had happened to her in the graveyard. To turn her thoughts elsewhere she quickly started looking through the other sacks from Lindsborg.

Phil had bought her a small wooden Dala Horse, a Swedish joke book, a jar of cloudberry jam, a pair of silver Viking ship earrings, and an adjustable one-size-fits-all silver heart ring.

She sat in the dark car and clutched the presents to her, tears in her eyes, feeling fonder of Phil than ever before. Then she slipped the ring on the third finger of her left hand and looked into the rearview mirror in order to put on the earrings. Her face startled her—haggard, drawn, eyes sunken and haunted.

She put the earrings on, then pushed the empty sacks behind the seat and sat waiting for Phil, holding the Dala Horse and joke book and cloudberry jam protectively in her lap.

Phil came out of the supermarket carrying a grocery sack. "Hope these will do," he said after he opened the car door and handed her the sack. In the sack were a pair of white gym shorts, a cellophane package containing three pairs of white sweat socks, and a pair of cheap white canvas tennis shoes. "They didn't have any underwear. It just about took the rest of our cash, anyway. So, now we've only got about five dollars cash left. They didn't take credit cards. But I can try using the credit card to get money if we find the right kind of bank machine. I see you found your surprises."

"Yes, Phil. Thank you," she said, then leaned over and kissed him. "They did make me feel better. How do you like my engagement ring?" she asked, holding up her left hand to show him the silver heart ring.

He laughed. "I'll get you a real one, Trudy."

"It couldn't mean any more to me than this one does."

"Then maybe I'll save my damned money," he joked.

"I love you, too, monkey," she whispered, and gave him another kiss. Then she slipped on the shorts and socks and shoes. The shorts were a little tight, and the shoes a little too big, but she told Phil everything fit fine. "And thank you, again, for the presents, and . . . just for everything."

He put an arm around her shoulders and pulled her closer.

Thoughts of the graveyard suddenly filled her head again. Tears welled in her eyes. She struggled to hold herself together.

Phil silently held onto her until she straightened in the seat and wiped at her eyes.

"Let's find someplace to use your credit card for a hot meal," she said. "Maybe food will help me get rid of my shakes. After that, I'll try to talk about what happened."

They stopped at an all-night place that had a credit card sticker on the window. There was a friendly sign on the door announcing *No shirt, no shoes, no food.* "Good thing they don't check for underwear," Trudy mentioned as they entered, making Phil chuckle.

"Are you sure those shorts fit all right?" Phil asked, noticing how tight they were, watching her walk.

"You don't like the way they fit?"

"Well, sure, *I* do, but—"

"Lecher."

"Seriously, Trudy, if they're too tight, we can drive back to that supermarket and—"

"They're fine, Phil. Really."

"Okay."

They sat down in a corner booth and started looking at the

menu. "They're having a special on fried shrimp," Phil noted.

"Caught fresh daily, I assume? Off the Wichita coast?"

They both ordered the shrimp special anyway.

"I think the food did help stabilize me some," Trudy said after they had finished the shrimp. She took a sip of coffee. "So, I'll try telling you about what happened." She took a long breath, then another sip of coffee.

"The Ally communicated, through me, with . . . a Dead One. The headstone said he'd been called Reverend William Johnson. The Ally sought him out because he had once fought a Pain Eater."

"How'd the Ally know that?"

"She sensed residual psychic energy from the battle, or something. The fight had happened a long time ago, in early pioneer days. It had something to do with an Indian curse on white settlers, the work of a Medicine Man powered by a Pain Eater.

"Reverend Johnson had fought the curse without being himself allied with a Pain Eater. So, the Ally thought he might know a trick or two we didn't. But Reverend Johnson was no help. The Medicine Man had killed him with Pain Eater sorcery early in the battle."

"You mean we went through all that shit in the graveyard for nothing? Christ. I keep expecting something to turn up that will be the answer to our problem, and I thought for sure that—"

"So did I, Phil."

Neither of them spoke for a moment, then Phil said, "Did you know your eyes glowed when you were in the graveyard?"

"No. But I'm not surprised."

"What scared *me* worst of all, though, was the way you came at me through the air afterward."

"I did *what?*"

"You don't remember it?"

"No."

"You floated above the grass. Glided toward me. Your mouth was open as if screaming, but no sound came out."

"God, Phil," she moaned as she ran her hands through her

hair. "I was . . . so frightened, all the time it was happening. When that . . . ghost thing began to come up out of the ground in answer to the Ally's summons, I . . . just kind of went away, in my mind, into a dark corner, trying to hide. But I couldn't hide, because the Ally made me stand there, naked, facing Reverend Johnson's ghost-skeleton, and I managed to endure it, somehow, until it was over, but then I just ran away screaming inside my head, and I guess that must have been when you saw me coming at you . . . like that."

While she had talked, Phil had reached across the table and taken hold of her hands.

"The next thing I remember," she said, "was being on my knees, screaming, then calling for your help."

"I would have stayed near you, Trudy, but something kept me standing where I was. It wouldn't even let me call out your name. It was like one of Liz's spells. I guess the Ally caused it, just like Demon Young caused Liz's."

"Yes. The Ally had to keep you from interfering. Partly for your own good. The awakened Dead can be . . . dangerous."

"Oh, really? What a surprise."

They finished their coffee. Phil paid the check.

"Can we get a motel? Or do we have to keep driving?" he asked as they left the restaurant.

"We've got to keep moving, because I've got to get back to work with Erzebet and the Ally, experimenting, which will attract Demon Young's attention, again."

"Trudy, you need rest. Especially after what you went through tonight. And so do I. We've got to stop and sleep sometime, for Christ's sake."

"For *our* sakes, Phil, we don't dare. At least not until I've mastered enough occult powers to protect us better."

"But it'll be too dark to see in the mirror."

"Not if I turn the inside dome light on."

They got into the car. "I'd better stop for gas," he noted. "It's after eleven, and I don't suppose there'll be many gas stations open in rural Kansas after midnight."

"Or before."

"You'll be navigating us in circles again, I assume?"

"I assume."

Phil filled the gas tank, then started driving. Trudy gave him directions to a road leaving Wichita, heading west. Then she turned the dome light on and got back to work with the mirror.

PART FIVE

Raw Pain Max

□

Darkness had no need of aid from them—
She was the Universe.

Lord Byron,
"Darkness"

40

Welcome Back

Seen from I-35 at three A.M., downtown Oklahoma City was silhouetted by orange heat lightning flickering behind it in the distant west. But Phil was not worried about more thunderstorms. He was not worried about anything.

Trudy was asleep in the passenger seat, her temples throbbing with a purple glow. Her sleep was not peaceful. She had been struggling to awaken since suddenly falling asleep in Kansas five hours before.

Phil stopped at a filling station and filled the Trans Am with gas. Then he got back in and started driving south once more. Several hours later, the dawn sun slanting down from the east, he crossed the Red River into Texas. Gainesville and the Z-ROCK transmitter went by shortly thereafter. But Phil did not think about turning the radio on. Phil was not thinking about anything.

When he reached Denton he exited from I-35 and drove west several miles to an abandoned farm. He stopped the Trans Am beside a station wagon parked near an old barn. Then his eyes closed and he slumped against the car door.

"Welcome back, kiddies," Liz said from the barn door, grinning unpleasantly. "Bring the man into the barn and strip him naked," she ordered Marcy and Kathy and Charles. "I'll deal with Darvulia myself."

41

Worms

Phil awoke to the feel of kisses on his bare chest. He gasped as someone teased his left nipple with tongue and teeth. "Trudy?" he called. In reply there was a nibble at his other nipple.

He was lying naked on a floor, his upper arms bound to his sides, his hands bound behind him, and his ankles bound together by what felt like strands of thick wire. A blindfold covered his eyes.

A tongue traced a line down his torso, lapping momentarily at his navel, then traveling lower, and lower.

Phil struggled with his bonds, suddenly feeling that something was terribly wrong. But as swiftly as they had come, his worries vanished. Nothing was wrong. Trudy was giving him fantasy sex. Everything was fine. Wonderful.

Warm fingers touched his testicles, stroked his penis, began manipulating him, bringing him closer and closer to orgasm. Warm breath bathed his sex as a mouth engulfed him. The mouth went away. Warm flesh replaced it as he was mounted and skillfully ridden, his rider's inner muscles gripping and teasing, until he climaxed, calling Trudy's name, panting with passion . . . but then he heard Liz laugh and a stench of rotting flesh clogged his nostrils.

The blindfold was ripped away from his eyes. A decaying hag whose flesh-tattered face was missing a nose and lips straddled him with worm-eaten thighs, her body deformed by cancerous oozing sores, drool seeping from the corners of her death-grin mouth.

"Brave little boy," the hag cackled. "Fucking me is dangerous. You could catch something . . . deadly. Hungry little worms could get inside your prick. Let's see if they already have, shall we?"

She climbed off him and knelt by his side. In horror he looked down at his softening penis and felt/saw tiny things moving inside it, heaving against the surface.

Terror panicked him. He screamed in horror, writhing on the floor, fighting his bailing wire bonds. Then the squirming/tickling sensation inside his penis vanished. He stopped struggling.

"No," the hag said, leaning closer, "I was wrong. No worms. Goody. Now I can have him stuffed after I cut him off. Or maybe I'll *bite* him off instead," she suggested, "right now."

She opened wide her broken yellow teeth. Cold saliva dribbled onto Phil's genitals. In repulsion and terror he tried to crawl away. She grabbed his testicles with one filthy hand and clamped her other hand around his throat, long nails digging into his neck, half-choking him, then held him against the floor and bent down toward his penis. He felt her breath against him, felt the scrape of her teeth, began to scream as her teeth began to clamp closed.

But she did not finish the job. Instead, she withdrew her mouth after only breaking the surface of the skin. She licked away drops of blood, then gave him a wink. "Your blood needs more pain," she told him. "But don't worry. I'll see that it gets it, eventually."

A purple glow bathed the hag's rotting flesh. Her skin rippled and heaved, began to reform. A moment later, Holly knelt beside Phil where the hag had been, her nakedness as sensuous as the hag's had been horrible. The whip welts Liz had given Holly in the playroom were still faintly visible upon Holly's flesh.

"Having fun, Phil?" Liz asked him. "Oh, dear. You look confused. It's simple. I had to take over Holly's body after Darvulia killed mine. Then Demon Young found you and made you drive back to Texas."

"Texas? But . . . I was driving in . . . Kansas . . ."

"Dodo, I'm afraid you're not in Kansas any more," Liz said, then laughed at her joke. "Get it? *Dodo*? I've been waiting to say that," she added, still giggling. "You're not laughing? Aren't you going to ask about Darvulia?"

He kept silent.

"Don't you care what happens to her?"

"All right. Where is Trudy?" he asked, feeling a faint hope she might, with the Ally's help, have escaped and still be safe in Kansas.

"You'll find out, soon enough," Liz answered. "But as I recall, I promised you a reward for betraying me. Do you remember that, Phil? Something to do with your balls? Now that I've let you use them one last time—wasn't that nice of me, by the way?—we might as well get on with it, or rather off with them. I think I'll make a little coin pouch out of the skin," she said, reaching behind her and lifting into the air the meat cleaver she had taken from Trudy's shoulder bag.

Phil struggled with his bonds as Liz slowly lowered the blade toward his genitals. Then she suddenly swept the blade downward to thunk into the wooden floor beside him.

"But you don't have to say goodbye to them right away. I've decided you'd enjoy it more if I didn't just *cut* them off. I'll show you what I mean."

Liz got up, yanked the cleaver free.

For the first time since his blindfold had been removed, Phil took his eyes away from his tormentor long enough to glance at his surroundings. It was a barn. Daylight came through an open door. The floor was strewn with remnants of dirty hay. No one else was there except Liz.

She reached up and pulled on a thin black fishing line which she had stretched across an overhead beam. There was a fishing hook attached to the end.

"I *could* stick this through your nose," Liz said, holding the fishing hook near his face, "or your lips, or tongue." She moved it down to his chest. "I could put it through a nipple," she suggested, "but that's always more fun with girls. With men, I've always found they get the point best in the prick or balls."

He suddenly drew his legs up, intending to kick at her, maybe reach her throat and somehow hurt her. And he did kick at her, but she easily evaded the blow and spoke purple-glow words that, moments later, had paralyzed him.

"Naughty, naughty," Liz laughed, turning him over on his stomach, then gave his buttocks several stinging spanks with the flat of the cleaver's blade.

She turned him back onto his back, then used the cleaver to cut the fishing hook off the line. She tossed the hook and the cleaver away into a shadowy cattle stall.

"I wasn't going to hook you anyway, Phil. I have something different planned for you."

She tied a slip-knot in the fishing line, then put the loop around his testicles and pulled it tight. She stood and pulled the line tighter still. A ring of burning pain seared him. He couldn't move, but he could cry out, and did.

Liz kept the tension in the line as she walked to the far wall with the other end. She jerked on the line, earning another cry of pain from Phil. Then she slowly put more and more pressure on the line.

The tightening line pulled the loop tighter and tighter around the base of Phil's testicles until finally, still unable to move, he lay screaming as Liz kept pulling.

She tied the line around a rusty harness hook and came back over to him. She plucked the line. He groaned. She revoked his paralysis. He reflexively arched his back, thrusting his hips upward to try and ease the pain. She hurried back to the hook and pulled the line even tighter, until he was bowed upward, supported by his shoulders and feet. But the line was now tighter than before, his pain many times greater.

Satisfied, Liz tied the line off again.

"How's that feel, Phil?" she inquired, leaning down to take a closer look. "Tight enough?" she asked, giving the line another pluck. He screamed.

"Aren't you going to beg for mercy?" she wanted to know. "Maybe you don't understand. I'm going to leave you like that until they die. They're already turning blue from lack of blood, see? But maybe they have too much blood as it is. What do you think? I could always bleed them a little. But no, I think I'll just let them die unpunctured, for now.

"How long do you think it'll be before they're dead?" she asked, then moved down to his feet and took hold of his ankles.

"What . . . are you . . . doing?" he panted.

"Watch," she grinned, then lifted his feet into the air.

Phil screamed, his body suddenly suspended from the shoulders down by the thin strand of fishing line cutting into his testicles. His abdominal muscles stood out in hard ridges as they tried, in vain, to pull his body up and relieve the pain. He kept screaming as blood started oozing from beneath the punishing loop.

Liz let go of his feet. Still gasping with pain, he immediatley used them to bow his body upward to reduce the pain to a less severe level.

"The physical pain won't last long," Liz promised. "Your balls will be numb, soon. Of course then you'll have a bit of psychological pain, knowing that they're slowly dying from lack of blood. Just think of it. They may already be damaged beyond repair. Wouldn't that be just too awful, Phil?"

She started to walk out the door.

"Wait!" he cried. "Where . . . are you going?"

"To see Darvulia," Liz answered. "Want me to tell her hi?"

"Please . . . Liz! Don't . . . leave me like . . . this!"

"Why not?"

"For . . . God's sake, Liz! Please!"

"Crybaby," Liz said, then laughed, and left.

"No! Liz! Please! Aaah! God! Liz! Come back!" he begged, staring helplessly at the empty doorway. His muscles were beginning to tremble and cramp, lowering him, making the pain even worse, hastening Liz's stated goal. Sweat ran from his body, dampening the floor. His heart hammered frantically in his chest. He gasped air in shuddering spasms. A muscle cramp clamped his straining abdominal muscles in a crushing vise. He screamed. And screamed.

Liz reappeared at the door. "Excuse me, Phil, darling," she said from the doorway. "I apologize for the interruption, but I forgot something *very* important."

She spoke a single word. Glowing mist traveled rapidly from her mouth and soaked into his penis. "There," she announced. "That should do it. Have fun."

Walking away from the barn, she laughed happily when she heard Phil begin bellowing with horror in the barn, tiny worms squirming inside his penis once more.

42

Blood and Barbed Wire

Liz approached the abandoned farmhouse. The yard around the decaying wood frame house was overgrown with weeds, and the inside was a dusty ruin, the remnants of more than one party thrown by trespassing college or high school students littering the scarred linoleum floor. But Liz didn't care about any of that. She was not going inside. Instead, she picked her way through the weeds around to the back.

Marcy and Kathy and Charles stood, staring glassy-eyed straight ahead, exactly where she'd left them near an old oak tree, all three as naked as she. Trudy, like Phil, was naked too. But Trudy was not standing near the tree. She was hanging from one of the tree's limbs.

Trudy's bare skin glistened with blood and sweat as she hung suspended from two ropes tied to twin loops of barbed wire twisted tightly around her breasts. A loop of bailing wire held her elbows together behind her back, and another bound her hands. Before she had been hoisted into the air, Liz had also wired each of her ankles to its respective thigh, so that now Trudy's knees, not her feet, were the closest part of her body to the ground.

The strands of wire were thin bands of fiery pain burning deeper and deeper into Trudy's flesh. She hung as still as she could, even the slightest movement causing her breasts new pain. Panting with shallow, pain-wracked breaths, Trudy's tear-reddened brown eyes looked down into the cold blue eyes of her torturer.

"Did I tell you that when I was a little girl, my grandpa tied a rope to a tree a lot like this one, but up in Kansas?"

Liz asked. "He tied an old tire to the rope, and I had so much fun swinging on that tire. Do you like to swing too, Darvulia? Like this?"

She gave Trudy a violent shove.

Trudy screamed as she swung back and forth, the limb creaking above her, the barbed wire chewing deeper into her breasts. Liz let her make several swings, then reached out and stopped her.

"But the thing I liked to do most, was spin. You too, darling?" she asked as she slowly began turning Trudy around and around, winding up the ropes.

In the distance, Phil bellowed another scream.

"Phil," Trudy moaned. "What have you . . . done to him? Please . . . stop hurting him. I'm . . . the one who—"

"How touching," Liz interrupted. "Don't worry about Phil. He's just hanging around like you, except by his balls."

"Oh, God . . ."

"But I let him use them first, one last time, in *me*. You don't mind, do you, Darvulia, dear?"

"I'm . . . not . . . Darvulia!" Trudy shouted angrily, the effort giving her added pain. "I am . . . Trudy! And you . . . are not Erzebet . . . Bathory!"

Liz just chuckled.

"I . . . know more now . . . than before, bitch," Trudy ground out as Liz kept winding her ropes tighter and tighter. "I . . . know about . . . Pain Eaters."

Liz's grin broadened. "Good for you, dear. Glad to see your memory is improving. Too bad it came too late to do you any good."

"And I know . . . who you are! You were . . . never a Countess, but . . . I was. *I* was Erzebet . . . Bathory, not you."

"Who was I then? Mary Poppins?" Liz laughed.

"You were . . . Darvulia, and . . . I, Erzebet, killed you . . . by allying myself . . . with a . . . Pain Eater too!"

Liz laughed louder. "You're still confused, Darvulia, darling. That Pain Eater of yours is playing tricks with your mind. *I* have Erzebet Bathory's memories. I can remember—"

"So . . . can I! If you have . . . Erzebet's memories, it is

. . . because you were attached to part . . . of my soul, after
. . . my Ally devoured your . . . Demon Young!"

"Yes, indeed. Your Ally's been playing lots and lots of
cruel tricks with your mind. Well, perhaps a little spinning
will help clear your head."

The ropes were wound tight, Trudy's head nearly touching
the limb from which she hung. She knew that when Liz
released her, the pain would be intolerable. She had to find a
way to stop Liz. She had to think of some way to save
herself from the threatened pain. She had to—

Liz released her and she began to spin. She screamed
steadily as the ropes unwound, whipping her around and
around, the barbed wire digging mercilessly into her breasts.

Happily watching from a few steps back, Liz let Trudy
spin first one way and then the other until finally the spinning slowly stopped.

Trudy hung bleeding and panting, sobbing brokenly.

"There, now, Darvulia, dear. Did that help, do you think?
No? Perhaps you want to spin again?"

"Fuck you . . . bitch," Trudy panted. She heard Phil
scream in the distance and thought about how he must have
just heard her screaming too.

"Phil is in good voice today, don't you think?" Liz asked.

"God damn you . . . to Hell!"

"Oh, good gracious. Such language. Looks like you do
need another spin after all."

Liz wound Trudy up and let her go.

When Trudy again stopped spinning several minutes later,
Liz held up two new lengths of barbed wire for Trudy's
inspection, then started to twist the end of one around the
middle of the other.

Trudy fought to concentrate through her pain, trying
again, as she had countless times since waking up naked and
bound, to contact Erzebet and the Ally. But both Erzebet and
the Ally seemed to have vanished from her mind. She assumed that Demon Young must be interfering, cutting her
off from the only help Phil and she had managed to acquire,
leaving them as frustratingly and terrifyingly helpless as
they'd been that first time days ago.

Liz positioned the new lengths of barbed wire so that the

place she had attached them was centered on Trudy's navel, leaving the halves of one wire sticking out to each side and the attached strand pointing downward toward the ground. Trudy immediately understood what was coming.

"Go . . . ahead," she said between gritted teeth, looking down at Liz. "Should . . . be fun."

"What bravado," Liz laughed. "Don't bullshit me, Darvulia. I can read your thoughts and emotions. You *did* get off on the pain a little at first, much to your disgust with yourself, considering the situation. But now all you're feeling is good old agony, and you certainly are *not* looking forward to having a strand of barbed wire between your legs. Right?"

Trudy lifted her eyes from Liz and said nothing.

"Come here, slaves," Liz ordered.

Marcy and Kathy and Charles came obediently to Liz's side. "Hold her arms up out of the way, Kathy," Liz commanded. "Marcy, Chuck, grab her thighs. Keep her well spread."

Trudy screamed with pain as the three obeyed.

Liz quickly belted Trudy's waist with the halved wire and twisted the ends together at the small of her back until she had a snug fit. Blood trickled from several gouges. Every breath Trudy now took drove the rusted barbs deeper and gave her fresh pain. Then Liz took hold of the strand pointing toward the ground and began bending it upward between Trudy's legs.

Trudy somehow kept the scream that wanted to come out to a prolonged groan.

"Think you could do that dance I saw you do at the club while wearing one of these?" Liz asked as she threaded the back end of the crotch wire beneath the belt of pain and bent it downward to keep it loosely in place. "Maybe we'll find out, later, after you're properly fitted. A barbed wire crotch strap might be just the thing to motivate even wilder gyrations. Bet the audience would pay lots more to see it, too."

Liz leaned down and reached between Trudy's legs.

Trudy wanted to beg Liz not to do it, but she kept herself from saying anything at all as she felt Liz's fingers manipulating the crotch wire into place. Then Liz reached around and began pulling it tighter.

Trudy did cry out as the wire sank deeper and deeper.

Liz kept pulling until satisfied it would not slip and loosen. That done, she twisted the belt tighter too, using her bare fingers like steel pliers, until the taut skin of Trudy's trim waist bled and bulged around it.

Liz stepped back and surveyed her victim. "Very fetching," she decided. "Blood and barbed wire suits you, Darvulia, darling. You should never wear anything else. But did you know you still have places where there's scarcely any blood? I wonder what we should do about that?"

Liz walked a few yards away to a hedge tree and broke off a supple, thorny branch. Then she broke off the needle-like thorns near the larger end of the branch and held onto that end as she walked back to Trudy. She motioned for her slaves to get out of the way.

Trudy saw what was coming. She closed her eyes and waited for the pain.

Liz struck her with the thorny branch three times across her thighs, twice across her shoulders, once across her face, only barely missing her left eye with a flesh-piercing thorn, then three times across each of her distended breasts, and six times up between her legs.

"Get the bitch down," Liz ordered after Trudy's new screams had devolved into panted sobs. "She's going for a little walk."

43

Roadwork

Trudy's ankles were unwired from her thighs before she was lowered to the ground. But the reduced circulation had left her feet and lower legs numb. She could not stand. So she was lowered until she knelt in the weeds.

Liz took hold of the two ropes that had held Trudy suspended and that were still tied to the strands of barbed wire twisted tightly around Trudy's breasts. Liz gave the ropes a slight tug.

"Aah!" Trudy cried.

"Get on your feet!" Liz ordered.

"Go . . . to fucking . . . Hell!"

"Get on your feet, *now!*" Liz commanded, emphasizing the order with a violent jerk on the ropes.

When Trudy's scream died away, she started struggling to stand up, the numbness in her feet and legs slowly being replaced by fiery pinpricks as feeling returned. She gritted her teeth and clenched her fists in anticipation of the pain she knew would come from the crotch wire when she moved her leg, then she shifted all her weight to her left knee and quickly moved her right leg up so that her right foot rested on the ground.

As she had expected, the movement brought a sickening flare of pain from between her legs. Then, after taking several panted breaths which brought pain to her barbed wire-cinched waist and breasts, she shifted her weight to her right foot and stood up, causing more pain to tear her crotch.

She swayed unsteadily, her feet and legs burning with returning circulation.

Liz walked away at a brisk pace, holding the two ropes like a leash. "Walkees, Darvulia," Liz called back over her shoulder without turning around or slowly down. "Marcy, Kathy, Chuck . . . you come too."

Before the slack went out of her breast-leashes, Trudy desperately staggered forward and nearly fell but somehow stayed on her feet and kept walking, each step grinding the crotch wire into her flesh, her own movements torturing her with jabs of pain from her belly down between her legs and up between her buttocks.

The inside of her thighs became slick with blood after only a few dozen steps. She tried to keep her panicked mind from thinking about the damage the barbs must be doing inside her.

As the walk continued toward the barn, the pain and exertion made her breathe harder, which in turn gave her more pain from the barbed wires that cinched her breasts and waist.

When they reached Phil's Trans Am, Liz stopped and turned to face her victim. "How long has it been since you did some decent roadwork, darling?" Liz asked. "How about a little jogging, say a couple of miles down the road and back?"

Trudy didn't answer, just stood panting in pain, her eyes half-closed.

"Answer me, you betraying bitch!" Liz ordered, and jerked on the ropes.

Trudy cried out, then said, "Only . . . two miles?"

"Smart ass. Maybe I'll tie these ropes to Phil's car and then drive ahead of you. If you don't keep up, you'll get dragged a few miles by your tits."

Trudy said nothing, trying to conceal her horror.

"Putting on a brave face, are we?" Liz laughed. "I *know* how the thought of jogging or being dragged by your tits horrifies you. It would anyone. No shame in that. So why don't you beg me, just a little, and maybe I'll cancel your run."

"Sure . . . when Hell . . . freezes over."

"Actually, Demon Young's Hell *is* frozen over. But with blood. You'll get to visit there eventually.

"But before that, before I'm finished with your flesh, you'll be a slab of raw meat with more resemblance to a side of beef than something that was once human. You'll no longer have a face, nor legs, nor arms, nor tits. But you *will* still be alive, because with Demon Young's help I am going to amuse myself with you for as long as I want. Only when you start to bore me and I feel my revenge is complete will I let you visit Demon Young's lake of frozen blood."

Trudy kept silent, except for her panted gasps of continuing pain.

"But before I decide whether to jog you or drag you, let's see how Phil's balls are doing. I wonder if they've died yet? If they have, I'll let you watch me cut them off with that cleaver of yours. Or maybe I'll make you de-ball him yourself."

Liz led her leashed victim into the barn.

"Oh, God . . . Phil . . ." Trudy moaned at the sight of him. He was lower than before, muscles cramping, but still bowed upward somewhat and fighting to keep from being totally suspended.

"Trudy . . ." he gasped, their eyes touching.

"Balls dead yet, Phil?" Liz brightly asked. Keeping hold of Trudy's ropes, she walked over to him and leaned down. She spoke a word of glowing power. The feel of worms writhing inside his penis went away. He had already decided that the effect was just another of Liz's tricks, and that there were not *really* worms doing him internal harm. He hoped.

"Now then," Liz grinned down at him, taking hold of the line, "just tell me when it hurts. Feel this?" she asked, then jerked upward on the taut line. Phil screamed hoarsely. "Guess it'll be a while longer before they're dead. They're tougher than I thought they'd be. Come, Darvulia, dear. Let's get that roadwork in while we're waiting. But you three," she spoke to her slaves, "stay here and keep Phil from getting bored. Take turns whipping him with bailing wire. And use pliers on him too."

"No!" Trudy cried.

"Don't neglect his balls and prick," Liz told them.

"No! Wait!" Trudy pleaded as she saw one of the female slaves obediently pick a short length of bailing wire up off the floor. The male slave picked up a pair of pliers. "Please . . . don't hurt him . . . any more!" Trudy begged.

Liz laughed as she tugged on Trudy's ropes, forcing her to leave the barn. "A little jogging should help take your mind off him, don't you think?" They emerged from the barn and headed toward the Trans Am.

"Phil!" Trudy cried, trying to look around as she heard him scream raggedly inside the barn. Liz jerked hard on the ropes, making Trudy scream too as she stumbled forward and fell onto her knees.

"Tell you what, darling," Liz said, looking down at her, "let's try a little jog without the car and see how it goes. *If* you do well, *maybe* I'll have them stop torturing Phil. Okay?"

Phil screamed again in the barn, and again.

"Have them . . . stop now, and . . . I'll do it."

"You'll do it *first*, love. Up on your feet," she ordered, and pulled hard on the ropes.

Gasping with pain, Trudy struggled back to her feet.

"Ready?" Liz asked. "I could use some exercise too, so I'll just run ahead of you for now. Then after you're warmed up, maybe we'll try it with the car. Sound fair? Here we go!" she exclaimed, and started jogging down the curving, overgrown driveway that led away from the barn, Trudy's breast leashes held firmly in her hands.

Trudy cried out again and again as she started trying to keep up, each jarring step sending agony through her body. As they kept going down the driveway past the decaying farmhouse, Liz began to speed up.

Sweat and blood streaming, Trudy fought to match Liz's faster pace. As they left the drive and started down the rutted country road, Liz speeded up again. The slack went out of the ropes. Liz pulled. "Keep up, slowpoke!" she warned.

Crying out with each step, each breath, Trudy struggled to go faster. And for several anguished steps she succeeded. But then she stumbled and fell, screaming when she hit the ground.

Liz came back and looked down at her. "What a lazy bitch. Lying down on the job. What am I going to do with you? I *could* wrap your ankles, individually, with wire too, then when you stand up again, the wires would dig deeply and encourage you to step lightly. Want me to do that, darling?"

Trudy heard the sound of an engine. Through tear-blurred eyes she looked up and saw a pick-up truck coming down the road toward them.

"He won't see us," Liz predicted. "But we'd best get off the road. Here, let me help you," she offered, then stepped into the weed-filled ditch and, before Trudy could struggle back to her feet, began dragging Trudy off the road by pulling on the ropes.

Trudy was still screaming when the truck went by. The driver never so much as turned his head.

"Back on your feet," Liz commanded. "I'm tired of jogging, but I can see that you're not. So let's go back and get the car."

44

Trojan Horse

Trudy was stagger-jogging behind Liz back up the driveway toward the barn when it happened. The Ally and Erzebet were suddenly back within her mind. And with them came understanding.

The Ally had *wanted* Demon Young to find and recapture Trudy for Liz. The Ally had *wanted* Trudy to be tortured. The Ally had used her as a Trojan Horse, then fed on her pain to get strength for the coming battle with Demon Young! The Ally had used her as an expendable human pawn. But her usefulness to the Ally was not over, and although learning how she had been used filled Trudy with rage, she had no choice but to do what the Ally wanted her to do next. If she did not, Liz would continue to torture them and Demon Young would win.

Trudy gritted her teeth and made herself stop running, letting her breast-leashes jerk tight, letting herself topple screaming to the ground. Then, as Liz laughed and walked back toward her, Trudy fought to concentrate through her pain on what Erzebet and the Ally said to do.

Trudy kept her face turned toward the ground so that Liz would not see the purple fire beginning to burn in her eyes.

"You're never going to get in shape lying about on the ground," Liz chided, and started to jerk up on the ropes, but suddenly Trudy whipped her head up, fixed Liz with her purple-fire stare, and shouted a guttural word of command.

Twin bolts of purple fire shot from Trudy's eyes and struck Liz's chest, hurling her backwards, flesh smouldering.

Liz screamed as she struck the ground and began writhing

in agony, the smoking holes where the bolts of energy had struck ringed with bright purple flames.

Trudy spoke other words of power. The wires that bound her began glowing with purple light. Agony gripped her when for a heartbeat the wires turned molten, searing her skin. Then the wires everywhere on her body vanished and she was free.

But Liz was fighting back, trying frantically to work a counter-spell to stop the flames from spreading, purple fire now hungrily eating away at her breasts and shoulders. Blisters were forming on her face. Her hair was beginning to burn.

Trudy raised her arms and let Erzebet take control in order to release the Ally from her flesh.

Demon Young, suddenly realizing the trick the Ally had played, did not wait for Liz to release him. Her body began glowing with a pulsing purple light. Out of her mouth billowed black smoke that streamed skyward, becoming boiling black clouds streaked with bolts of purple lightning. Thunder moaned. Black thunderheads towered skyward, blotting out the sun. Lightning strobed the land with flickering purple light. Along the edges of the moaning clouds wispy patterns like screaming human faces formed and vanished and reformed.

Trudy kept letting Erzebet do as she wanted, releasing the Ally, while Liz's body continued to burn, no longer moving, a discarded husk.

The spell to release the Ally began to work as Trudy's body began pulsing with a purple glow. Then deep inside her Trudy felt a gate jerk open. A stream of violent darkness tore through the opening, ripped upward through her, billowed out of her mouth like boiling black smoke, burning her like acid, eating away at her flesh.

Trudy tried to scream, but not until the last of the Ally's force had left her did she succeed. She crumpled to the ground, blood oozing from her mouth. Her stomach heaved. She vomited blood. She realized with horror that with such internal damage she was soon bound to weaken and die.

From the sky overhead, daggers of burning purple light hurled downward toward the rising darkness of the Ally. The moaning mass of the Ally answered in kind, billowing higher, rapidly matching Demon Young's towering black columns of lightning-laced energy.

Trudy struggled to her feet, body in agony, blood still pouring from her mouth. She sought Erzebet's advice, thinking that perhaps there was a spell to stop her bleeding, a way to yet save her life. But neither Erzebet's presence nor her memories told Trudy of any such spell.

Trudy began staggering toward the barn, determined to at least help Phil before loss of blood drove her unconscious.

Violent winds suddenly sprang up, gusting from all directions at once. Trudy fought to keep on her feet, to keep moving forward toward the barn. Bolts of purple lightning arced overhead as the battle in the sky continued.

She had nearly reached the barn door when the female slave with bleach-blond hair appeared. She held a crowbar. "Surprise, Darvulia, dear," the slave said, then laughed Liz's laugh.

Demon Young had helped Liz possess Marcy's reanimated body, but now he was devoting all his energy to the fight against the Ally, leaving Liz to face Trudy using only her own wits and the no-more-than-human strength of Marcy's muscles. But Trudy was badly weakened, staggering, blood oozing from her mouth. The fight, Liz was certain, would be a short one.

Liz ran forward, raising the crowbar to strike.

Trudy fought to clear her blurring vision as she saw the slave Liz had possessed attacking. At the last moment she managed to clumsily raise her left forearm to block the blow.

The crowbar splintered bone, crushing Trudy's forearm with pain.

Trudy cried out and staggered back. Liz struck again. Trudy sacrificed her left forearm again to block the blow as she suddenly threw herself toward Liz, letting her body's weight carry them both to the ground.

Her left arm hanging uselessly at her side, blood-soaked bone peeking through her forearm's punctured flesh, Trudy sat astride the possessed slave, clamped her right hand around her throat, and began to squeeze, hard-trained muscles bulking into rock-hard masses beneath her blood-streaked skin.

Liz had dropped the crowbar when she fell. Now, as Trudy kept squeezing harder and harder, Liz frantically tried to reach the crowbar, but it was just beyond the grasp of her clutching fingers. Her vision began to darken as Trudy's strength slowly crushed her windpipe.

Helpless with panic, Liz suddenly knew that she was going to lose. Her terror touched Demon Young. He sent energy to her. She used it.

Trudy felt the invading presence of Liz's will enter her mind like a shaft of ice-cold steel.

Trudy screamed out a curse of frustrated hate and fear as the strength left her muscles and her vision darkened. Then the darkness became her universe, and she sprawled unconscious upon the ground.

45

Monster

Trudy was lost in darkness. And silence. She was moving, running, desperately running, but she felt nothing, not her legs moving, not the impact of the ground beneath her feet, not the stirring of air against her skin. Yet she kept running, terrified, sensing that danger was closing in.

Pain. She remembered being in pain, but she could not remember why. And there was no pain now. Not even pain to interrupt the nothingness through which she ran. But should the pursuing danger catch up with her, there would be pain again, so she kept running, panic and horror pushing her on.

Time passed, she thought, but how much she did not know.

She kept running, terrifying thoughts pressing her on-

ward, questions that had no answers. She could not remember how she had gotten there. She could not even remember who she was, other than a name which had no
meaning. But she clung to the name, desperately. Trudy. Her
name was Trudy. Trudy. Trudy...

Minutes, years, centuries, all meant the same in the nothingness through which she ran, until...

There was a sound. So faint she could but barely hear it.
A woman's scream. Followed by a woman's laughter.

The sounds came again—another scream, more laughter
from no direction and all directions, even from below, surrounding her, pressing in on her, more screams, more laughter, growing louder, louder, until soon she was trapped
within an echoing center of screaming, laughing madness,
cringing in terror, screaming soundlessly herself, on and on
and....

Light appeared, two ovals of light, far above her, tiny in
the distance, flickering dimly with orange-red light, shaped
and spaced like eyes, the eyes of some demon, perhaps,
towering above her in the darkness.

She began to run away, but somehow the eyes always
stayed in front of her and each step she took brought them
nearer, as if she were ascending a vast stairway that led to
the eyes, the burning eyes, the screams and laughter all the
while growing louder and louder around her as the eyes drew
nearer and nearer.

She reached the eyes, and discovered that if demon's eyes
they were, she was within the demon's head. Because the
eyes were windows, and through them she saw Hell. A moment later, the eyes through which she looked became her
own.

Around her, flickering orange-red torchlight illuminated
damp stone walls. Hanging from the ceiling by its wrists was
a raw-fleshed thing that had recently been a woman, now a
corpse, freshly dead, blood still seeping from countless
wounds.

Three women, two gray-haired and one younger, their
faces and hair and clothing and hands stained with blood,
stood near the corpse. One held a barbed whip. One held a

wooden-handled poker, its smoking tip glowing cherry-red. The other held a device resembling an iron claw, strips of flesh dangling from its crimsoned points.

Trudy felt horror, but elsewhere, around her, she sensed irritation that the young woman had survived torture so short a time.

"I thought her stronger," Trudy heard herself complain in a voice that was not hers. It was a cold, aloof voice speaking a foreign language Trudy nonetheless understood. But though she had never before heard that voice, she recognized it, because she recognized the feelings that went with it, Erzebet's feelings. And then, in a sickening rush all the rest of Trudy's memories came back too, all the horror and desperation of the past few days leading up to the battle with Liz by the barn.

She was dead. She had to be dead, but not dead. Lost in Erzebet's memories. Or. . .could it be more than that? Erzebet felt *alive* around her, as if she had been somehow thrown back into Erzebet's time and was perhaps now trapped in Erzebet's mind as Erzebet had been trapped in hers.

Then Trudy remembered something she had read in one of the occult books while in the motel in Lindsborg, a theory of reincarnation that said all times were one, that the past and present and the future were mere illusions. And if that were true, perhaps it *was* possible for her to actually be present in Erzebet's mind while the Countess was alive. Perhaps she could even find some way to influence the Countess, to change the direction her life would take. And if she could do that, might not it also change the course of Trudy's own life? Perhaps the horror of the past few days could be avoided entirely. Perhaps . . .

Trudy stopped her wild and groundless speculations, suddenly imagining what Phil would say if she had voiced the thoughts to him. He would have probably said he had seen it in a horror movie, or read it in a science fiction book, or. . .

Phil, Trudy thought. And with the thought came an ache of emotional pain. She had been unable to help Phil. Was Liz continuing his torture at that very moment? Was he, perhaps, already dead? Only one thing seemed certain. She would never see him again.

Alone in the shadows of Erzebet's mind, Trudy wept, and the eyes of the Countess Erzebet Bathory suddenly blurred with tears.

Trudy noticed, and felt elation. *Her emotions had touched Erzebet's! Influencing Erzebet might be possible after all!*

But *was* she in Erzebet's time? Or just somehow lost in Erzebet's memories? Was there some way to find out? Perhaps, Trudy reasoned, there was.

The collection of Erzebet's memories had held the entirety of the Countess' life. The Countess' memories in the midst of her actual life, however, would not yet know about events waiting in her future.

But how could Trudy find out if that were the case? Was there a way to probe the Countess' memories in order to compare them with the memories Trudy remembered?

Then Trudy suddenly realized that there was another, more obvious answer. The *presence* she had come to think of as Erzebet's consciousness was no longer *within* Trudy's mind, only the collection of Erzebet's memories. Instead, the feeling of Erzebet's presence now *surrounded* Trudy, and she could no longer feel the Ally's presence at all.

Trudy knew that the feeling of being surrounded by Erzebet's consciousness was not positive proof that she had been thrown back into Erzebet's time. The effect could no doubt be explained in other ways. But she decided that until evidence to the contrary said otherwise, she might as well proceed as if she actually were in the Countess' time, and as if she might actually have a chance to change the course of Erzebet's life, and possibly her own, for the better. It was a goal, something to do to keep her from feeling completely helpless, something to keep her, she hoped, from going hopelessly insane.

Trudy felt the Countess frown at the sudden tears Trudy's thinking about Phil had caused. But then the Countess shrugged off the unexplained feeling and turned her attention back to her disappointingly short-lived victim.

"Dorka, have Ficzko dig a new grave and dispose of it,"

she said, motioning with a bejeweled hand at the hanging corpse.

"Yes, Milady."

"Katarina, Helena Jo, you will aid me with the next one."

"Yes, Milady," they chorused and followed in her wake.

The Countess went down a torchlit corridor, her brocade gown rustling against the damp stone floor.

Other sensations were reaching Trudy now. She could feel the cold and damp subterranean air upon the skin of the Countess' face and hands. And she could smell its mustiness. But she could also smell, as the Countess walked past a group of wooden, iron-banded cell doors, behind some of which were sounds of weeping and agonized whimpering, the stale, acrid odors of vomit and urine and feces.

The Countess entered a large torchlit chamber and walked across to a young woman, naked save for the remains of her shift, a few scraps of tattered cloth hanging precariously from her hips.

The young woman's face was plain, the nose large, lips thin, an inconsequential face, Trudy felt the Countess think with aloof disdain, the face of a peasant. Then the Countess swept her gaze downward, examining the peasant woman from bottom to top.

Her bare feet were small and highly arched, and her thighs were well-formed, but her ankles were thick and the calves stoutly muscled. Above her flaring hips and narrow waist, her breasts were large, the aureolae small, the nipples protruding provocatively. Her neck was short, her long blond hair thick and tangled.

Trudy realized that the Countess found the peasant woman's unrefined beauty attractive in an innocent yet vulgar, earthy way. Indeed, the Countess felt that way about most of the young peasant women from whom she chose her servants, and her victims. But most important to the Countess, the young woman before her had a body that appeared strong enough to survive many nights of pain.

Through the eyes of the Countess, Trudy looked into the frightened blue eyes of the young woman the Countess intended to torture. The victim was, Trudy estimated, probably no more than sixteen or seventeen years old.

Bare-breasted and all but naked before the coldly appraising gaze of the richly gowned aristocrat and her two ominously blood-splattered helpers, the young peasant woman shamefully lowered her eyes, panting with fear.

The young woman's arms were held above her head by a rope that chewed into her wrists, her clenched fists a blood-starved blue. The rope from her wrists was threaded upward through a thick iron ring embedded in the stone ceiling and then stretched downward to circle a large wooden cylinder that was part of a racking mechanism bolted to the stone floor.

The bound woman's legs were spread obscenely wide, held there by chains attached to heavy iron manacles clamped around her ankles. She was straining upward on her tiptoes because of the tension in the rope. The mocking remnants of the tattered shift that still clung to her hips did more to accentuate her nakedness than to cover it.

"What are her duties?" the Countess asked.

"My . . . name is Anna, Milady," the young woman hesitantly said, keeping her eyes lowered, "and I am—"

Helena Jo slapped the servant's face. "You were not asked your name, girl."

"You were not asked anything at all," Katarina added. "You will not speak again unless spoken to," she warned.

"In answer to your question, Milady," Helena Jo said to the Countess, "she is a seamstress."

"And her crime?"

"She was late with her sewing this morning, Milady," answered Katarina.

"Then she needs a sewing lesson. Bring a large needle and a long length of stout thread, Katarina."

"As you wish, Milady," Katarina said with a knowing grin, then turned and went to do as the Countess had requested.

Trudy suddenly understood that the Countess saw the peasant woman as only barely human. To the Countess, the young woman was little more than a transient possession, an amusing object to torture to death as she pleased, and then discard as she had done a great many others, without ever so much as a twinge of conscience, never once suffering a guilty, sleepless night.

With a shock of revulsion Trudy realized the truth. The Countess Erzebet Bathory was, indeed, a monster. And Trudy was trapped within her mind.

46

Sewing Lesson

Trudy felt the Countess' lips twist into a smile as she raised a brocade-clad arm and reached toward her victim's breasts. A blood-red ruby in an intricately carved gold ring glittered in the torchlight upon the middle finger of the Countess' hand.

As she gently touched the heavy curve of Anna's right breast, the young woman blushed and inhaled sharply and strained in her bonds, reflexively trying to evade the embarrassingly intimate touch.

"Why were you late with your sewing, child?" the Countess asked like a concerned mother as she rubbed her thumb gently back and forth over Anna's stiffening nipple.

"I ... had most of it done, Milady," Anna answered, her voice trembling with fear, "but, they ... gave me so much to do that I ... ah ... oh, Milady, must you do that ... to my ... aah ... to my ... breast?"

"Would you rather I do this?" the Countess sweetly asked, then viciously grabbed the taut nipple between the nails of her thumb and index finger and began to pinch, harder and harder while Anna gasped and heaved in her bonds, then began crying out, begging the Countess to stop.

Trudy desperately tried to do something to stop the Countess, but nothing she tried worked. And worse, from Erzebet's memories she knew what was going to happen to the young seamstress next, and then after that too, on and on, and to countless other helpless young women in the years to come unless she found some way to influence the Countess.

Eventually, after tears had begun to run from the captive's eyes, the countess stopped pinching and resumed stroking the reddened nipple with her thumb.

"You were late because you are lazy, is that not so?" the Countess asked.

"No, Milady!" Anna sobbed. "I worked most of the night! I have done so for several nights in a row! If I had not fallen asleep last night, I would have finished on time again. Please, Milady. Let me go! I have worked hard for you! I will work harder still, if only you will let me go!"

Trudy again tried to stop what she knew was coming, but again without success as the Countess began to pinch Anna's nipple again. Then she reached out with her left hand and did the same to Anna's other breast, pinching and twisting and pulling both of her victim's nipples, laughing at the young woman's screams.

When the Countess finally stopped, there was blood beneath her nails.

"You've dirtied my hands," the Countess noted accusingly. "I might have forgiven your laziness, but not an affront such as this," she added, holding her immaculately groomed but now bloodied nails near Anna's tear-streaked face. "Bring me a basin, Helena Jo."

"Apologize to Milady for your thoughtlessness," Helena Jo ordered, hooking a hand in Anna's sweat-dampened hair. "Do it, girl, or I'll punish you severely."

"Forgive . . . me . . . Milady," Anna sobbed brokenly.

"We shall see," the Countess replied with cold aloofness. "The basin, Helena Jo?"

Helena Jo hurried away just as Katarina returned.

"Needle and thread, Milady," Katarina said, holding out a large, thick needle and a long length of stout black thread.

"She has earned added punishment for dirtying my nails," the Countess said. "Before you begin her sewing lesson, stretch her tighter. Make her toes leave the floor. Then sew up her lips."

"No!" Anna cried in panic, muscles tensing, bloodied breasts heaving.

"As you wish, Milady."

"First the lips on her face," the Countess said, "and then," she continued, suddenly reaching down and ripping away the scrap of cloth clinging to Anna's hips, "her lips down there."

"Yes, Milady."

"No! I beg you! Please! Milady! No!" the terrified young woman cried as the Countess turned and walked a few paces away to a large, throne-like chair.

The Countess turned and sat down facing the victim, ready to enjoy the coming spectacle.

Trudy was becoming more and more frantic to stop what was about to happen. There had to be a way to influence the Countess. But how?

Katarina began working the racking mechanism, each notch clicking loudly into place as the rope was drawn slowly tighter.

Anna fought her bonds, looking wildly over her shoulder at Katarina as she felt the increasing strain beginning to burn in her shoulders and elbows and wrists.

"Please!" she gasped. "Milady! I am not lazy! I am a hard worker! Stop her! Please! Please! Stop her!"

Katarina grinned at the terrified young seamstress' pleadings as she kept stretching her tighter. The Countess merely watched without comment, her aristocratic features an emotionless mask.

"Aaaah!" Anna cried.

"Her toes, Milady," Katarina said from the racking mechanism. "They have left the floor."

The Countess took a moment to make a show of leaning forward slightly in her chair to examine Anna's bare feet. Then she looked up at the young woman's pain-twisted face. "Are you uncomfortable, child?" she asked.

"Oh! . . . Milady!" Anna panted. "It hurts . . . me! Please . . . make her . . . let me down!"

"You're *hurting* her, Katarina," the Countess said in a scolding tone.

"Yes, Milady."

"You must make her more comfortable. So . . . stretch her tighter."

"Nooo!"

"Yes, Milady," Katarina chuckled and began working the racking mechanism again.

Helena Jo returned with a small basin of clear water.

Apparently oblivious to the young woman's new entreaties and screams, the Countess dipped her bloodstained fingers into the basin and swirled them around, turning the water pink while Katarina kept clicking the rope tighter and Anna kept screaming and Trudy kept desperately trying to find a way to stop what was happening.

The Countess removed her hands from the basin. Helena Jo offered her a clean cloth.

The countess leisurely dried her fingers upon the cloth, then said, "Stop now, Katarina. She looks much more comfortable. But she looks a bit cold, all naked like that. See how she's broken out in a . . . cold sweat? Warm her up a bit, Helena Jo. I want to hear how well she sings before you sew up her mouth."

Helena Jo took a torch from a wall bracket and approached the racked nude.

"Milady! Please . . . stop her!" Anna frantically begged, watching the approaching flames with disbelieving horror. "I work . . . hard! Ask anyone in . . . my village! Please . . . don't let her . . . torture me!"

"Is anyone from your village here in this chamber tonight to vouch for you?" the Countess asked.

"No, Milady! But—"

"Helena Jo, have you noticed her laziness before?"

"Many times, Milady," Helena Jo lied with a grin.

"Then proceed, Helena Jo."

"Nooo! Don't! Please! Please!"

"Silly girl," Helena Jo said, holding the torch behind the panicked woman, bringing it slowly toward her buttocks.

"You were brought to Milady's Torture Chamber to be punished for your laziness. And punished you shall be."

"The fire! Not so close! Aaaah! Not so close!"

Trudy was sick with frustration and panic. Nothing she did got through to the Countess. All of the Countess' attention was focused upon the terrified young woman. Erzebet's growing sexual excitement was creating an impenetrable wall of sadistic concentration behind which Trudy was trapped, helpless to stop the young servant's ordeal.

A small chuckle escaped the Countess' half-parted lips as she watched Helena Jo tease the naked victim by darting the torch between her spread legs so that, looking down the column of her suspended body, Anna caught terrifying glimpses of flames licking upward toward her crotch.

"Aah! Milady! I'll...do...anything! Aah! Please! Make...Aaah!...her stop!"

In response, Helena Jo started moving the torch slowly enough to redden Anna's inner thighs and genitals and to singe her pale blond pubic hair.

"No! Aaiee! Stop her!" she sobbed. "I'm...burning! Aaieee! I'm burning!"

"Not yet, you aren't," Helena Jo chuckled, then finally did the unthinkable and for a heartbeat that seemed an eternity to the captive held the torch unmoving between the wide-spread legs.

Anna threw back her head and screamed raggedly and kept screaming long after Helena Jo had pulled the flames away.

"She sings well, Milady," Helena Jo commented when Anna's screams had devolved into heaving sobs. "And with hardly any cause. Her skin is scarcely warm to the touch," she noted, running a wrinkled hand along the smooth skin of Anna's reddened inner thighs. "Although it is a little bit warmer...here," she added, looking up at the captive as she held her hand between Anna's legs.

"Please," Anna sobbed, "no more! I work hard! I—"

"Shall I inspire a longer and louder song, Milady?" Helena Jo asked.

"I would enjoy that, I believe. But her breasts look cold too," the Countess noted.

"Yes, Milady," Helena Jo said and obediently raised the torch toward the tortured woman's breasts while Trudy silently screamed in frustration within the Countess' excitement-deafened mind.

Anna's blue eyes were wild with panic as she watched the flames near her breasts. "Nooo! Stop her! Aaah!"

Helena Jo began teasing the victim with the flames again, pushing the torch close for a moment and then jerking it back.

"No closer! Milady! Please!"

Helena Jo chuckled and slowed her movements.

"Aaaah! Milaldy! Help . . . meeeaaieeee!" Anna screamed and kept screaming as Helena Jo moved the torch its nearest yet and held it there for one heartbeat, two, three—

"Stop, Helena Jo," the Countess ordered, staring at Anna's reddened breasts, thrilled by her victim's erotic writhings and anguished screams. Sweat had begun to glisten upon the Countess' forehead. "Are you warmer now, child?" she asked when Anna had stopped screaming.

"Answer Milady, girl," Helena Jo ordered, "or I'll do some *real* damage with these flames."

"Now, now, Helena Jo," the Countess chided. "I fear you are frightening the poor child. Put away the torch and help Katarina show our lazy seamstress how to sew."

"Yes, Milady."

Katarina threaded the needle near Anna's face, then Helena Jo held Anna's head as Katarina brought the needle toward her lips.

"Is there any last thing you wish to say, before your sewing lesson begins?" the Countess asked.

"Please . . . Milady!" Anna sobbed.

"You will pay close attention, I trust," the Countess responded. "I expect you to be a better seamstress after this lesson. Proceed, Katarina."

Through the eyes of the Countess, Trudy watched, helpless to prevent it, while the torture of the young peasant woman resumed.

As Anna's torture continued and the Countess' sexual excitement kept building, to her shame Trudy began feeling excited too, her own dark passions rearing within her. But she fought desperately to control them as she tried again and again to reach the Countess, to make her stop the torture. But again and again she failed to earn even a glimmer of attention.

Anna fainted before the second set of stitches was finished.

"When you have finished sewing her up," the Countess said, stifling a yawn as she rose from the chair, "put her naked in the small cell at the bottom of the stairs. Do not bind or chain her in any way. And do not leave her a candle or a torch. But make certain she sees the spiders and rats before you take your torch away.

"I also want you to leave more sewing in the cell for her to do, then warn her that I will punish her more severely tomorrow night if she proves lazy again. And before you lock her in the dark, tell her that you have hidden a needle and thread for her to use in one of the rat holes along the walls. Of course there will not really be a needle and thread hidden there at all. Do you understand?"

"Yes, Milady," Katarina and Helena Jo answered, grinning.

"I do hope she has learned her lesson," the Countess said, stifling another yawn. "I would hate to have to punish her again tomorrow night, but laziness amongst my servants cannot be tolerated, and when found it simply *must* be punished."

"Yes, Milady."

The Countess walked forward to the unconscious woman and examined her stitches, starting with the ones lower down. Trudy felt the Countess smile. Then the Countess examined Anna's bleeding mouth, which was already badly swollen around the black thread that held it tightly and totally closed.

"Leave some milk and sweetbread for her in the cell, and make certain she sees it before you take away the light," the

Countess ordered. "She will probably be hungry after her sewing lesson."

"Yes, Milady," Helena Jo and Katarina replied, their grins broadening.

The Countess chuckled at the jest she had made, then leaned forward, kissed the captive's mutilated lips, and touched the blood-soaked stitches with the tip of her tongue. With revulsion Trudy felt a shiver of excitement run through the Countess at the taste of Anna's blood.

The Countess drew back, licking blood from her lips. "Proceed with your sewing," she told them, then left the torture chamber, brocade rustling, and turned her steps toward the upper reaches of Castle Csejthe, thinking about other pleasures she intended to enjoy before making her way to her bed.

47

Raw

The Countess relieved the sexual tension her visit to the torture chamber had spawned by making use of a suitably frightened servant girl she had selected and trained for just such special times. Then she prepared herself for bed.

Trudy made plans while she waited for the Countess to fall asleep, hoping that when the Countess' conscious mind was submerged in sleep, she might be able to reach it, if not directly, at least through a dream.

Causing a dream to form seemed a hopeless task in itself. But Trudy had decided to begin trying by simply visualizing what she wanted the Countess to know. She doubted that a mere dream would make any difference in the Countess' life. But it might at least form a psychological wedge to open the Countess' consciousness to more direct attempts when she was awake.

Trudy had not yet allowed herself to think much about her own predicament, trapped in a time and a body not her own. Whenever her thoughts turned in that direction, panic threatened to take over. So she had chosen, for the moment at least, to concentrate on reaching the Countess in order to try to prevent more scenes of sadistic horror such as the one she had witnessed below the castle.

Trudy had found, however, one encouraging piece of information. By comparing the events surrounding the torture of the young seamstress with the entirety of Erzebet's memories, she had discovered that it represented a time in the Countess' life *before* Darvulia had been recruited. Therefore, if Trudy could find a way to change Erzebet's future, Darvulia and all the horror that would come in her wake, including Erzebet's eventual summoning of the Ally, might never become part of Erzebet's life at all.

The Countess fell asleep. Trudy had decided to start with the nightmare of Erzebet's death, reasoning that Erzebet was most likely to respond to that extremely emotionally charged image. Perhaps dreaming of the horror that would befall the Countess, if her life continued as history described, would make Erzebet more open to ways to avoid it.

Trudy concentrated her thoughts and pictured the richly furnished tower bedroom in which the Countess now slept as it would one day be, the door bricked up, dim light squeezing through narrow slits at the tops of the bricked-up windows, the floor thick with dust and accumulated filth, the countess' expensive gowns soiled and tattered.

Then Trudy recalled the panic and terror the Countess had felt while waiting for the Ally to devour her soul. Again the storm drew nearer outside, again lightning flickered through the narrow slits and thunder crashed closer while the Countess cringed in the corner, watching the bare patch of wall where the mirror had once been.

Now the storm had reached the castle, the mirror had reappeared, the Ally was drawing the Countess toward it, then emerging, engulfing her with tentacles of soul-searing pain, suffocating her with terror, ripping her consciousness from her flesh, pulling her soul into the realm beyond the surface of the mirror.

Trudy tried to pull back, to stop the memories, to go no farther. But they were too strong this time, would not obey her will.

Now Trudy felt pain herself, Erzebet's pain, pain that was already unendurable yet grew even worse as the memories carried her through the mirror, wrenching her away from the realm of Earth into the realm of the Ally, a place of hollow darkness, searing heat, freezing cold, mindless agony, hopelessness, unending terror.

Then the darkness began to lift. The horizon on all sides slowly changed from black to gray.

Trudy found herself standing naked upon a vast plain of dark ice the color of blood. Arching overhead boiled black clouds laced with writhing snakes of purple lightning. Thunder rumbled and moaned.

Beneath the surface of the blood-ice Trudy saw the faces of countless humans, all screaming in silent agony, clawing at the surface, trying to break through, to escape the pain in which they were submerged. But then suddenly Trudy's own pain mercifully vanished.

A few yards away, the ice bulged upward. It reformed. A naked, cancer-skinned hag with stringy white hair stood grinning at Trudy, purple fire blazing in her sunken eyes.

"Don't you recognize your old lover, Darvulia, dear?" the crone asked with Liz's voice. "I trust you enjoyed your visit to Erzebet's time? You see, now, that you and I are not so very different after all. But you betrayed me, and for that you still have much to pay. So, let me welcome you to Demon Young's Hell! You'll be staying here a while, until I choose to send your soul back to your Earth-flesh. Come, let me show you the ropes, or rather . . . the wires."

Liz's laughter boomed out of the crone's lipless mouth as Trudy suddenly found herself again bound in torturing barbed wire, except worse than before, because now, in addition to the barbed wire twisted around her breasts and between her legs, her elbows and wrists were held together behind her with barbed wire, and punishing strands also encircled her throat and, inside her mouth, her tongue.

Trudy gagged on the pain. Crimson drool dripped from her barbed wire-filled mouth, and when she screamed in agony a moment later, the sound emerged bubbling through muffling blood.

The hag began moving toward Trudy, gliding over the blood-ice upon her decaying feet.

Trudy took an instinctive step backward, pain tearing between her legs from the movement. But she only took one step, because then the blood-ice beneath her suddenly grew soft, and she began to sink downward.

The blood-ice reformed an instant later, trapping her legs from the knees downward in a flesh-freezing vice that slowly began crushing Trudy's legs and feet. Her shins began to splinter and crack.

Trudy gag-screamed again and again with the pain in her legs. Then she felt new pain, looked down, and saw that those trapped beneath the blood-ice near where she stood had been allowed to reach her feet, and from her ankles down were now gnawing the flesh from her broken bones.

The hag reached her victim. She hooked a hand in Trudy's dark hair and jerked her head back, making the barbed wire around her neck dig deeper into her flesh. Blood began pumping in thin spurts from a pierced artery. The hag leaned down and caught a couple of spurts in her mouth, then moved her cancer-eaten face near Trudy's and kissed Trudy's blood-drooling lips.

"How do you like it so far, darling?" Liz asked. "Don't worry about dying. Not here. Because you're sort-of already dead. But that doesn't mean that you don't have a kind of flesh to torture. Souls are flesh in Hell, you see? Are you comfortable? Are your wires perhaps too loose?" she inquired, then reached down and jerked upward on the barbed wire that went between Trudy's legs.

Trudy gagged another scream, her eyes rolling wildly in agony.

"Yes, it seems a bit loose to me. The nice thing about having you here, is that my magic works so much better. Let me show you what I mean."

An instant later, the strands of barbed wire began glowing with purple fire, sizzling Trudy's flesh while they also began tightening around her breasts, between her legs, around her elbows and hands and throat and tongue.

She bubbled scream after hopeless scream.

Her tongue went first, burned/squeezed off by its closing loop.

"Your breasts will probably be next," Liz told her, leaning closer for a better look. "Or maybe your head."

With a sickening jerk Trudy felt something give way between her legs. Barbed wire ripped upward into her intestines as blood poured down her thighs.

"And just think, Darvulia, darling, this can go on as long as I want. Isn't it just absolutely wonderful?"

Trudy was spasming with agony, blood pouring from her deepening wounds as the searing loops of barbed wire squeezed smaller and smaller, smoke rising from her burning flesh.

"Won't be long now," Liz predicted, examining Trudy's breasts. "Want to make any bets about which one will go first?"

Then it all changed. Trudy stopped spasming. Her pain was suddenly gone, and she was filled in its stead with a deep, soul-penetrating calm, replaced moments later by an all-consuming rage.

Confusion spread over the hag's face. She looked upward at the boiling black clouds as if she expected them to provide an answer.

The blood-ice cracked around Trudy's crushed legs. She rose into the air, her legs healing, the flesh reforming on her feet, her tongue regrowing within her mouth, her body absorbing the blood which covered it.

Clothing appeared, covering her nakedness, rich clothing, lace and brocade, an aristocrat's clothing, the clothing of a sixteenth-century Hungarian Countess.

The hag cowered back.

"You lost before, Darvulia," Erzebet said from Trudy's mouth. "And you are going to lose again. Like your magic, my magic is also more effective in this place beyond Life."

Erzebet's/Trudy's hands gripped the hag's arms. "I am stronger in this body than in the one you knew," Erzebet grinned as she effortlessly lifted the hag into the air. "I have Trudy to thank for that." She pulled the hag's cancerous face close to hers.

The hag tried to speak, but she no longer had the power to move or make sounds.

"My soul is stronger now, too," Erzebet continued, her breath laced with purple fire as it bathed the hag's face, slowly melting the flesh from her skull.

"My soul no longer needs to hurt people to have pleasure," the Countess continued. "My soul is no longer that of the monster I once was. I have Trudy to thank for that, too. She has learned to satisfy our dark passions with fantasy."

The hag was screaming now, her head being rapidly reduced to a smouldering skull.

"The soul I share with Trudy and all the other women we ever have been is growing, Darvulia, evolving. But you are not evolving, and your stagnating soul is reflected in this decaying hag's body you have earned. You will never be a Countess, Darvulia," Erzebet said as she pulled the hag's fleshless mouth closer. "You will always be a slave to Demon Young and your own twisted lusts. And so I, through the power of my Ally and through the power of my soul and Trudy's, condemn you, slave of pain, to that which you worship so well!"

Erzebet's/Trudy's mouth clamped down upon the smouldering mouth of the hag. Deep within her Trudy felt a gateway jerk open, and through it emerged the dark force of the Ally, hungry for pain.

Erzebet/Trudy vomited the ravenous force into Darvulia's mouth, then she hurled the skull-headed hag onto the blood-ice. The hag began to move, to spasm, to scream. Tentacles erupted from her breasts and belly and mouth, spewing blood and chunks of dripping flesh as the Ally began to consume her.

"You never knew my Ally's name," Erzebet/Trudy said, smiling down at the screaming hag at her feet, "and neither did I. But Trudy knew without even being told. So if you

want a name for your conqueror, you can call her Raw, or
you can call her Pain, or you can call her Max, *or you can
just fucking scream!*"

Darvulia sank downward through the blood-ice, spasming
and screaming into the masses of those whom her centuries
of cruelty had condemned to Demon Young's Hell.

In the sky overhead new lightning lashed the boiling black
clouds. From the blood-ice, at the spot where the hag had
vanished, bolts of purple fire shot skyward, cracking the
surface upon which Trudy stood.

Those trapped beneath began to stream upward, their
screams no longer silent, hungry for freedom, hungry for
revenge.

Trudy felt herself being pulled upward into the Ally's battle with Demon Young too, but suddenly into her mind came
Erzebet's voice. They had done what was needed. And now
it was time to go home.

48

Alive

Trudy was alive. The pain told her that. But she did not
think she had much life left. The pain told her that, too.

Overhead, the black clouds were dissipating, sunlight
breaking through.

She was lying on the ground where she had fallen outside
the barn. Nearby lay the steaming, decomposing corpse of
the slave Liz had possessed during the battle.

Phil. She had to get to him and help him while she could
still move. *If* she could still move.

She tried to sit up. She cried out with pain and slumped
back, tried again, managed to turn over and raise herself
onto her knees. She made it to the barn using her knees and

right arm, then she used the barn door to pull herself up onto her feet.

A stench of decaying flesh filled the barn. She saw the two slaves Liz had left to torture Phil lying on the floor near him. Flies buzzed around their rapidly dissolving remains.

Phil was still breathing, she saw, but was unconscious, suspended by the loop of fishing line around his testicles. Patches of coagulating blood had pooled on the floor beneath his blood-streaked body.

Gasping with pain, vision swimming, her weakness growing, Trudy pulled herself along the wall of the barn until she reached the harness hook where Phil's fishing line was tied. Her fingers were still half-numb from her bondage, making it even harder. But the numbness in her fingers told her that in spite of how long she had seemed to stay in Erzebet's time and on the plain of blood-ice, a much shorter amount of time had passed in the world to which she had returned.

She got the line untied and used her rapidly fading strength to gently lower Phil to the floor. Then she got down on her knees and crawled toward him. When she reached him, she saw that most of the blood upon his skin came from relatively superficial wounds. But shock and loss of blood could still prove fatal if he did not get medical help soon. And the same went, Trudy knew, for herself, if it wasn't already too late for her, which she was very much afraid it was.

Trudy started trying to untwist the wires with which Liz had bound Phil's arms and hands and ankles, not allowing herself to think too much about how impossible getting medical help for Phil or herself seemed. They were probably miles from help, miles from even a telephone, and neither of them in any shape to drive a car. One step at a time, she kept telling herself, fighting to remain conscious. Freeing Phil was the only thing she must think about. Free Phil.

Working one-handed, fingers struggling with the twisted bailing wire, she finally freed his hands and arms. But she began to black out before she finished unwiring his ankles.

Fighting unconsciousness, she finished freeing his ankles, then pulled herself close to his face.

"Phil," she whispered weakly, "you've got to . . . wake up, Phil. It's . . . up to you . . . now . . ."

Then she slumped unconscious and all was silent in the barn, except for the lazy buzzing of the flies.

49

Kinks

Heavy metal music blaring from its radio to keep its driver awake, a battered black Trans Am careened down a Denton, Texas city street, its driver fighting to stay conscious just a little way more. But now he was losing the fight and knew it. His last conscious act was to try braking to a stop and he almost made it, but when he slumped unconscious over the wheel, the car was still moving.

The Trans Am leisurely swerved to the right, climbed a curb, and collided with a streetlight.

Inside the car was a naked man and a naked woman, both unconscious, both covered in blood, but not from the minor car crash. Witnesses called an ambulance and the police.

The doctors finished with Phil in less than an hour and pronounced him in stable condition. They worked on Trudy much longer, then put her on the critical list.

Phil regained consciousness later that night, and though heavily drugged to dull his pain, he managed to mumble an inquiry about Trudy.

The nurse hesitated. Phil knew it meant Trudy had not made it. His eyes blurred with tears. Then the nurse told him it was too soon to tell. Trudy had a fifty percent chance of pulling through. Internal bleeding, loss of blood, and trauma had taken their toll. Phil told her Trudy was going to make it, that Trudy was the strongest person he knew, and not just physically. If anyone could make it, Trudy could.

The nurse nodded, but Phil could tell she didn't believe him. He prayed some. Then some more.

Before Phil went to sleep the following night, he was told that Trudy's chances were now better than fifty percent.

Trudy's odds kept improving over the next twenty-four hours. Phil was by her bedside when she regained consciousness the following afternoon. She reached out her right hand and he took it, held it tightly. She weakly squeezed his hand back.

"You're not going to believe this," Phil said, smiling, "but Marv heard about us on TV and sent flowers. Look," he said, then lifted a small but colorful arrangement off the bedside table. He opened the attached card. "The card says," he read, "Have too much fun on the honeymoon? Come back to work. Please? I still want to see those rings."

She smiled weakly, then her drugged system returned her to sleep. Phil put the flowers back on the table and then held Trudy's hand until the nurses made him go back to his own room to rest.

"I had given up," he told her the next day when the doctors pronounced her strong enough for a short visit. "I mean, *really* given up. I figured I was going to hang there by my balls until they rotted off, before which I would be dead. But you know what? I laughed. It hurt. But I laughed. Because when I saw those two who had been torturing me start to decay like you'd described Donna and Liz doing in your playroom, I knew that whatever happened to me, and whatever had happened to you, at least we'd taken Liz with us. Because, why else would her slaves decay?

"Then when I came to, you were sprawled next to me, your right arm across my chest. I tried to get up. I knew I had to somehow drive us to a doctor. I passed out twice just getting us to the car.

"You told me one time that muscles weighed more than fat, and you were right, because I thought I'd never get you dragged those last few feet. Getting you inside was even worse.

"When I finally had you inside, I didn't know which way to drive. Liz had told me we were back in Texas, but I didn't remember shit about arriving at the farm.

"So I turned on the radio and there was Winston Zeppelin on Z-ROCK, the signal loud and strong. I hoped that meant we were near Dallas. I just picked a direction, then, and started driving, hoping the music would keep me awake until I found help.

"I swerved a lot, I remember, but evidently didn't hit anyone or thing. Finally, I saw a big white water tank with green arches painted on it and knew I'd found Denton."

Trudy, though still weak, wanted to tell him her side of what had happened, so she briefly decribed her battle with Liz outside the barn. Then she told him what had seemed to happen to her after that.

"And I think it somehow really did happen, Phil. I should be dead, because before I passed out I was vomiting blood and all. But the doctors say they found no damage to that part of me. My stomach and inside my throat and all were not harmed. Yet I know that they *were* harmed, badly, when the Ally came through to attack Demon Young. So I think that maybe Erzebet used some of the Ally's power to help me when she sent me back, healed me just a little, just enough to give me a chance to live. And, I think, she maybe also healed you a little, too."

"But, Trudy, that would mean the Ally cared about you, and even about me, and that doesn't sound like her, not after the shitty way she used you as a Trojan Horse without your knowing, first at the farm, then in Demon Young's Hell itself."

"Yeah. But, Phil, if she had told me what she was planning, Liz could have read it in my mind and it would not have worked. Know something else? That business in the old graveyard with Reverend Johnson? That was a trick, too. The Ally herself was the one who was allied with the Indian Medicine Man cursing white settlers. The Ally herself killed Reverend Johnson."

"Shit. No wonder she knew where to find his grave."

"Well, it was just a trick, anyway, to make Demon Young think she was searching for help, unable to deal with him on her own, and to make him think Erzebet would not simply turn the Ally loose to try devouring him again. It was all so that he would believe it was possible to attack and win, like he tried in the storm on the hood of your car, then later when the Ally let him make you drive back to Texas."

"Well, I may understand why the Ally did it, but I'm not about to forgive her, letting you be tortured to feed on your pain. Christ."

"I'm not talking about forgiving, Phil. You think I'm going to forget and forgive her for letting Liz do all that to me? The doctors saved my breasts, and I'm going to be okay lower down, too, they say, but I won't be much of a beauty queen with my clothes off."

"You will be to me," Phil assured her, gripping her hand.

"But you haven't seen—"

"You will be to me, and besides, they do wonders with cosmetic surgery these days, right? I'll help pay for whatever it costs. Okay?"

She was silent a moment, then nodded her bandaged head slightly. "We'll see. But thanks, monkey," she said, eyes glistening. Phil decided to change the subject.

"The funny thing to me, Trudy, is the way Pain Eaters bother with us at all. Why not just battle it out on their own and leave us humans the fuck alone?"

"But if humans *made* them, somehow, way back when, do they have any choice? They're our fault, sort of. Right?"

"I suppose, if any of that stuff about our making them was true."

"Well, assuming for a moment it is, here's something else to think about. *Why did the Ally send me back at all?* I've been thinking about that, and I see two possibilities, one I like and one I don't.

"First the one I like. Maybe, because Erzebet's and my soul is evolving and growing, maybe we're somehow making the Ally better too, more caring, you know? Or, maybe that's not it. Maybe, and here's the other possibility, maybe the Ally is just . . . not finished using me . . . yet."

Phil squeezed Trudy's hand. "No, Trudy. We *have* to believe the whole mess is over."

"But, Phil, I don't know for sure that the Ally won the battle that was going on when I came back. I don't even know that . . . that Liz won't walk through that door any second in another body. I had a nightmare last night, Phil. I

dreamed that . . . one of the nurses came in with my medicine, and she turned into that hag."

"Don't worry about bad dreams, Trudy. Please? I've had
one or two myself since we got here. And we'll probably
keep having them for years. I've heard that Vietnam Vets
have nightmares about the shit they survived years and years
later. Best way I can think of to deal with it is if we always
sleep together from now on. That way, if one of us wakes up
from a bad dream, the other one will be there to—"

"Give me another kiss," Trudy interrupted, smiling as she
raised her bandaged right arm.

He winced with pain as he moved too fast, then leaned
down and kissed her.

"I like your plan, Phil, about always sleeping together. I
like it a lot. Does this mean the engagement's still on?"

"It sure as hell had better be. I've got to find out if all my
equipment works after what Liz did to it, and the doctors for
it. You know?"

"Everything's going to work just fine," she assured him.

He kissed her again, then sat back down on the edge of
her bed. "Trudy, I've been thinking about something else
that never bothered me much before. But maybe you can
give me a clue, being through what you have with Erzebet,
and having her memories, and all."

"I . . . don't have them anymore," Trudy said. "I can still
remember some of them, the ones I actually touched. But
the feelings that went with them and the feeling of Erzebet's
presence, and the Ally's, is gone."

"Oh. Well, *good*. Right?"

"Definitely. But what did you start to ask?"

"What makes us like we are, Trudy? What put the kinks in
us? I'm talking about our fantasies, whips and chains, all
that. What made the Countess start wanting to torture other
women? She was evidently that way long before Darvulia
and Demon Young arrived, and long before she herself became allied with a Pain Eater of her own. So, why? You
know? Just fucking *why?* Why did she become a monster?
Did something happen to her as a kid that made her that
way? Or was she born one?"

"You tell me. I'd like to know, too. People always want to

know things like that. Maybe they think it will ward off the same thing happening to them or something. I mean, *why* did that nice-looking guy next door shoot his wife and kids and then himself? *Why* did that man on the evening news torture women? *Why* do whips and chains excite people like us? I remember nothing from Erzebet's memories about anything *making* her want to hurt people. Her sex drive got twisted somehow, but—"

"But don't you think your kinks might have been because of hers? I mean, what with your maybe having *been* her?"

"Yeah. I've thought of that. But maybe there was someone *before* I was Erzebet that made *her* have sexual kinks. And someone before that, and before that. Maybe eventually, in some life, we'd find a reason. Or maybe not."

"So, maybe something happened to me in a different life that gave me my kinks, too," he responded.

"But I'm sure there are headshrinkers who would say reincarnation is just a bullshit way to avoid taking responsibility for our actions. And those same headshrinkers could undoubtedly give us explanations about why we are how we are just by using things that happened in our childhoods. Right? So, do you think that maybe we should see a headshrinker, together?"

"Feeling well enough to make jokes, I see?"

"We could even tell him, or her, all about everything that happened to us over the last few days."

"Laughing hurts, or I would."

"Don't you think we should get ourselves all straightened out and, you know, normalized? If we're still going to get married?"

He gave her a kiss. "Marv would never forgive us. And neither would we." He kissed her again. "Your eyelids are drooping. I'll go back to my room and let you get some sleep, after I ask you just one other thing. Have the police questioned you yet?"

"Yeah. But the doctor didn't let them stay too long. You too?"

"They stayed longer with me. What did you tell them?"

"Pretty much the truth, up to a point, and it seemed to

satisfy them for now, though they said they'd probably have more questions later. How about you?"

"Well, for once I decided to pretty much tell the truth, too, up to a point, as you say. I told them we'd been taken to some farm and tried to give them directions. And I told them that we'd been tortured by a woman and her gang. I gave them a description of Liz as she *originally* looked, but—"

"Me too."

"—but I didn't tell them she decayed like Dracula a few days ago."

"I forgot to mention that, too."

"You also forget to mention about Donna?"

"Yeah. Our memories are really slipping, Phil. Darn."

"How about Holly?"

"Forgot her too, though I didn't feel right about it. If she was not one of Liz's slaves to begin with, and I still don't think she was, she'll be another unsolved case in the missing persons files. Those three at the farm will be too, I guess, unless that station wagon belonged to one of them, but even if it did, without any body being found, the person will still be considered missing."

"Sounds like our stories agree well enough, though," he decided, relieved, then kissed her again. "Now get some rest, Trudy. I'll see you later, okay?"

"Okay, monkey," she replied, her eyelids drooping lower by the moment.

Phil headed for the door. When he turned around to give her a wave before he went on out, she had already drifted back to sleep.

Happy dreams, Trudy, he thought, *and maybe I'll have some now, too.* Then he went on back to his room.

EPILOGUE
Castle Csejthe, Hungary

The Countess Erzebet Bathory cried out in her sleep and awoke. She sat up in bed and gave another cry of terror. Her bedroom had become the hideous prison in her nightmare, the windows and door bricked up, sealing her in, entombing her alive. But the after-image from her dream lasted only a heartbeat, then her room returned to normal.

Moonlight flooded through the tall windows. The little lamp she always left lit at night glowed cozily upon the highly polished top of her ornately carved bedside table.

Erzebet took a deep breath to try and calm her nerves, then she lay down again and turned on her side, facing the wall on which, above her dressing table, hung a large mirror.

Seeing the mirror awoke another image from her dream; a naked woman, taller than most men and muscled like a warrior, pointing at the mirror, trying desperately to warn her about something, but . . . what?

Erzebet looked away from the mirror, suddenly afraid she would see something moving within it. The sudden, unexpected fear made her frown.

The Countess thought about the nightmare only a few moments more before turning her thoughts to more pleasant things, such as who did and did not deserve to be invited to her eldest child's birthday party, and about her plans for the naked, half-tortured seamstress who was spending the night searching rat holes in the dark for a needle and thread that were not there.

Erzebet's lips twisted into a smile. She chuckled softly, closing her eyes and imagining the seamstress' terror.

She was soon sleeping soundly once more.

But for the next several days, the nightmare of the bricked-up bedroom hovered in her mind, arising to irritate and upset her in the midst of her daily, and nightly, activities.

Eventually, however, the dream receded into the shadows of her mind and she did not think about it again until, years later, she sat watching in horror, pretending to be aloofly unconcerned, as workmen bricked up her bedroom, making part of the nightmare come true.

The rest of it came true nearly four years later, and on that night, she died.

But only, of course, for a while.